DON'T READ THE COMMENTS

**Books by Eric Smith
available from Inkyard Press**

*Don't Read the Comments
You Can Go Your Own Way*

ERIC SMITH

DON'T READ THE COMMENTS

Recycling programs for this product may not exist in your area.

ISBN-13: 978-1-335-20996-2

Don't Read the Comments

First published in 2020. This edition published in 2021.

This edition published by arrangement with Harlequin Books S.A.

For questions and comments about the quality of this book, please contact us at CustomerService@Harlequin.com.

Inkyard Press
22 Adelaide St. West, 40th Floor
Toronto, Ontario M5H 4E3, Canada
www.InkyardPress.com

Printed in U.S.A.

For my dear friend Darlene Meier,
a strong female character who has never needed saving.

And for my wife, Nena, and son, Langston,
who saved me.

1

DIVYA

"Mom. We've been over this. Don't read the comments," I say, sighing as my mother stares at me with her fretful deep-set eyes. They're dark green, just like mine, and stand out against her soft brown skin. Wrinkle lines trail out from the corners like thin tree branches grown over a lifetime of worrying.

I wish I could wash away all of her worries, but I only seem to be causing her more lately.

"I'm just not comfortable with it anymore," my mom counters. "I appreciate what you're doing with…you know, your earnings or however that sponsor stuff works, but I can't stand seeing what they're saying about you on the Internet."

"So don't read the comments!" I exclaim, reaching out and taking her hands in mine. Her palms are weathered, like the pages of the books she moves around at the library, and I can feel the creases in her skin as my fingers run over them. Bundles of multicolored bangles dangle from both of her wrists, clinking about lightly.

"How am I supposed to do that?" she asks, giving my hands

a squeeze. "You're my daughter. And they say such awful things. They don't even know you. Breaks my heart."

"What did I *just* say?" I ask, letting go of her hands, trying to give her my warmest it's-going-to-be-okay smile. I know she only reads the blogs, the articles covering this and that, so she just sees the replies there, the sprawling comments—and not what people say on social media. Not what the trolls say about *her*. Because moms are the easiest target for those online monsters.

"Yes, yes, I'm aware of that sign in your room with your slogan regarding comments," Mom scoffs, shaking her head and getting to her feet. She groans a little as she pushes herself off the tiny sofa, which sinks in too much. Not in the comfortable way a squishy couch might, but in a this-piece-of-furniture-needs-to-be-thrown-away-because-it's-probably-doing-irreversible-damage-to-my-back-and-internal-organs kind of way. She stretches her back, one hand on her waist, and I make a mental note to check online for furniture sales at Target or Ikea once she heads to work.

"Oof, I must have slept on it wrong," Mom mutters, turning to look at me. But I know better. She's saying that for my benefit. The air mattress on her bed frame—in lieu of an actual mattress—isn't doing her back any favors.

I'd better add a cheap mattress to my list of things to search for later. Anything is better than her sleeping on what our family used to go camping with.

Still, I force myself to nod and say, "Probably." If Mom knew how easily I saw through this dance of ours, the way we pretend that things are okay while everything is falling apart around us, she'd only worry more.

Maybe she does know. Maybe that's part of the dance.

I avert my gaze from hers and glance down at my watch. It's the latest in smartwatch tech from Samsung, a beautiful little thing that connects to my phone and computer, controls the streaming box on our television… Hell, if we could afford smart lights in our apartment, it could handle those, too. It's nearly 8:00 p.m., which means my Glitch subscribers will be tuning in for my scheduled gaming stream of *Reclaim the Sun* at any minute. A couple social media notifications start lighting up the edges of the little screen, but it isn't the unread messages or the time that taunt me.

It's the date.

The end of June is only a few days away, which means the rent is due. How can my mom stand here and talk about me getting rid of my Glitch channel when it's bringing in just enough revenue to help cover the rent? To pay for groceries? When the products I'm sent to review or sponsored to wear—and then consequently sell—have been keeping us afloat with at least a little money to walk around with?

"I'm going to start looking for a second job," Mom says, her tone defeated.

"Wait, what?" I look away from my watch and feel my heartbeat quicken. "But if you do that—"

"I can finish these summer classes another time. Maybe next year—"

"No. No way." I shake my head and suck air in through my gritted teeth. She's worked so hard for this. *We've* worked so hard for this. "You only have a few more classes!"

"I can't let you keep doing this." She gestures toward my room, where my computer is.

"And I can't let you work yourself to death for… What? This tiny apartment, while that asshole doesn't do a damn thing to—"

"Divya. Language," she scolds, but her tone is undermined by a soft grin peeking in at the corner of her mouth. "He's still your fath—"

"I'll do my part," I say resolutely, stopping her from saying that word. "I can deal with it. I want to. You will not give up going to school. If you do that, he wins. Besides, I've... got some gadgets I can sell this month."

"I just... I don't want you giving up on your dreams, so I can keep chasing mine. I'm the parent. What does all this say about me?" My mom exhales, and I catch her lip quivering just a little. Then she inhales sharply, burying whatever was about to surface, and I almost smile, as weird as that sounds. It's just our way, you know?

Take the pain in. Bury it down deep.

"We're a team." I reach out and grasp her hands again, and she inhales quickly once more.

It's in these quiet moments we have together, wrestling with these challenges, that the anger I feel—the rage over this small apartment that's replaced our home, the overdrafts in our bank accounts, all the time I've given up—is replaced with something else.

With how proud I am of her, for starting over the way she has.

"I'm not sure what I did to deserve you."

Deserve.

I feel my chest cave in a little at the word as I look again at the date on the beautiful display of this watch. I know I need to sell it. I know I do. The couch. That crappy mattress. My dwindling bank account. The upcoming bills.

The required sponsorship agreement to wear this watch in all my videos for a month, in exchange for keeping the watch, would be over in just a few days. I could easily get $500 for it on an auction site or maybe a little less at the used-electronics shop downtown. One means more money, but it also means having my address out there, which is something I avoid like the plague—though having friends like Rebekah mail the gadgets for me has proved a relatively safe way to do it. The other means less money, but the return is immediate, at least. Several of the employees there watch my stream, however, and conversations with them are often pretty awkward.

I'd hoped that maybe, just maybe, I'd get to keep this one thing. Isn't that something *I* deserve? Between helping Mom with the rent while she finishes up school and pitching in for groceries and trying to put a little money aside for my own tuition in the fall at the community college… God, I'd at least earned this much, right?

The watch buzzes against my wrist, a pleasant feeling. As a text message flashes across the screen, I feel a pang of wonder and regret over how a display so small can still have a better resolution than the television in our living room.

THE GALAXY WAITS FOR NO ONE, YOU READY D1V? —COMMANDER (RE)BEKAH

I smile at the note from my producer-slash-best-friend, then look up as my mom makes her way toward the front door of our apartment, tossing a bag over her shoulder.

"I'll be back around ten or so," Mom says, sounding tired. "Just be careful, okay?"

"I always am," I promise, walking over to give her a hug. It's sweet, her constant reminders to be careful, to check in, especially since all I generally do while she's gone is hang out in front of the computer. But I get it. Even the Internet can be a dangerous place. The threats on social media and the emails that I get—all sent by anonymous trolls with untraceable accounts—are proof of that.

Still, as soon as the door closes, I bolt across the living room and into my small bedroom, which is basically just a bed, a tiny dresser, and my workstation. I've kept it simple since the move and my parents split.

The only thing that's far from simple is my gaming rig.

When my Glitch stream hit critical mass at one hundred thousand subscribers about a year and a half ago, a gaming company was kind enough to sponsor my rig. It's extravagant to the point of being comical, with bright neon-blue lighting pouring out the back of the system and a clear case that shows off the needless LED illumination. Like having shiny lights makes it go any faster. I never got it when dudes at my school put flashy lights on their cars, and I don't get it any more on a computer.

But it was free, so I'm certainly not going to complain.

I shake the mouse to awaken the sleeping monster, and my widescreen LED monitor flashes to life. It's one of those screens that bend toward the edges, the curves of the monitor bordering on sexy. I adjust my webcam, which—along with my beaten-up Ikea table that's not even a desk—is one of the few non-sponsored things in my space. It's an aging thing, but the resolution is still HD and flawless, so unless a free one is somehow going to drop into my lap—and it probably won't, because you can't show off a webcam in a digital stream or a recorded sponsored video when you're filming with said camera—it'll do the trick.

I navigate over to Glitch and open my streaming application. Almost immediately, Rebekah's face pops up in a little window on the edge of my screen. I grin at the sight of her new hairstyle, her usually blond and spiky hair now dyed a brilliant shade of blood orange, a hue as vibrant as her personality. The sides of her head are buzzed, too, and the overall effect is awesome.

Rebekah smiles and waves at me. "You ready to explore the cosmos once more?" she asks, her voice bright in my computer's speakers. I can hear her keys clicking loudly as she types, her hands making quick work of something on the other side of the screen. I open my mouth to say something, but she jumps in before I can. "Yes, yes, I'll be on mute once we get in, shut up."

I laugh and glance at myself in the mirror I've got attached to the side of my monitor with a long metal arm—an old bike mirror that I repurposed to make sure my makeup and hair are on point in these videos. Even though the streams are all about the games, there's nothing wrong with looking a *little* cute, even if it's just for myself. I run a finger over one of my eyebrows, smoothing it out, and make a note to tweeze them just a little bit later. I've got my mother's strong brows, black and rebellious. We're frequently in battle with one another, me armed with my tweezers, my eyebrows wielding their growing-faster-than-weeds genes.

"How much time do we have?" I ask, tilting my head back and forth.

"About five minutes. And you look fine, stop it," she grumbles. I push the mirror away, the metal arm making a squeaking noise, and I see Rebekah roll her eyes. "You could just use a compact like a normal person, you know."

"It's vintage," I say, leaning in toward my computer mic. "I'm being hip."

"You. Hip." She chuckles. "Please save the jokes for the stream. It's good content."

I flash her a scowl and load up my social feeds on the desktop, my watch still illuminating with notifications. I decide to leave them unchecked on the actual device and scope them out on the computer instead, so when people are watching, they can see the watch in action. That should score me some extra goodwill with sponsors, and maybe it'll look like I'm more popular than people think I am.

Because that's my life. Plenty of social notifications, but zero texts or missed calls.

The feeds are surprisingly calm this evening, a bundle of people posting about how excited they are for my upcoming stream, playing *Reclaim the Sun* on their own, curious to see what I'm finding… Not bad. There are a few dumpster-fire comments directed at the way I look and some racist remarks by people with no avatars, cowards who won't show their faces, but nothing out of the usual.

Ah. Lovely. Someone wants me to wear less clothing in this stream. Blocked. A link to someone promoting my upcoming appearance at New York GamesCon, nice. Retweeted. A post suggesting I wear a skimpier top, and someone agreeing. Charming. Blocked and blocked.

Why is it that the people who always leave the grossest, rudest, and occasionally sexist, racist, or religiously intolerant comments never seem to have an avatar connected to their social profiles? Hiding behind a blank profile picture? How brave. How courageous.

And never mind all the messages that I assume are supposed to be flirtatious, but are actually anything but. Real original, saying "hey" and that's it, then spewing a bunch of foul-mouthed nonsense when they don't get a response. Hey, anonymous bro, I'm not here to be sexualized by strangers on the Internet. It's creepy and disgusting. Can't I just have fun without being objectified?

"Div!" Rebekah shouts, and I jump in my seat a little.

"Yeah, hey, I'm here," I mumble, looking around for my Bluetooth earpiece, trying to force myself into a better mood. *This is why you don't read the comments, Divya.*

The earpiece is bright orange and yellow with white outlines, inscribed with the logo from the game *Remember Me*, a kick-ass sci-fi adventure with a lady protagonist that I adore.

I don't care if the series got canceled; I wear my earpiece to show my solidarity.

I *will* remember you, Nilin, you underrated heroine. You deserved better.

"You were really zoned out for a second," Rebekah says. "Let's go. It's time."

I hear her tapping a few buttons, and suddenly her little screen goes quiet, the video stream of her now bearing a circled microphone with a line through it in bright red. I can still see her, but she's muted. She won't appear in video on the stream, preferring to stay behind the scenes for personal reasons that belong to her.

I chuckle as she reaches off-screen and her hand comes back gripping a giant clear Starbucks cup with a huge froth of whipped cream on top, the beverage most definitely filled with pure chocolate and sugar. "Game fuel," she likes to call it.

I swivel in my chair to make sure my room's door is closed and take a quick peek at my window. Curtain drawn—check.

We're good to go.

For a minute, I debate breaking out my Oculus. It's way more fun to explore the universe in *Reclaim the Sun* when you're using the VR feature, but then I'd have a giant virtual reality headset covering up my face, hiding my expressions while I'm playing. And all of that, blended with the gameplay, is the point of this. Plus, I want to see Rebekah in her side window. Maybe I'll plug it in later, when I'm gaming solo.

I look up at my webcam and shift around, trying to find the perfect angle for where I'm sitting, the old camera wrestling to adjust the light balance within the room. I keep my outfits on the stream simple—today I've got on a dark green T-shirt with a bright white *Halo* logo in the center, which makes my green eyes look even greener on the camera. Perfect.

I hit Record.

"Hey, lovers and dreamers and streamers!" I exclaim, plastering a bright smile on my face. "It's D1V, coming to you live from the vast universe of *Reclaim the Sun*. Today we're going to be exploring the galaxy and seeing what we can find out here in the cosmos. Hopefully, as I'm out adventuring, I run into some of you! Feel free to hit me up on the *Reclaim the Sun* messaging network at letter 'D,' number '1,' letter 'V' and join the Armada as we claim planets for our own.

"As always, the fantastic and talented and beautiful Commander (Re)bekah is on the stream with us."

I point at the camera. There's an audible click, and the video stream switches to Rebekah, who gives a faux salute to the camera for just a second, and then switches back to me. Even in that quick clip, you can't see her face. She saluted while looking down. She's not a huge fan of the attention and prefers to stay behind the camera, even though she's got tens of thousands of followers on her various social networks from working on this little show of ours. She mostly posts pictures of her coffee, her cat, Garrus, or books. She's big into bookstagram, making beautifully artsy arrangements to photograph and showcase her current reads.

And no matter what game we're playing, if there's a customizable vehicle, she'll name it after a book she's really into. I've seen her share screenshots with authors on social media, and they always seem over-the-moon thrilled.

"She'll be on deck running around with us in her brand-new vessel, the *Heart of Iron*, and recording our exploration from another angle to catch all the action. You can flag her ship, as well as mine, the *Golden Titan*, and track us as we travel the universe—and, of course, please feel free to join our fleet! Though be warned, if you fire on us, we will be forced to unleash upon you the fury of a thousand suns, as well as the fury of the thousand fans who are traveling with us. Your ship won't survive against my darling Angst Armada."

I glance over at Rebekah on the screen and catch her giving me a smile. She's the one who named our quickly growing fleet, which largely consists of teenagers like us, eager to do a little exploring outside the real world we're trapped in. And a lot of venting sure does happen on our hashtag and in the game, almost none of which has anything to do with video gaming. School. Breakups. Parents. The usual.

#AngstArmada it is.

Rebekah's been working on getting patches and pins done up for when we make our appearance at GamesCon later in the summer. She says we can potentially make a ton of money, even if we're only selling them for a few dollars at our table. I wince at the thought of it—not the patches or pins, which frankly sound awesome and like what I'm all about, because how cool would it be to see someone randomly in the mall rocking our fleet badges? And extra revenue to put away for college and help Mom? Yes, please.

But manning the table. Being in public. Sitting in one place where people can come up and talk to me, shake my hand, take pictures. The trolls and their emails and messages... They get so brutal. And the idea of being someplace in real life as D1V and not just as me, Divya, is terrifying.

But if Rebekah can be brave enough to do it, so can I. She's been through far worse than I have.

"Turn up the enthusiasm," Rebekah murmurs from her little window, on mute for everyone playing with us and for the stream, but still audible to me. "You sound like you don't want to be here today."

She's awfully perceptive.

"And...we're in!" I shout, lifting my hands up in the air, fingers wide and open. I beam directly into the webcam.

"Alright, alright, dial it back there on the performance," Rebekah snipes, and I grin, putting my hands back on the keyboard and mouse. The universe of *Reclaim the Sun* is welcoming and beautiful on my massive screen, an expanse of sprawling black dotted with faraway stars, each a destination that's possible to fly off to. The fact that there's no beating this game, no end goal—that it's just nonstop exploration—makes it all the more fun. There's no real competition here, unless you're looking for a fight. We're all in this together.

I look down at the controls on my ship and take quick stock of what's on the readouts. I'm still feeling a little bitter that I can't have my Oculus headset on, as I have to navigate everything with my mouse instead of just physically looking at this stuff. I click on the little video window that contains Rebekah's floating head and drag it over, placing it atop one of the more useless control screens, there mostly for decoration. Seeing her there makes me feel like she's my real navigator and in this ship with me. And really, she is—without her, there wouldn't be a proper show with sponsors and actual revenue or any of that. It'd just be me floundering around in front of an audience, one that wouldn't be nearly as big as the one we have now.

Or maybe I wouldn't be doing this at all. I'm not sure *what* I'd be doing right now without Rebekah's help, what with Mom and our finances the way they are.

I give my friend's video window an affectionate little click with my mouse and turn back to the open universe.

"It's that time, Angst Armada! Our coordinates are as follows… Quadrant Seti Six, 51.7, 92.2, 62.7, in the Omega Expanse. We'll wait here for approximately five minutes, and then take off and try to find an undiscovered planet. With any luck— Whoa!"

The radar screen goes haywire, and Rebekah's video screen

next to it shows her looking far more excited than I've seen her in recent memory. A smile explodes on her face, and her voice erupts in my headset, though her video is getting choppy as she talks.

"O-Oh my God, —ere has got to be like, a thousand ships in he—" She screams in my ear, making me wince. "How's your la—? I swear my sys— go— to cra—"

I check the latency bar, which monitors our connection, and it looks like everything is holding up okay on my end, even as vessel after vessel warps into view in front of my ship. Rebekah's video stream cuts in and out, her voice getting garbled and then clear and then static again. Spaceships of all kinds and shapes and sizes thunder in and out of warp from wherever they were before in the cosmos. Bright neon colors contrast with numerous ships in cold metallic shades, some colored so black, so dark, they practically blend in to the open space. Ships of gold and silver shimmer from the reflecting light of a nearby star, and my radar screen is full to bursting with small glowing dots, each representing a nearby player.

The Angst Armada has arrived.

2

AARON

There are many planets in the universe, but this one is mine.

As my small ship bursts through the atmosphere, hurtling toward the planet's surface, the wind roars outside of my vessel, the chassis rattling with an intensity that makes me feel as though the cockpit is set to fall to pieces.

Two sights demand my attention. One, the control panel before me, consisting of a small screen tracking my speed and angle of descent, accompanied by a large surface map of what's below. But as the ship shifts to manual controls and I grip the flight stick, my hands firm against the rubber handles, my gaze is inexorably drawn to the second sight, looming out the cockpit window, filling my eyes with color.

The actual planet. Undiscovered. New. Mine.

The sky glows with bursts of ruby, purple, and blue, like paint that's been carelessly spilled over an impossibly giant canvas. To the right, forests bloom in what *look* like autumnal colors, although there's no way to know what the seasons are on this planet, and a large mountain range interrupts the foliage with light browns and beiges. On my left, a long bright blue river cuts through the wilderness, swaths of white streaking through the water.

Reluctantly, I drag my focus back to the controls. Rate of descent, good. Speed, good. Fuel—more than enough to get off the planet if there's any hostile wildlife. Readings dictate no humanoid life, which is important, as I'm not here to disrupt anyone's place in the universe or steal their home.

I take a deep breath and steady myself for the landing as a suitable clearing appears on the map display in front of me, followed by a glimpse of the landscape through the large cockpit window: a massive field of green, marred by a handful of large boulders scattered across it, like large gray marbles tossed by a child. I try to focus on them as my ship gets closer, lower to the ground. I'd like to avoid damaging my ship and getting trapped here if I can help it.

With a hum, the landing pads extend, emitting a soft rumbling under my feet. They click loudly into place with a hard snap, and my ship slows and slows until it comes almost to an standstill above the clearing, hovering in place. The roar of the wind is gone now, replaced by the hum of plasma engines behind and below me as they pulse softly, controlling the sway of the ship as I lower it to the ground.

I land gently, the ship jangling around just a little and letting out a soft hiss of air, decompressing. I peer out at the meadow for a moment, then scan the screens under the flight stick for any sign that the terrain before me might be dangerous. Breathable air? Check, just slightly thinner than back home or here in the ship. I'll need to be careful when climbing or running too much. Need to keep up my stamina. There's a water source not far away, though, so I shouldn't have to carry that much in the way of supplies.

But that wilderness out there. Those mountains.

I hit a panel under one of the screens, and it slides open,

revealing a small blaster that I picked up on my latest supply run. I toss it in my pack, along with a canteen and some
purification tablets for the water by that river. Then I push a
button on the digital tracker on my wrist, and a menu pops
up, displaying a dizzying array of options. I shake my head
and quickly push the map button, eager to figure out where
I am so I can start exploring. Details be damned. With a soft
chime, the menu closes, and a small white light pulses on the
edge of the screen.

Good. It'll map the terrain while I walk.

I stare out the cockpit window one more time, at the field
and the boulders stacked around. A splash of color flickers in
the corner of my vision, and I turn to see a flock of birdlike
creatures taking to the skies, their wings a bright emerald
shade of green, their bellies the yellow of fresh corn and full
of glimmering scales.

I press a few buttons on the screen near the flight stick and
the cockpit opens, my heart pounding with anticipation as the
glass slowly slides away, the view of the landscape sharpen-
ing. I hop out, the gravity normal, my feet cushioned by the
grasslike plants beneath me. The sky shimmers with an odd
mix of vivid colors, and the soft light from two suns dances in
lens-flare patterns through the glass on the ship's open door.

I gaze hungrily toward the mountains in the distance, then
glance around for the rushing river that's apparently just a few
leagues away. I can just barely make out the roar of the water
as I check my canteen—half-empty. It looks like a visit to the
river is in order, so I can stock up on supplies and see what
kind of food this new landscape offers before I trek out into
the total unknown.

With a soft blip, I load up the menu on my wristlet, the
display beaming up a holo of light orange text on a darkened
background.

CLASS FOUR PLANET [ESTIMATED]
Status: Uncharted, Undiscovered
Life Support Capability: Positive
Detectable Resources: Timber, Water
Would you like to claim and name this planet?
[YES] [NO]

My heart races, and I feel warm all over. I've been waiting for that last option since I started exploring this galaxy. And a Class Four? Awesome. Not going to run and gun it—I'm going to take my time here, do things right.

With a wave of my hand, a keypad appears in the air above my wrist. But before I can decide on a name for my new planet, static rings in my ear. A flicker of worry runs through me as I adjust the small earpiece tucked inside. Did someone else land on the planet? Communication from my guild at our headquarters?

A more hopeful thought occurs to me. Maybe a supply vessel is in the area, which would be perfect. I could use some building material, maybe some food supplies until I figure out what I can and can't use—

Then the static breaks, and the sound comes in clear.

"The planet," a familiar voice says. "Name it Butts."

I put my controller down and turn around to see my six-year-old sister, Mira, standing behind me, her hands over her mouth, eyes sparkling, a surefire fit of giggles set to explode. She hops back and forth on her feet, her curly black hair bouncing with her frantic, silly movements. I take my headset off, the music from my exploration-meets-real-time-strategy game, *Reclaim the Sun*, quickly replaced by the sound of Mira's irrepressible laughter.

"Mira, come on," I groan. "Get out of here."

"Planet... Butts!" Mira shouts, her hands leaving her face

and quickly coming back up, as though she's trying to hide that *she's* the one who just screamed "butts" at the top of her lungs.

Resigned, I smile and motion for her to come sit with me. She scurries over and squeals gleefully as I pick her up, then settle her on my lap in front of my computer. It's a massive gaming rig that I've slowly built piece by piece over the years, collecting parts off eBay and from discarded machines around my neighborhood—the latter much to my parents' disapproval. No parent likes seeing their kid drag home old, beat-up computers they've found in the trash, no matter how often they tell you to experiment and explore and all that.

But *this*—it's the perfect beast to explore galaxies in *Reclaim the Sun*. It's a massive game, with worlds that are randomly generated for exploration and a universe so big no one will ever be able to see all of it. And when you're playing a first-person exploration game that micromanages even the tiniest things— like upgrading vehicles, customizing armor, establishing trade routes, and slowly creating your own character to look way too much like yourself—you need a lot of power. And even though I have the graphics turned down a bit to keep things running smoothly, it still looks great. Plus, my rig is great for working on the games I'm trying to write with my best friend, Ryan, at our part-time job with ManaPunk, a local game developer.

And I managed to build it without bothering anyone for upgrade money.

Not that my parents would give it to me, anyway. We might have money, but none of it is being used to support something they refer to as a "hobby," a frequent point of contention whenever I come home with parts gleaned from dumpster diving at Penn or Temple, the nearby universities, or discarded computers our wealthy neighbors toss outside, even though you're not supposed to toss computers in with the general trash. RAM, hard drives, better speakers… My rig is the Frankenstein's monster of PCs, only I nurture my creation.

When most people hear that I write video games, I think they imagine coding. Programming and all that. But no, I *write*. Story-type stuff, dialogue, instructions. Ryan does the art, Laura handles the coding, and Jason, the publisher, does a mix of all of it.

We're a scrappy little team, and I love it.

My monster-machine of a computer helps process the beta code of the games-in-progress better than my regular old laptop, which I drag around to coffee shops when working on the story. But this beast also helps me play games like *Reclaim the Sun*—because not all of us can afford a fancy game-developing PC on our own, like Jason and ManaPunk can.

Though maybe I would be able to buy some new parts if he'd just pay me for our last project already.

"Beeeeeeee…" Mira gibbers, staring down at the keyboard. She leans over the smooth white desk as she glances at all the keys, a single finger on her tiny fist sticking out, ready to jab the letter of her choosing.

"Here," I say, unplugging my headphones from the PC. The music of the game blasts from the speakers behind the monitor, an epic classical score that sounds like it's ripped straight from a *Star Wars* film, mixed with the sounds of my unnamed planet. The rustling plants, the din of the roaring river, the odd calls from those flittering lizard-birds that have begun to circle overhead, and the hum of my ship's cooling engine.

Mira moves her hand out of the way as I reach for the keyboard next, painstakingly typing out the planet's name.

Would you like to claim and name this planet?
[YES][NO]
What would you like to name this planet?
PLANET BUTTS
Are you sure you want to name this planet
PLANET BUTTS?

Once a name is chosen it cannot be changed.
[YES] [NO]

I click Yes, securing Planet Butts's place in *Reclaim the Sun* for as long as the game exists, set in a universe of trillions of planets. It's unlikely anyone will ever find it again, but if they do, I guess they'll be in for a treat of a name? Though it's more than likely scores of younger kids playing this game have come up with similar—likely far more creative and lewd— planet names.

For a moment, I wonder just how many Planet Butts there are out there. I grin, thinking about how much fun it'll be when Mira is old enough to play games like this on her own. How I could take her exploring. How we could name endless planets together.

The view of the landscape pulls away for a moment, bringing up the planet in its entirety, stars dotting the sky as the big green-and-blue Earth-like sphere spins slowly in front of us.

PLANET BUTTS

Discovered by Aaron Jericho

"Yay!" screams Mira, bouncing up and down, and then begins cheering like she's rooting for a sports team. "Pla-net Butts! Pla-net Butts!"

"Um, what's going on in here?"

I spin around in my computer chair and see my mom leaning in the doorway, her black hair tied up in a bun. She's dressed in a blue blazer, with thin glasses on the bridge of her nose. An ID tag dangles from her neck on a lanyard, though I have no idea why she wears it. She runs her medical practice in the tiny building connected to our house. She's the boss. Everyone knows who she is.

Mom stares at us, shifting the bundle of magazines under her arm, some of them still wrapped in the plastic covers they arrive in with the mail. Her eyes flit back and forth from me and Mira to the computer screen, an amused look on her face. Mira's mouth is clamped shut, a thin line barely holding back her laughter, and it's easy to see so much of my mother reflected back in her. She's got my mother's Honduran looks, while I look more like Dad. Like we're little clones that just budded off them.

"Just exploring the universe." I shrug.

"Okay, well… I left some money on the fridge. Maybe get a pizza or something for the two of you? I shouldn't be too late today," she says, and I catch her absently fiddling with her ID badge. It's her tell, and I know that she *will* be late again, even though it's her office and it's connected to our actual house.

And judging by her expression, I know what's coming next.

"Aaron, you promised this summer—" she starts.

"Mom, can we just… Not now?" I ask, my heart sinking. *Reclaim the Sun* has been out for a few weeks now, but this is the first day I've had any time to myself to do some intense, proper exploring, between end-of-the-year homework and babysitting-despite-Mom-and-Dad-being-right-next-door and my attempts at script writing for ManaPunk. It's finally summer vacation, and I want to do what everyone wants to do with bright clear skies, warm beautiful weather, and all the freedom in the world.

Stay inside and play video games.

"Your father and I think it'll be good for you, especially for…you know. When it's your turn, and all." She presses her lips together, and I fight the urge to audibly sigh at her mention of "your turn," like she's suddenly going to finish being a doctor and I'm magically going to take her place. Like it's a kingdom and she can just pass me a scepter or something, and that taking over her practice doesn't involve me spending an actual decade of my life studying something I don't want anything to do with.

"Just a few hours a week, that's all we're asking," Mom says pleadingly. "And then you can continue to work on your games and exist on…" She squints at the screen and smiles indulgently, shaking her head. "Planet Butts."

Mira erupts into a fit of giggling, effectively ruining any chance of having a serious conversation about all this. That *this*, these virtual worlds that I get lost in—it's all serious. That I want to make games. Write them. See my name in the credits at the end. That I don't want to be the next Dr. Jericho.

"Plus, your father could use some time to himself, away from all that paperwork," Mom says. "He's been in there really late at night and terribly early in the morning lately."

"Okay, okay," I grumble. "Guilt me with Dad, that's a good tactic." She gives me a look, and I shake my head. "But we're going to have to define what 'a few hours' is. And I get to write on my downtime in the office."

Mom makes a face and fusses with her ID badge, and I can tell a "no" is coming.

"I can use Google Drive or Dropbox on that ancient computer at the reception desk," I add hastily. "No one will even know. Otherwise, I'm just going to do it sneakily on my phone or something, and I know you don't like me using my phone behind the desk."

"That's not it—you can work on your games. It's just…" She pauses. "Aaron, has that boy paid you yet?"

I don't want to say "no," but I can't exactly lie here. I'd wrapped up some freelance copyediting for ManaPunk right before the school year ended, and I have yet to see a check for it. Ryan, too. But I know Jason's good for it.

"He will," I insist. "And there will be even more money when the new game sells."

My mom eyes me for a moment, then gives a small nod. "Okay, well, you can fuss over your games as long as he's settling up soon. I don't want you getting taken advantage of," she says, looking away and down the hall. "Time to fly. Have fun exploring the universe."

She walks off, and I can hear her making her way down the stairs, her heels loud against the hardwood floor of our home. Her retreat is replaced by the sound of soft footsteps approaching my door. Dad leans in next, peering over from the side. He's in some loose-fitting sweatpants and a T-shirt, a mug of coffee in his hand.

"Hey, Doctor," he says, flashing a sleepy grin. His accent is thick, unlike everyone else in the family. His Palestinian looks certainly rubbed off on me, though, our faces both full of sharp edges and stubble.

"Not funny." But I smirk anyway.

"Just...do me a favor? Humor your mother?" he ventures, stepping into my room while sipping on his coffee. He walks over and ruffles Mira's hair, and she responds with a chorus of laughter. He's close enough that I can detect the faint scent of his cooking, the aroma embedded in the fabric of all his clothes, even though he doesn't work in a restaurant anymore. It's like he's keeping tamarind, garlic, and rice in his pockets.

"Dad—" I start.

"Just keep her happy," he says. "And in exchange, I'll watch the desk once in a while, give you a break."

"Thanks, Dad." He's always so much more supportive of these dreams of mine—making games, writing them—than Mom is. I smile, though the small victory feels bittersweet as

I take in the sight of his threadbare shirt, his overall disheveled appearance. "How late were you there last night?" I ask, curious.

"Ah, don't worry about me," he says, brushing me off with a wave of his hand. But I know he can't enjoy being in the office that late, trying to cover for me so I can focus on what I actually care about, and I certainly don't like being the reason he's working so hard. Life would be so much easier if Mom would just give up on her pipe dream of me as a doctor and hire someone else to work the front desk.

"Is this that new one?" Dad asks, staring at the computer screen. "All that modern stuff… I don't know how you kids do it."

"You could totally figure this one out." He loves to make these jokes, even though he's perfectly capable of handling a computer.

"I'll stick with *Minesweeper*."

"Dad."

He tussles my hair like he did Mira's, and I squirm to get away. While I might not have inherited all his good looks, like his jawline, sharp enough to cut the veggies he preps downstairs, we do have the same hair—thick, black, and wavy.

"Anyhow," he says, walking toward the door. "I'll get to look up recipes when your mom isn't looking, and you'll get to enjoy your summer. Everyone wins." ·

"Dad, come on," I groan. "You have to get Mom to bring on an intern or something—"

"Deal?" he asks pointedly.

"Deal," I huff, knowing I've lost this particular battle for now. "You know that's just a temporary solution, though, right? Next year is The Year of College Applications, remember?" I glance over at the horrifying stack of college brochures on my desk, one that teeters dangerously—or perhaps fortuitously—toward falling into the trash bin on the floor.

"Yes, yes," Dad says, taking a sip of his coffee. "Who knows, maybe by then you'll want to become a doctor."

I glare at him.

He laughs, his smile as warm as that coffee in his hand. "We'll figure it out," he says with a wink. "In the meantime, I'll take care of the office today. You go do…whatever that is. I want you to teach me how to do it one of these days. These spaceship games of yours look kinda fun." He waves at the computer with his free hand, then disappears back to his and Mom's bedroom, his footsteps soft on the hardwood floor, a major contrast to my mom's. It's always so easy to tell who's coming and going around here.

I spin the computer chair back around and, much to the delight of Mira, let it rotate a handful of times before stopping it in front of the screen. I place my hands back on the keyboard.

"You ready, copilot?" I ask Mira, and her face lights up, her wide smile revealing the dimples in her cheeks.

"I'm the copilot?!" she exclaims, her hands coming together again in front of her face.

"Always," I tell her. I grab the mouse and give it a shake, the since-gone-black screen returning to life with bright colors and the sight of my newly discovered planet.

Planet Butts still needs to be explored.

And I'm the one to do it.

3

DIVYA

My breath catches as more ships appear on the screen, and I'm awestruck by the digital expanse before me. Just knowing that each little ship, from the ones close enough for me to really see, to the ones that are little more than a pixelated blip in the distance, is a person.

Someone who cares enough to be along for this ride with me.

This is far more people than we've ever had, and something about it has tears pricking at the corners of my eyes. I shake it off and exhale.

"Well, well," I say, stretching in my computer chair, my neck cracking as I loosen up. I open the channel to our group. "I see you're all here."

A chorus of loud cheering erupts in my headset, the voices of hundreds from all over, and my heart feels full to bursting. While the money to help Mom out is great, and the extra funds I'm putting away for college are almost as good, *this* is the reason I keep streaming. Despite my mom's worries, despite the trolls... It's these moments that make this an absolute joy. That make it all worthwhile.

No wonder Rebekah is having latency issues on her end—there's definitely hundreds of gamers in our channel and on the screen. I'd likely be having the same problems if not for my Cabletown sponsorship. Thanks to them, I've got a wildly powerful connection in exchange for sharing a link to their website on my channel. As Rebekah's video flickers in and out, I make a mental note to email my sponsor and see if I can't get a hookup for her, too.

Far off in the distance, one star glimmers a little brighter than the rest, a shimmering blue color among all the white. I point my ship toward it, so the star is right in the center of my display. It must be a planet. It just has to be.

"Rebekah, how you holding up?" I ask after quickly muting my public mic, glancing at her video feed, which is starting to look a bit clearer.

"Better," she says, her voice not coming in choppy anymore. "Might have some issues when we warp, but if I get disconnected it won't be the end of the world. Just make sure you're recording everything on your end, so I have something to work with. I'll find you."

"Okay."

"Are you recording?" she says, nudging.

"Yes, *Commander*." I stretch the word out, making Rebekah grin.

I turn my attention back to the Armada, switching my mic back on.

"Alright, everyone, we're heading to this potentially undiscovered planet up ahead. Take note of the coordinates and get ready to jump!"

I select the planet, and several strings of numbers race across my screen before appearing on one of the little navigational displays in my control panel. After several weeks of intense gameplay, I've finally got the upgrades to detect far-off stars and planets like this. When we first started up, everyone was just slowly trying to find something in all the endless space. Straight-up level grinding, fighting random little monsters on desolate planets, and recording footage of wildlife and plants to earn experience points, to upgrade this, update that.

Now, it's almost too easy, but these upgrades definitely make the content of my videos more interesting. I wait a few seconds so everyone watching can plug in the coordinates, and scowl as a few ships make the jump without me.

"Hey!" I shout into the headset. "I see you guys jumping ahead. If that's an undiscovered planet and you name it without me, we are so getting into a dogfight." I hear several people on the stream laugh, and I smile, too. Because it doesn't really matter in the end. There are trillions—*literally* trillions—of planets in the galaxy of *Reclaim the Sun*.

When you think of that number, a trillion—I mean *really* think about it—it's pretty mind-boggling. A trillion is one million of one million things. I always thought a billion—a thousand millions—was a big number. But a trillion is one thousand billions.

It's enough to make your head explode and make you feel as if concepts like money or numbers aren't real. Like when you see a news headline about a company acquiring another company, and the purchase amount is something impossible, like "one hundred billion dollars." I read someplace once that Sony, the people who make PlayStation—the console this game is on in addition to the PC—is worth something like eighty billion dollars.

You're still short nine hundred and twenty billion to equal a trillion there.

I just can't with those numbers. Going back and forth from thinking of impossibly large quantities like that to thinking about the dwindling checking account me and Mom live out of… It almost hurts. How a seemingly insignificant amount of money, like $200, has the power to make or break my little family, and yet there are people out there throwing billions at one another like candy.

So, if someone scoops up and names that planet before me, whatever. I'll find another one. And another one. And another one.

There's so much possibility here, and no one can stop me.

"Jump!" I shout, pushing a button and sending my ship hustling toward the unknown planet. Once again, I find myself frustrated that I can't use my VR headset. Gorgeous beams of multicolored light blast by the cockpit window as my little ship breaks through time and space to traverse the cosmos at a speed mankind is still light-years away from figuring out.

But here, in the world of one of the most advanced video games out there, you can break the laws of physics to reach unheard-of destinations.

You can summon an armada of people from around the world, connecting virtually to play a game that brings us all so much joy.

You can pay the rent when your shithead of a father leaves your family behind for someone younger and refuses to help support you or your mom, who is working two part-time jobs while in the last year of finishing her dream of graduate school, being a kick-ass woman who has sacrificed too much to give up now.

Maybe get a job, his last text message read, when I asked him if he'd think about helping, when me and Mom were really struggling in the new apartment, before my sponsorship funds started kicking in. Before I deleted him from my phone and my life forever.

The new planet briskly approaches, morphing from a small blue speck into something larger, big and swirling. My ship settles into orbit around it, and I watch as the rest of the Angst Armada lines up alongside me. Hundreds, quite possibly a thousand or more ships, waiting on my every word.

The display in front of me brightens up, detailing infor-

mation about the planet. There's a lot I can tell just by looking at it, though. It looks like it's almost entirely water, with
little white patches here and there. Ice? Frozen land? Tundra?
Enormous mountains that jut out impossibly high from an
endless ocean, the depths of which hide creatures of unfath-
omable size and power?

More and more fantastic speculations spin through my mind
as the computer finishes up.

CLASS TWO PLANET [ESTIMATED]
Status: Charted, Unclaimed, Remains Unexplored
Life Support Capability: Probable
Surface: 89% Water [Frozen], 11% Land Mass
Detectable Resources: Water, Otherwise Unknown
Would you like to claim and name this planet?
[YES] [NO]

I scowl at the "charted" mention in the planetary status,
thanks to those eager gamers who sped off ahead of us. And
a Class Two planet wasn't exactly something to get terribly
hyped about, but whatever. I'll find my own planet solo, without the Armada, the next time I'm playing alone. Headset on.
The vastness of space spilling out in front of me in VR. The
galaxy to myself.

"Well, looks like we found ourselves a wasteland, my dears,"
I say, laughing into the microphone, prompting a chorus of
chuckling in response.

I hear a few people shout, "Let's go!" into the stream, and
I grin at their enthusiasm, even though the excitement might
be for nothing. A Class Two usually has few resources, though
water is always useful.

"Shall we claim this one for the Armada?!" I shout, throwing my hands in the air and raising my eyebrows in question. My headset blares with cheerful shouting from the other

players. This was only the sixth planet that we'd be claiming for our Armada, despite several game sessions of exploring. Some just weren't worth it, and players that traveled with us had scooped them up for themselves. Like Class Ones, which were basically just patches of dirt or useless asteroids without any minerals. But this planet, with all that water?

I've got a good feeling about it.

Rebekah chimes into my headset, on our private channel.

"Hey, when we sign off, an offer just came in from Samsung for them to sponsor you for another month with a different watch," she exclaims happily. "And they'll pay you this time, instead of just giving you the product. Which means I get paid, too, and don't just have to sit around writhing in my own jealousy."

My dad's last text flashes through my head.

Maybe get a job.

Fuck you, too, Dad.

The option to claim and name the planet still floats in front of the cockpit. As I type, the Armada roars in my headset, and I'm glad they all approve.

Would you like to claim and name this planet?
[YES][NO]
What would you like to name this planet?
BEKAH
Are you sure you want to name this planet
BEKAH?
Once a name is chosen it cannot be changed.
[YES] [NO]

I click Yes.

"Oh, aren't you just adorable." Rebekah laughs.

"For my first mate!" I shout into the microphone, for both Rebekah and the Armada. "Without her, there's no show, no Armada, and much like this planet, she's as cool as ice."

"Damn right," Rebekah growls.

"Descend!" I exclaim.

I tilt my ship forward, and the blue sphere with swirls of white rushes toward me as I speed down from the blackness of space. It's silly, but I worry for a moment about what my viewers are going to think if this rock is a total waste of time. Which it very well could be. The water resources will be great, sure. For trading, for building. But explorationwise, which is the best part of playing this game, it might be a total buzz-kill. That's one of the unique joys of adventuring in *Reclaim the Sun*—the possibility and the disappointment that comes with trying to discover something new.

Which, you know, mirrors life quite well. Maybe that's why people love it.

My ship rattles as we break through the atmosphere, the sky echoing with a loud sonic boom, the hundreds of other vessels thundering through the cloudy sky. The sound is like someone beating on a bass drum way too quick and sharp. I glance out the side of the cockpit, where rows of ships fly beside me, heading for the icy planet below.

This close, I can see that the frozen landscape is dotted with patches of sea greens and purples, blooming and shifting beneath the hardened surface. I wonder if that's just the color of the water, or if there are creatures living under the ice. *Reclaim the Sun* spontaneously generates planets and galaxies, but it also creates the environments *on* the planets. The ecosystem, the wildlife, the weather. Part of me wants to know exactly how it all works, and there are countless articles floating around on the Internet that'll dish all that technical stuff out, on sites like *Polygon* and *IGN* and *Engadget*. But most of me doesn't want to ruin the wonder of it all.

It's far more fun to think of it as magic than bits of code.

The scanners on my dashboard pick up a section that looks suitable for landing, and I punch in the coordinates.

"Let's go!" I shout, my little ship soaring across the frozen tundra, the shimmering colors of the ocean speeding by as some of the little mountains start to peek up in the distance. Those mountain ranges give way to what look like bits of land frozen beneath the ice, and I press a few buttons, taking my ship down toward the ground, the landing gear extending with a loud hum and snapping into place.

I hear the other ships buzzing in my ears, their gear and landing procedures all the same as mine. The ships in the *Reclaim the Sun* universe are varied in terms of colors, shapes, and upgrades, but everyone has the same kind of weapons, same navigational gear, all that. The upgrades help, but they don't give you an extreme advantage. A little one, sure, but nothing major. Keeps it fair, particularly when fights break out— which they do, per the many videos trolls have been posting online, taking out other players for kicks. Tricking them into thinking they're going to get a free resource drop from a helpful player, only to be blasted apart. Stuff like that.

Bunch of tools, those ones.

My ship nestles down on the terrain with a satisfying crunch, the landing gear pressing against the hard ice and snow underneath. The crunching of snow, programmed into a game. I can't help but smile. Those little details always get me.

I take a quick look at the display and note that the air is breathable and doesn't require any kind of helmet or mask, which is great, considering we might have some new players in the Armada who haven't explored or scavenged enough to buy the needed gear. I push a few buttons, and the cockpit opens with a hiss.

I'm immediately overwhelmed by the intense wind pummeling me from outside. I push against it as I climb out, the roaring loud and breaking apart my signal to the Armada. When I reach the ground, I turn to see several cockpits open and my people wrestling with the same issues, their avatars all looking fairly similar to mine, save for custom-colored outfits and little changes to their gaits and facial appearances. Customization isn't huge in *Reclaim the Sun* for the pilots, which makes for a massive army of people all looking somewhat the same. You can certainly dedicate an hour or two to making your character look more like you, but I seldom find anyone who has the time or patience for that.

Mine... She's close, but different enough that no one would look at the avatar and me and think we're the same person. Not that it really matters, anyway. I have a Glitch stream— you can see my face on video. Not much to hide.

"Sorry, you guys!" I shout over the wind, which dies down a little bit, then picks up again, shifting back and forth in loud blasts, sweeping bits of snow and frost with it. Players and their avatars are sliding across the white ground, bodies pressing against their ships. I turn to look up at the mountains and notice bits of green hidden among the white and beige. Maybe all the life on this planet isn't just underwater.

I glance over at the other players and give them an encouraging wave, one of the few physical gestures you can do in this game. All of them wave back simultaneously, the movements identical, and unintentionally hilarious coming from a hundred-plus people at once. I hear a bunch of people laughing in my headset, including Rebekah, who is currently walking right next to me.

I'm not sure it'll ever not be weird, having her as a second camera. It's not like her in-game character can carry an actual video camera or something, so she walks facing me, to pick me up for the second video from her character's perspective, which is streaming off her actual screen. It's like having a friend who won't stop staring at you the entire time you're out together, no matter what you're doing. Watching a movie? Looking at you. Walking down the street? Eyes all on you.

"Can you like, get some video of the mountains?" I ask, turning to look at her.

She wiggles her body right to left, like that's a good way of saying no instead of talking to me through her headset, and keeps her eyes on me. We could just use the in-game recording system to capture stuff, but Rebekah insists it looks better like this. More like an action movie.

"You're so weird," I say, looking back at the Armada. A few ships are still landing, but if we waited for absolutely everyone, the streams would take several hours instead of just one or two, and we'd never get anywhere.

"Let's go see what's hidden in those—"

The loud thundering of ship engines interrupts me as several vessels tear across the sky from behind the mountains, slowing to hover above me and the rest of the Armada. Rebekah directs her gaze away from me and up at them, and then her voice chimes into my headset.

"Whoa, these guys aren't registered in the Armada. What are the chances of someone else showing up on this planet at the exact same time?" she asks excitedly. "This is good footage. *Really* good. We can send this to the blogs. You should try to connect to them, see where they're from."

Behind me, I hear the members of our Armada talking among themselves, voices from all over the world trying to figure out who our guests are, and echoing Rebekah's words about how weird it is for them to be here, right now, out of all the trillions of planets across the digital galaxy.

"Hey!" I shout into my headset, waving at the ships. I offer to open a channel with them, sending a request over. "Open a private channel!"

There's a soft buzzing sound, followed by a number of sharp clicks, like something snapping into place.

I know that sound.

"Oh." I hear Rebekah in my headset. "Oh no."

Blaster fire hammers down on the planet's surface, lighting up the ground, taking out ships and avatars all around me. An explosion erupts just a few feet away, and I throw myself to the side, the flying debris missing me by mere inches.

The bastards are *firing* on us.

Rage wars with disbelief as I climb shakily to my feet. The rest of the Armada is scattering all around me, clamoring back to their ships.

"What the hell is this?!" I shout, sprinting toward my ship, joining the rest of my Armada in the scramble for safety. The blasters of the dozen or so ships above us pummel the icy terrain, breaking holes in the ice. I suck in an angry breath as several of my people are vaporized by the blasts, while still more flail about in the frozen ocean. Rebekah is still running by my side, though at least she's looking ahead and not at me, her avatar capturing the carnage all around us.

"Rebekah, who—" Blaster fire takes out more of the ice around me, and I'm forced to veer off course to avoid plunging into the freezing water.

"The social fee— are explo— over —ere!" Rebekah shouts, the latency making her voice break up. There's way too much going on, too much incoming and outgoing data for her crappy Internet connection to handle. I spare a glance at her video feed in the corner of my screen. The image is choppy, but I can make out her face, harried and stressed, as she looks from the game to a tablet she's now got propped up next to her.

"It's some o— the trolls —ave been going off on—"

She cuts out completely. Her avatar comes to a standstill on the ice and is promptly blasted away, along with the ship she's worked so hard on.

People are screaming as they run by me, intent on reaching their ships, but for a moment, I find myself unable to move.

Rebekah is gone. I'm alone.

Because when you die in *Reclaim the Sun*, you die in real life—

Okay, no, that doesn't happen, just kidding. This isn't *Tron* or something.

But when you die in the game, you *do* lose all your stuff. Which is almost as bad. You'll respawn someplace in the universe with a basic ship and blank avatar. Your former body and the ship you likely spent however many hours customizing and upgrading are left behind, potentially across the cosmos, waiting to be collected and scavenged by anyone lucky enough to stumble on the wreckage first...or by the jerks who shot you down.

And as the people in my Armada fall around me, I can practically hear the cackling of the people shooting at us, eager to reap their spoils.

Actually.

I do hear it.

They *are* laughing.

I want to scream at them, curse, shoot at them with the little blaster in my inventory bag. But my small gun won't do anything against an entire fleet of ships, and probably wouldn't even damage one in all this madness.

So I flee with the others, intent on reaching my ship. It's there, just up ahead. If I can get inside, I can jettison off, maybe get away, maybe save my vessel. Otherwise, I'll be starting all over again.

The paint. The small upgrades that make it pilot a bit better. The scanners that help me detect faraway planets. And all the stuff in my inventory—the weapons and the gadgets that help me navigate on the ground. The boosters that make running across terrain easier, giving me a little extra speed. And there's the mini jets in my pack that help me jump just a tiny bit higher. Not a huge advantage. But just enough.

And hopefully just enough to get away.

Dozens of ships are taking to the sky, the Armada blasting off. I watch two get shot down and explode in a massive fireball across the bright white sky, while others warp out, several sonic booms thundering in the wind. Elation at their escape wars with the soul-crushing disappointment and rage I feel for those who have not been so fortunate today.

All these players. All this effort. Wasted.

I wish logging out was as simple as just turning off the computer or console. Pulling the plug. But the developers thought of that when creating the game, kindly leaving you active for a few minutes in case it was an accidental disconnect.

Plenty of time for someone attacking you to finish the job. Like they did to Rebekah.

The cockpit window of my ship opens, the glass rising high as I get closer, another little upgrade I paid handsomely for. Well, paid for using in-game currency from running missions and discovering things. Not actual money. But paid for with something far more precious than funds.

My time.

The more you play, the more experience points you get, and the more stuff you can purchase with said points. But when those things are lost or destroyed…there's no just buying them back. You have to go back to the grind, leveling up more and more to get that stuff all over again. Doing menial tasks, like fighting alien monsters or cataloging plants or discovering small planets.

Just as I move to hoist myself into my ship, the blaster fire begins to die down. And then I realize it's not dying down just a little—the attack has ceased completely. I pause, turning to look at the enemy ships, the players that came to take out all my people. They're just…sitting there, floating in the air, ominous and silent. No laughter, no talking. They must have switched to a private chat channel.

"Divya!" My headset explodes with Rebekah's voice, and I see her reappear in the small video window on my screen. "I got disconnected. Lost all my stuff, damn it."

I glare up at the sky, at our attackers. There are at least a dozen of them, all painted the same colors. All on the same team, the same clan. The ships are a solid white and would almost disappear against the clouded sky and snowcapped mountains if not for the angry red zigzag pattern tearing through the sides of the vessels, like claw marks across skin.

"Why don't you come down here and face me?!" I shout, wondering where the hell my entire Armada went. There were hundreds of us making our way to that mountain. I get them running back to their ships, as one direct shot from a blaster would take you out. And trying to get away from the crumbling environment, sure. But now that there's this odd cease-fire…why was no one coming back to help me?

What's the point of all this if no one has my back?

"Man, fuck this bitch," a voice suddenly shouts out. A guy, his voice masked by something that makes him sound like a deep-voiced robot.

"Dude, don't!" another one yells, his voice unhidden, soft and young, like a kid in junior high, maybe. "We need her in the ship!"

"We need her off the streams," the deeper voice growls. "It doesn't matter how we do it."

"It'll look cooler if we—" Yet another new voice; another male.

"I'm not waiting any longer," the masked voice says.

The blaster fire hammers down from a single ship, which swoops in low toward me, the plasma weapons battering the ground around me. I hear his blasters hitting my ship, loud against the steel chassis. Warning alarms sound in my headset as lights flash red, and I dash away before—

The ship explodes.

Flames of red and orange billow up from the snowy white ground, and a plume of black smoke pools into the clear sky. The explosion echoes across the frozen tundra, and the ice beneath me starts to crack and splinter. I glance down at my feet, wondering if I can make it back to the mountains, just as the ice splits open, giving way to an ocean of water tinted blue and green and purple.

I plunge in, my vision fading.

"Bye, bitch," I hear the deep masked voice snarl, a thick chuckle following.

Then everything goes black, and the *Reclaim the Sun* title screen comes back up, inviting me to start all over again.

"Fuck!" I shout, slamming my hands against the keyboard.

"And…the stream is over," Rebekah announces, her voice coming in crystal clear. She's in her little video screen box, no chop or lag or anything holding her back now that the chaos is finished.

"What was that? *Who* was that?!" I demand, raking my hands through my hair in frustration. "My ship. All my upgrades. Where the hell was the rest of the Armada when I needed them? Goddamn it, that's going to take me weeks to build back up."

"We'll figure it out," Rebekah says, trying to calm me down. "But as for who… Some army of trolls calling themselves the Vox Populi, per the social feeds. They're…" She clears her throat. "They're celebrating. There's already a GIF of your ship blowing up and you falling through the ice."

"Do I want to see it?" I ask, dread already creeping up my spine at the very thought.

"I sure wouldn't," she counters. "I mean, it's just a digital version of you, but still. It'll hurt. But I know you're going to look anyway, so why are we even having this conversation?" She sighs loudly into the headset. "I know this isn't going to make it sting any less, but that stream, everything that happened… Once I'm done processing the live footage into a recap video to upload tonight… I mean, it's going to be really gripping. Viral content on our hands here, Div."

"Yeah, probably," I say glumly.

I can think of a lot of other ways I'd like to see myself go viral, though. In a video for something I'm *proud* of. Some kind of grand accomplishment, instead of going down in pixelated flames, at the hands of a bunch of Internet trolls. A joke.

"A couple game sites are already posting about what happened on their socials, and a few microblogs are linking to some collected social posts," she continues, and I can see her typing away furiously. "Damn, I gotta get ahead of this thing and finish compiling the video. Sucks, Div, I know, but we're gonna get a lot of traffic here. And that does mean more revenue, potentially."

"Right, right." I know Rebekah's trying to get me to see the silver lining, but all I can think about is the staggering amount of time it'll take to level back up. To where I was, playing since launch? Weeks.

Will people stick around to watch me trying to rebuild? Will I lose subscribers?

I think about the rent check.

And I hate that being able to help my mom is so goddamn dependent on my subscriber count.

"Keep your head up," she says. "And hey, it's still early. You can probably dive in for a bit tonight and start upgrading."

"This is true," I admit, stretching in my chair. "Shoot me a text when the video is up, so I can post about it without having to watch the damn thing."

"Without—"

I cut her off. "I'm not about to relive my own destruction all over again and listen to those toolbags talk about me like that twice over. Just…find a way to make this waking nightmare look good?"

"Deal."

Rebekah signs off, her little video window going blank, and I spin in my computer chair for a couple of rotations, looking around my room, coming back to reality. Rocketing back, even. While all that chaos was going on in the virtual world, in literal digital space, I was just here. In my room. My tiny room, with my bare furniture and lackluster…well, everything.

I pull my smartphone out of my pocket, another sponsored gadget that's way nicer than anything I'd be able to afford— one of the few things I've allowed myself to keep—and load up my email. The new watch sponsorship offer is in there, and an absolutely mind-boggling number of interview requests regarding what just happened literally five minutes ago. *Polygon. Engadget. Giant Bomb.* The list goes on. And my social media notifications are insane—the ones I allow myself to be emailed, anyway. Direct message alerts and the like. People sending love, people sending support, people sending—

I stop scrolling, staring at one email subject that stands out among the rest.

Rebekah Cole	FWD: Sponsorship opportunity with Samsung	8:30 p.m.
The Vox Populi	This is just the beginning...	8:28 p.m.
H. Siddiqui	Sponsoring a new VR set?	8:12 p.m.
Polygon Digest	PlayStation Deals This Week & More	7:43 p.m.
ManaPunk Newsletter	Sign up for the open beta of Knights...	7:40 p.m.

The trolls. That clan. They *emailed* me.

I think about deleting it. That's been our strategy since Rebekah and I first started streaming last year. Any contact with trolls was always filtered through her. She even has access to my personal inbox to avoid situations like this one. I should just leave it there for her to tackle later, or better yet, delete the email myself so she has one less thing to deal with.

But their clan name. I know what it means.

The Vox Populi.

The popular opinion.

Man. Fuck these guys.

I give it a click.

[INBOX]
(15 minutes ago)

This is just the beginning...
The Vox Populi [[legion@thevoxpopuli.net>

to me

We cannot be stopped. Strike us down, and more will rise. Report us, ban us, and more will take our place.

People like you have no place in our world. This isn't about gender or race. It's actually about talent in the streaming community, and you're taking up space for those far more deserving.

Leave. You aren't welcome here.

The Vox Populi

That line. That fucking "actually" line. That makes me scowl at it even more. It isn't about gender or race, huh? That's enough to tell me that it *is* about that. It's the "I'm not racist but—" of passive-aggressive conversation.

There's an attachment, too. The file's named Warning.jpg. Gmail's usual scan for viruses comes up blank, and when the small thumbnail loads up in the window, it looks...strangely familiar. My heart races as I click it.

It opens.

And I see a photograph of my apartment building.

My breath catches in my throat. *How?*

How could this have happened?

I've been so careful. I never use my real last name. The location and hometown on my social media accounts is "The Internet." My personal accounts are just that—personal. My Facebook, Instagram...all locked down to just my real friends, few that there are, and family.

My heart is pounding so hard that I can feel it in my temples, thrumming in my ears.

I inhale sharply, bolt to the window in my living room, and cautiously peer out the blinds, just a crack through the thin, cheap plastic. It takes me a minute to remember the picture in the email was of my building in the daytime, and right now, the sun is gone.

They'd already been here.

And who knows when.

I hustle back to my desk and close out the email, placing my hands on the surface. I take a deep breath, several of them, trying to calm down. Anxiety churns through me, the muscles in my back tensing up.

They aren't saying it directly, but this is a threat. A doxing threat. To reveal where I live. To set me up to be attacked. To be stalked. To be harassed in person. It's one of those moments when you can't say, "It's just the Internet," and wait for it to go away. A viral tweet that people share, a photo that gets too much attention...

This is real. And so are the consequences.

I glance up at my computer screen, reopen my email, and forward their message to *Reclaim the Sun*'s harassment support team. The people over there must have a file for me by now, but this...this one is different. This isn't just a hateful email. Or a racist or sexually explicit tweet or message on the game's server. It's the first step in doxing. They know my address. They know where I live. They could blast it out to the whole of the Internet.

I move to forward the email to Rebekah as well, then stop. I can't let her see this. I can't do that to her. Not after what happened to her last year.

Not after *him*.

Instead, I archive it and click over to my social feeds, to see if the Vox Populi has followed through on their threat, but I don't see anyone posting details about where I live or pictures of my building.

Not yet.

The crushing anxiety in my chest feels like it's set to collapse my body inside itself, like a star gone supernova. Knowing that something *might* happen, and waiting for the axe to fall, is almost worse than it happening.

I click away and open *Reclaim the Sun* again, the loading screen waiting for me. After briefly closing my eyes in resignation, I hit start and find myself back at the beginning, at a space station, a few basic ships available to acquire. No upgrades, no paint jobs, no anything. My inventory is empty. My body and gear are at the bottom of a nameless sea on a planet across the digital universe.

Assholes.

But I refuse to be made afraid. I've got work to do.

4
AARON

ACT 2 (FOREST, EVENING)
[Transition seamlessly to Cut Scene]

The party stands around a campfire in the wilderness, warming themselves by the flames. The trees are silhouettes, dark and ominous, and a few pairs of yellow eyes can be seen peering out from the brush.

MAGE
If we don't reach the bandit captain's settlement at the end of The Dark Highway by sundown, they're going to kill the Elvish Queen.

The MAGE waves their hands, and a purple haze materializes. In the foggy clouds, a vision of the Elvish Queen, Randielle, can be seen by the entire party. Randielle struggles against her binds, spitting in the face of an unknown bandit warrior.

ROGUE
I don't see why *those people* won't just pay the ransom. It could all be over so quickly.

The ELF takes an enraged step forward, shifting around the fire, and draws two daggers that glimmer in the firelight.

ELF
What do you mean, those people?

ROGUE
Whoa, now, I didn't mean—

"Aaron!"

I look up from my laptop, just in time to catch the Mana-Punk crew pulling up some seats. The café is a hodgepodge of miscellaneous furniture, enormous plush sofas with intricate carved wooden frames next to postmodern steel bar stools and tall tables. The team pulls up several wooden chairs, each a different bright color, each clashing against the other, squeaking loudly on the hardwood floor of LaVa. It's my favorite spot to write—close enough that I can walk or bike, and not too crowded with tourists, being at the north end of South Street.

The roar of a coffee grinder whirs to life while Jason, Laura, and Ryan get settled, the smell of roasted coffee grounds wafting through the air, thick and sweet, blending in with the aroma of Mediterranean food. During the day, the place mostly does coffee, breakfasts, and light lunches, but for the dinner hour it closes down to café goers and becomes a restaurant.

"How's everything going?" Jason asks. He launched Mana-Punk three years ago, when I was just starting off as a freshman at Central and he was a senior wrestling with serious senioritis, with no time for anything that had to do with our high school. Despite nearly failing out of school, he's now off changing the mobile gaming world—and he's brought a few of us geeks along for the ride.

Laura, who just graduated this year, takes a seat next to Jason, and Ryan snags the chair beside mine. The cushion lets out a loud *whoosh* when he leans back against it, and we all chuckle, Ryan the loudest. He's a year under me, and we've spent most of our lunches this year dreaming up video games or playing them.

Well, our lunches and our entire lives. We've been gaming together since we were in grade school.

"Not bad, working on the—" I start, and promptly stop as Jason stretches. He's got a tattered jean jacket on, covered in punk rock–looking pins of bands he insists we all listen to and often blasts whenever we're working at his small studio space. He threatened to fire me and Ryan when we didn't know who MxPx or Goldfinger was, so now I know their entire respective discographies. But the buttons aren't what's giving me pause—it's his T-shirt. It's ripped all over the place, but not in some stylish way. In a this-is-an-old-T-shirt-and-it's-time-to-throw-it-in-the-garbage kind of way.

"What?" Jason asks, and then looks down at his shirt. He laughs. "Oh, what can you do?"

"You're literally a millionaire," Ryan says before I can, pointing at Jason and his ripped-up T-shirt then glancing back at me, an exasperated look on his face. "Why do you always dress like you've just crawled out of a car accident or something?"

"Whatever, man," he huffs. "People like my style."

"What people?" Laura asks, smirking.

"There…there are people!" Jason argues, but he fusses with a few buttons on his jean jacket, closing off the view of the torn fabric and grumbling under his breath. "Focusing on clothes and all that crap takes away from my creative process, okay? I have games to make. I have a vision. Physical aesthetics just get in my way and take up brainpower I could be using for—"

Ryan, Laura, and I just stare at him.

"What? Mark Zuckerberg does the same thing."

I give Ryan a look, and Laura purses her lips, eyes bright with amusement.

"Man, fuck you guys, it was laundry day," Jason admits, and all of us burst into laughter. I feel the pressure from my mom washing away a little in moments like these, with the ManaPunk gang, away from the suffocating atmosphere of my house. Jason pushes the three of us to create what we care about: me, with my scripts; Ryan, with his gorgeous illustrations and storyboards; and Laura, with her coding, hammering away on her keyboard in a language I could never hope to understand, like she's speaking right to the computer's soul.

Jason shakes his head and gets up from the table. "What do you guys want?" he asks. "I'm buying."

"Yeah, you are," Ryan says with a smirk. "We're still waiting to be paid, you know."

"It's coming, it's coming." Jason waves him off and catches my side-eye. "Don't give me that look. I'm working on it."

"Black coffee for me," Laura cuts in.

"She likes her coffee like she likes herself—bitter," Ryan quips, smiling across the table.

"False. Dark and strong," Laura claps back. "And don't compare me to food. Isn't your best friend a writer? That's cliché as hell."

"Point goes to Laura," I say.

"Always does." She grins. "Grab me a plain muffin, too, or lemon. Surprise me."

"And surprise me with a check," Ryan says, tilting his head and drumming his fingers on the table. When Jason scowls at him, he adds, "Though some tea and a blueberry scone wouldn't go amiss, either."

"Always grumbling about money. Isn't your dad a lawyer?" Laura huffs and looks at her nails. "You'll be fine."

"That's not the point," Ryan snaps. "And you know it."

"So, um… I'll get a hot chocolate?" I venture. Ryan turns and glares at me, and I shrug, the tension diffusing as Jason heads toward the counter. I'm just as irritated, but I just need this to be…*this*. Us, making games, not worrying about what my mother can't stop stressing over.

Jason is going to do right by us. I just know it.

Ryan sucks air through his teeth as we all pull out our smartphones, gearing up for my favorite part of these meet-ups of ours.

Every week, we try to find the absolute worst game we can in our respective app stores, me and Ryan the die-hard Apple iOS users, Laura and Jason unstoppable Android fans. We take screenshots of gameplay, the title, and the like, and download the game to share. Screenshots are key, as the games some-times disappear from the app stores before we meet up. Poorly made titles where the developer has to pull the program, or clones of other games that get shut down directly by Apple or Android… There are plenty of reasons why something might vanish within a week or so.

It's the most ridiculous tradition and rule of every meet-ing, but we'd likely do it even if it wasn't a required team-building, lesson-learning type of thing handed down to us by Jason. It's always good for a laugh, and whoever has the worst game gets to pick our next meetup spot.

I flip to this week's hilarious find, then lean over to try and sneak a peek at Ryan's phone.

"No way!" he says, angling the screen away from me. His blue eyes flash with mischievous glee, and he's smiling so big I can see the snaggle tooth he pretends to hate, but I know he really doesn't. I've overheard several girls talking about it being cute at our school, and his boyfriend, Alberto, always makes it a point to get him to smile as broadly as possible in their selfies.

"My pick this week is way too good," Ryan boasts. "Neither of you stand a chance."

"Hah!" Laura chuckles. "We'll see about that. Mine was buried so far in the app store that I had to downgrade my OS to even install it. I made my phone practically useless for this thing."

"Damn," Ryan says, clearly impressed, his smile fading away. "That's a lot of effort for a not-so-great prize. I guess we'll see."

Last week, I'd won with a terrible *Angry Birds* clone, *Furious Chinchillas*. It looked almost the same as *Angry Birds*, only instead of catapulting the iconic brightly colored birds toward those green piglets, there were these supposed-to-be chinchillas? That flew for some reason? The physics programming in the game was all wrong, and the things either flew off the screen or just didn't go anywhere. It had a single-star rating from thousands of aggregated reviews—clearly from people just downloading it for the sake of novelty—and the game was absolutely riddled with obnoxious advertisements everywhere.

But when you think about it, thousands of people took the time to leave reviews for this game. I read an article once that something like only 3 to 5 percent of users ever leave a review for something, so there are likely tens of thousands more people who also paid a dollar to download this thing. And with all the ad revenue…that chinchilla developer is likely rolling in cash the way chinchillas roll around in dust baths, bad reviews or not.

Jason saunters back over as I get my game loaded up, hiding the screen from my friends. He's carrying a hefty tray with a wide array of muffins, doughnuts, scones, and other various pastries piled all over the place haphazardly, plus several cups of something that doesn't at all resemble tea or hot chocolate.

"What is—" Ryan starts.

"I forgot what all of you said the second I got up there, so I just got a few of everything." Jason shrugs. "Oh, and black coffee. You guys can go put in sugar or whatever."

Ryan grumbles out something and the two of us get up and make our way to the fixing station. We sweeten our coffee to the point where it'll taste like candy, the only way either of us can stand the stuff. Laura stays behind, and as Ryan dumps a ton of cream into his cup, I turn around and see her take a satisfied sip, then lean against Jason's shoulder, looking content.

Ryan bumps my arm playfully just as I finish securing a plastic lid on my coffee.

"You good?" he asks.

"Yeah, yeah," I say.

"She's too old for you, anyway," he says, shrugging. "She's off to college in the fall. And he's a millionaire. Kinda hard to compete with all that."

"Oh God, it's not like that." I laugh and shake my head. I turn to Jason and Laura, who are both fixated on their phones, not even looking at each other. It makes a little piece of me ache inside. If I ever find the right person, that won't be us. I'll be present, the way Ryan and Alberto always are with each other—hanging out on Ryan's porch after school, fussing over their sketch pads together, consistently snuggled up and talking about their dreams and the future. I've seen them in action, like something out of a rom-com, more times than I can remember since they got together two years ago.

I've also seen Jason in action.

When we've gone to conventions. To events. How he goes through girl after girl. Always someone new on his arm, accompanied by looks from people milling around the Mana-Punk table or booth. And I can't bring myself to watch Laura make the same mistake, even if we aren't exactly close. I'm going to have to say *something*—the sooner, the better.

"Alright!" Jason exclaims suddenly, finally putting his phone down on the table. His eyes are wide, and he's got a mischievous smile on his face, the one he wears when he's been up to something. Which he always is. "Who wants to go first? The reigning champion, perhaps?"

I grin and slide my phone across the table, feeling a little rush at Jason's words, despite what I think about his approach to dating. He's still my hero, however flawed, in the gaming space. He's a local icon.

Ryan and Laura place their phones in the center with ours, and the game begins.

The game I've chosen is a nightmare of a thing, and even though I know it's not nearly as good as the chinchilla game, it'll do. You play as a slice of cheese, trying to find a hoagie to live inside. It's some weird, promotional game tied to a chain of delis here in Philadelphia—Ilagan & Weir Hoagies. The animation is terrible and janky, and even when you find the right sandwich, it's almost impossible to get the cheese in there. It's a weird puzzle game that makes almost no sense, and is no doubt extra infuriating to people who live near those delis. Apparently if you win, you get a dollar or two off a sandwich. I wonder how many people have actually won and scored the coupon. Judging from the handful of reviews in the app, probably not many.

I've definitely got Ryan beat, though. He's got some odd platforming game about a sentient piece of candy on a mission to collect a bunch of gems, which looks like *Candy Crush* meets *Super Mario Bros.* It's a little suspect, as if it might have been accidentally released by one of those publishers, unfinished. We spend a few minutes debating that idea, until Laura silences us with a wave of her hand and shows us the game she found.

It's magnificent.

It's one of those gamification creations that attempts to get people to exercise in exchange for points and leveling up a character. The more you work out, the more chores you get done, the more experience you earn, etc. In theory, a wonderful idea. There are a bunch of games like it, and they encourage kids and adults to get outside. But this one uses augmented reality, and gives you things to chase. Bad guys and the like. Sort of like *Pokémon GO*.

Great idea.

Except someone had hacked into the game, and instead of villains to chase, there were…

Well, there's no polite way to say it. There were pictures of penises. Lots of them. Looking as though they were poorly photoshopped over whatever the original graphic was supposed to be.

None of us can stop laughing. Laura holds her phone up so the augmented reality kicks in, and there, in the coffee shop, is a giant penis, waiting for us to chase it away. Tears are streaming down my face, and I spot numerous people in the place staring at us. I try to choke back my laughter, and the four of us slowly calm down.

"Jason?" Laura asks, nodding at his phone, still facedown on the table. "Can you beat that?"

"My dear," Jason begins, and I feel myself exhale as Ryan glances at me, shaking his head "no" quickly. The affection level with these two has very quickly gone from their occasionally weirdly flirty notes to each other—in our group emails and Discord and Slack channels, mind you—to occasionally snuggling up in public and whispering sweet nonsense to each other.

"My pick is nothing compared to that," Jason concludes. "I'm abstaining this round. Victory is yours."

"The Autofocus Café on Thirty-Seventh and Walnut!" Laura exclaims triumphantly, grabbing her phone and raising her hands up in the air, wielding the smartphone like a little sword. Ryan and I groan. Laura is on the completely other side of town, out in University City near Drexel University and Penn—as is that coffee shop, surrounded by expensive stores and boutique restaurants and nowhere to park. And I could live forever without seeing the photography gallery in that shop again, all weird experimental stuff by local college kids I don't understand.

"That's right, deal with it." She leans back in her chair, a victorious smile on her face, and winks at Jason. "Now let's get to work."

"Yes!" Jason exclaims, slapping the table excitedly. "You have new script pages for us, Aaron?" He gestures at me, and I open my computer back up, hitting a couple of keys.

"It should be in the shared Dropbox now," I say, trying to mask the bundle of nerves I feel myself becoming, all their eyes ready to look at what I've been writing. "Load it on up, and let's do a reading."

Everyone around the table grows quiet, and I watch their eyes staring at their glowing screens. Jason is reading on his iPhone, while Laura reads on a tablet she's pulled out of her bag. I glance over at Ryan, who is looking at his phone, thumbing through quickly, and I can tell he's just skimming the pages. He's already read this more times than I can count.

I hear Jason scoff and look up to see him glaring at his screen.

"What is it?" I venture. I know it's a bad idea to ask for feedback in the middle of a reading, but all signs are pointing to him not liking whatever he's scoping out.

"It's just..." His mouth flattens into a thin line. "I don't know, Aaron, does it always have to be some race thing?" He swipes at something and turns the phone to me, highlighting a few lines. It's the moment when the Elf is berating the Rogue for using a microaggression.

"Listen, you can use a fantasy world to discuss bigger issues going on in the real world," I protest. "That's what makes good fantasy, in my opinion. It says something about our world, while exploring a made-up one—"

"Aaron, it's a video game," Jason says, putting his phone down.

"So?" It's my turn to scoff. "Games like *Mass Effect* and *Dragon Age* explore racism, xenophobia... The *Elder Scrolls* series absolutely digs into classism and—"

"It's a *mobile* game." Jason rubs his forehead. "I'm not trying to change the world here. It's something for people to play on long train rides. On the bus. On the toilet. It doesn't have to be art."

"I'm trying to—"

"Exhaust me?" Jason suggests, grinning. "Come on, keep it simple. Let's cut out all this filler—"

"Racism isn't filler!" I exclaim, leaning over on the table. "How can you—"

"Aaron, do you want to write this game or not?" Jason asks, his tone growing cold as he leans back in his chair. "'Cause I need something simple. I'm not trying to alienate my audience with subliminal messages or political statements."

I take a deep breath and look over at Ryan, who shrugs. He's not trying to be unhelpful or unsupportive, I know that. He just knows where this conversation is going—we've been down similar routes before, and we're not going to change his mind here.

"Well?" Jason presses.

"I'll edit it when you cut me a paycheck," I snap.

I can almost feel the air being sucked out of the room, as all of us sit there in silence. After a few tense moments, Jason turns to Ryan, collecting himself.

"Any new drawings?"

The cobblestone streets leading back toward my house feel like they stretch on forever as Ryan and I walk along them in silence. They push into the bottoms of my too-thin sneakers, the curved rocks digging into my feet, in this weird, comforting-but-kinda-painful sort of way.

"Dude, you can't let it get to you," Ryan finally says, breaking the silence we've been strolling in for the past ten minutes. "Especially if this is what you actually want to do with your life. Writing and all, for video games or anywhere, really. Criticism is part of the game, so to speak."

"I don't mind criticism, it's just... I mean, damn, if Jason doesn't want to play games that engage in meaningful conversation, why try to make an RPG?" I ask, mostly to myself. I know the answer. We both do. Money. "He made fun of all the dialogue, and he was so harsh with your storyboards and illustrations, and I just don't—"

Ryan cuts in. "Are you upset over that, or is it Laura?"

"Can't it be a little bit of both?" I ask, offering up a weak smile. He grabs my shoulder and gives me a shake. "I know, I know. I just worry about—"

"Not every woman is a princess who needs saving," Ryan says. "You have to let her make her own decisions."

"I just—"

"Look. Focus on the game. The money will be good, if he ever pays us." Ryan laughs, but there's something hollow to it, and I agree with the feeling. "You can use it for whatever school you want to go to, or maybe for actually buying a real computer instead of that..." He trails off, struggling for a definition. "That *monster* you have in your room. Just think about that. And besides, it's a taste of the real world. People in big ol' corporate video game studios probably aren't going to be nice."

"Yeah, yeah, I know. At least they'll pay us on time, though." Still, I can't stop thinking about Laura. And Jason's harsh words about my writing. And how the two of them just don't belong together.

There's this part of me that absolutely knows Ryan is right, and that this is none of my business. And I hardly even know Laura that well, just from a few interactions at school and our gigs with ManaPunk. But it's just irking at me, and I can't fight it.

"Well, when Jason finally publishes this game and pays up, you'll be too busy spending all that money to worry about other people's relationships," Ryan points out, slowing his pace as we reach the side street leading to his house. "I'd come hang or game, but Alberto is coming by."

"Nice, tell him I said hi," I say. We shake hands and pull each other in for a hug. "I'll see you later, man."

"Sure will," he agrees, then pulls back and smacks me lightly on the shoulder. "In the meantime, be a little less Paragon and a little more Renegade. You're allowed."

With a smirk, Ryan hurries off down his street, whistling to himself. I smile ruefully at the *Mass Effect* joke and continue the walk toward my house, the summer sun still bright and burning. It's edging toward late afternoon, the day still full of so much possibility, but really, only one thing is on my mind.

Video games.

And that potential money from Jason and ManaPunk.

The check that is supposedly coming, both in the future, and the one he already owes us.

Last year, we made a little bit working for Jason. Nothing crazy, but it was enough to pay to upgrade my gaming rig with gear not found in the neighbors' trash or at local flea markets. Jason and ManaPunk as a company, though? He'd made so much money. And I know we're not going to get much for the work we've done lately—I'd only done some co-pyediting for his latest game, this puzzler where you have to match different-colored shapes to the pulse of music. Writing things like the instructions, tutorial text, stuff like that. And Ryan had only worked on a couple of vector graphics, but still. It felt like we deserved more. A bigger cut of the profits or something, you know?

But this role-playing game, the one he seems to hate so much, has the potential to net us so much more. Because Jason hadn't just agreed to pay us a fair wage this time—he'd promised us a share of the profits.

And maybe, just maybe, if the game does well—hell, if it sells even *kinda* well—I'll be able to pay to go to whatever college I want. Far away, maybe. Not someplace that my mom makes me apply to. Not a place where I'll have to be a doctor or whatever dream it is she's got plotted out for me. It's a plan I kick around with Ryan all the time. Philadelphia has some great colleges; I've gone to enough events at Drexel, Penn, and Temple to know that. But there's no way I'll be able to afford any of those places without taking out a staggering number of student loans. A straight-A scholarship student I am not.

Jason said it was possible. Laura, too. Still, the idea of pulling in…what, over six figures? From my little slice of what the game makes? It doesn't feel that realistic.

But earning a little bit to get myself started making my own games…that feels more possible. I don't even need to make that much, comparatively speaking, to what Jason ends up netting with his games. Give me like, $10,000. I could buy a proper computer to develop my own games on, not something cobbled together. I could invest in the software and add on effects I'd need, in something like Unity. Work on my own studio while readying myself for graduation. Have a backup plan.

My house appears, waiting down the street, the little side office of my mother's private practice sticking out of our home like an unwanted redbrick growth. It's a strange effect, the old historic Philadelphia brownstone exterior, with the ivy that's probably older than I am and the bricks that most certainly are by a couple hundred years, contrasted with the inside, the doctor's office part of the place. Without Mom's sign, you'd never know that a sterile waiting nook and patient rooms lay tucked away beneath the warm bricks and dark green vines.

If I became a doctor like she wanted, maybe I could surgically remove it.

But I'd rather make video games. Make a digital version of that house. And that little side building. And maybe blow it up with a laser cannon. Or a dragon. Anything, other than sitting in there looking at papers and checking in patients.

I look at the time on my phone and sneak a quick peek inside the front window, and see Dad talking to someone. Whoever the patient is, it's not going well, and Dad is shaking his head, looking down, while this person is clearly flipping out. I can hear the muffled shouting all the way out here, and I hurry around to the office's side entrance to see what I can do to rescue Dad.

I walk in and close the door a little harder than necessary behind me. The patient turns around, his expression full of irritation. I don't recognize the man, and he narrows his eyes at me as I walk past him toward my dad. In the faded fluorescent lights of the waiting room, Dad looks a lot older than Mom does, even though he's barely two years older. Thick lines are worn into the corners of his eyes, giving him a perpetually tired look.

He doesn't talk much about the years before he met my mom. When he does, it's often with rue and regret, talking about this bad retail job or that, gigs he'd taken over the years since moving to America, struggling to save money to send back home. Sometimes he'd joke about how all those places and jobs had aged him prematurely, and I could see it, every single time, in the eyes of a man who was only in his forties but looked like he was nearing sixty years old.

Those weary eyes meet mine, and I move behind the desk to stand beside him. "Why don't you go on break?" I suggest.

"Oh good. Someone who speaks English," the man spits.

My blood turns to fire in my veins, furious heat warming me all over as I inhale sharply and clench my teeth. How *dare* he. Never mind the fact that my father speaks perfect English, but for the man to insult him, my family, in our home?

My dad gives me a look before I can tear into this guy. "Aaron, it is fine," he says, but I can tell that it isn't. Whenever Dad gets harried and upset, his accent comes thundering back, way thicker than it usually is. I've seen this happen with Jason sometimes, when he gets all worked up, only his accent is more South Philadelphia, saying "water" like "wudder" and whatnot. And on top of that, my father sounds exhausted.

"Your mom will be back any minute," he insists. "You have your games. It's the weekend. Go work on your—"

"Are one of you going to get me my damn prescription, or should I come back when the actual doctor is here?!" the man growls.

I turn my head to stare at the man. He's older, white and bald with thick jowls that seem to quiver a little as he eyes me in return.

"Is this your first time here?" I ask, crossing my arms.

"Yes, I was referred by—" he starts.

I cut him off. "You're aware that the *actual doctor* is my mother, right?"

"Aaron," my dad says, a subtle warning tone in his voice.

I ignore it, continuing to address the patient. "And did you also know that the man you're currently berating is her husband?" I glance back at my dad, who looks away, fixing his gaze on the computer screen. "My father?"

The man's eyes narrow, his mouth a thin line, like he's trying to think of something not awful to say, and it's breaking his fragile racist mind.

"Dad," I say gently, speaking to my father while still glaring at the man. The patient looks away, exhaling heavily. He knows he fucked up. "Go ahead. I'll take care of all this."

Dad gets up from his seat, groaning a little. I swear I hear his back crack as he stands upright, and his hand pats my shoulder. It's moments like this that make me think maybe I should give up the gaming thing, become a doctor, just so I can get him out of here.

"See you at dinner," he says, giving my shoulder a quick squeeze without looking at me or the man in the office. He makes his way through the door that leads into our house, and I sit down at his desk, hitting a couple keys on the keyboard to get the ridiculously old computer going. It makes no sense that we have this thing, a relic of who knows when, but Mom and Dad are both stubborn. We'll replace it when it breaks, they say.

The screen lights up, and I'm taken aback by what's on it. It looks like some kind of...video game? There's a wizard-looking person on the left-hand side, and in the center the avatar is in some kind of a tavern. But the scene is shown from above, letting you see through the walls, in this old-school isometric view.

I shake the mouse, but nothing happens. I tap on the keyboard. Again nothing. Whatever it is, it's frozen.

"Just a minute," I mumble to the patient, who is practically burning holes in me with his stare.

There are some names in light blue and others in yellow above the different frozen characters. But the one that catches my eye is the one in the center, surrounded by a bunch of other avatars.

Souschef the Bold.

Sous-chef? I squint at the name and suppress the urge to laugh. Totally sounds like something Dad would make up for himself if he was a gamer. I give the mouse a final shake before discreetly pulling my phone out and taking a picture of the screen, making a mental note to do some digging later.

Turning the computer off and on again, I clear my throat and say, "Sorry, looks like our system froze up. It'll take just a minute to reload."

The man grunts in response. While we both wait, I adjust a photo of my parents on the desk—young, pre-me, Dad still looking older, Mom looking much the same as she does now, blessed with genes that make her seem eternally ageless.

The computer finally finishes booting up, and I exhale with relief. "Now," I say, "how can I help you?"

As the man rattles off his requests, I can't help but let my mind wander. The money might not be here to take me where I want to go. Away from this office. Away from people like this man standing in front of me. No. Not yet. But there's a game upstairs in my room that certainly can.

(RE)BEKAH: You ready yet? We could do some streaming today.

ME: Not even a little. My new ship is as basic as a pumpkin spice latte.

(RE)BEKAH: How dare you. You know I'm counting down the days until fall.

ME: ♥

ME: How's your new ship looking? Pick a bookish name yet?

(RE)BEKAH: Eh, getting there.

(RE)BEKAH: And yes, the Savage Song.

ME: Awesome.

(RE)BEKAH: Well, let me know when you're done leveling and resource grinding. Or if you go exploring.

ME: I'm not terribly eager to see myself get blown up live again.

(RE)BEKAH: Noted. Can't hide forever though, D1V. Your fans are waiting.

My new ship is devastating.

Not in the way that I want it to be, either.

No, a devastating ship in *Reclaim the Sun* would be as sleek and beautiful as it is fast and deadly, but right now, my ship is just emotionally devastating. Even after tons of grinding the other night—running quest missions, blowing up asteroids, clearing out space trash around my pilot's assigned home planet—I've barely got enough credits for a new paint job. Forget improved blasters or faster warp travel or advanced sensors or anything even remotely helpful.

It would have been easier to level up and get more supplies if I hadn't spent the past few days answering emails galore regarding what happened in the attack during my last stream. Feels like every damn video game outlet has reached out, a majority asking the same questions again and again:

Why do you think it happened?

Is it because you're a female in the gaming community?

Does it have to do with race?

Are you going to give up?

What are your plans for your appearance at New York GamesCon—

I curse to myself, resisting the urge to kick my ship as it sits in my space dock. Not that I actually could kick it, anyway. A large window maws open at the end of the dock, with impossibly infinite space waiting outside. So much to explore, and so much work to do.

I thought video games were supposed to be fun.

I glance at my ship again, scowl, then load up my on-screen menu. The option to name my vessel appears, and blank spaces meant for letters dot their way across the side of the ship, waiting for me to put something in there.

Damn it, the *Golden Titan* was such a good name. Such a good ship. Renaming it the *Golden Titan II* or something seems ridiculous. *2 Golden 2 Titan*? *Golden Titan: The Titaning*?

The name of the clan that attacked me springs to mind. The Vox Populi. Popular opinion, voice of the people, my ass. And *Latin*? Assholes probably played through *Assassin's Creed* one too many times and think they know their stuff.

And if they were real gamers, they'd know about the Vox Populi in *BioShock Infinite*. Underground rebels who fight for equality and social justice. Daisy Fitzroy would be furious.

I can play the Latin phrase game, too, trolls.

I type a name out, the letters appearing on the screen.

What would you like to name your ship?
CEDERE NESCIO
Are you sure you want to name this ship
CEDERE NESCIO?
Once a name is chosen it cannot be changed.
[YES] [NO]

I practically smash the yes button.
I know not how to yield.
Damn right.

The Latin words sear themselves onto the side of my vessel, the game rendering it in black against the golden hue of the ship. I turn away from my computer screen to grab my VR headset, since I'm going into the game solo. I slide it on, securing the straps, the soft foam plastic along the edges fitting snuggly against my face, cushioned like a pillow. I blink a few times to adjust to the lens as the world of *Reclaim the Sun* renders in, and the sounds fill the stereo speakers inside. I fumble a little for my controllers, two sticks with triggers for my fingers and directional pads on top for my thumbs, then settle back into my chair.

I look around the hangar, at all the details. The paint, the rivets in the steel, the expanse of space waiting for me. This is the way *Reclaim the Sun* was meant to be played. It's like no other game out there, and so easy to get lost in.

I open the cockpit and climb aboard. The control panel inside the ship is plain, nothing as fancy as the one I used to have. The digital displays are gone, replaced with dials and gauges, as though steampunk exists in space or something. It's disappointing to look at, even more so in VR, the letdown of it all right up close in my face. But I get it. The game is trying to make it look as basic as possible, which I get. It's how the studio makes money, encouraging gamers to spend money on fancy upgrades. Or, in my case, time.

I reach out and press a button, and the engine fires up, a soft hum emanating from it as the ship hovers in the air and glides out of the space dock into the black sky and shimmering stars. Flying normally delights me, especially in VR, but the sound of the chassis rattling and the ponderous pace of the ship utterly spoils the experience.

It's so slow. So very slow.

I turn around and watch my assigned home planet and the space dock gradually disappearing behind me. With my old ship, both would have been long gone by now. A distant thought. Barely a glimmer in the background. I grit my teeth and clench my fists, feeling my real hands tighten on the VR controller sticks as my virtual fingers grip the flight controls in the game in front of me. At least with the headset on it feels like I can physically let loose my frustrations in real time, as opposed to just angrily shaking my mouse.

I lean back in my chair and look at my watch. The VR headset registers my real-world smartwatch, thanks to some neat features in the game and a couple of plug-ins courtesy of Samsung. I tap the digital version of the watch, and the tiny screen grows larger, taking up half my vision. A handful of emails have come in since I turned on the computer, and my social feed is still abuzz with everything that went down in the last stream. Blogs and media outlets keep linking to articles about what happened, too, all being oh-so kind as to include my name in the links and tweets.

Great. Now more people can find me.

For every like, six dozen awesome fans commenting with their support, there's some douchebag hanging out with no profile photo and a gusher of racist, sexist bullshit at the ready. At least it's just my gamertag and my social media handles out there, and not my real name. I've been very careful about that. Deliveries of any sponsored material get shipped to the local library or to Rebekah's dorm, and are always addressed to D1V, not the real-life Divya Sharma.

Something beeps, drawing my attention back to the game. With a wave of my hand, I swipe away the digital display from my smartwatch and scan the control panel before me. The sonar is picking up a little something, off to the left of where my ship is aimlessly traveling. My heart flutters excitedly, and I shift course slightly, straining to make out more details.

There, in the distance—a discolored star among all the white spots in the dark.

A planet.

I lean forward in my chair, as though that will somehow make the ship go faster, and watch with anticipation as the off-color speck slowly grows bigger and bigger, shifting from a pale reddish hue in the distance to a beaming, burning orange as it gets closer. If I was in my old ship, I would have been there by now, and the tediousness of traveling at this crawl is killing me. For a moment, I'm ready to rage-quit the game, thinking that it targeted a star and confused it for a planet for some reason. But then the planet finally registers, and a light orange display appears on the windshield of my cockpit.

CLASS ONE PLANET [ESTIMATED]
Status: Uncharted, Undiscovered
Detectable Resources: Ore
Life Support Capability: Positive
Would you like to claim and name this planet?
[YES] [NO]

I drop my head into my hands and groan. A Class One. Hoo-*freaking*-ray. I'd probably find just enough ore to upgrade my ship a smidge, or maybe get some better armor or a new blaster. But likely not much else.

Here's the problem with *Reclaim the Sun*. While upgrading ships and spaceports and weapons is all technically free, from the paint jobs to the boosters, it costs a hell of a lot of in-game currency and experience points. Takes an eternity to upgrade anything. Mine an entire planet? Cool, now you can upgrade your gun to the next level. Oh wow, you harvested all the wood on a continent? Neat, here's a jacket for your character that does absolutely nothing. Shit like that.

It's probably the single biggest criticism that reviewers have been hitting the game with. Sure, you can buy in-game currency with real-world currency and *pay* to get things upgraded. But where's the fun in that? Also, some of us have bills to pay, and I'm not about to drop fifty dollars on a thousand space bucks or whatever.

And for me, all this extra work I now have to do kinda ruins the fun, no matter how much it adds to the so-called story our streamers get to experience. The "narrative," as Rebekah likes to say. Girl gets taken out by a bunch of online trolls and struggles and wrestles her way back to the top, to seek out justice and revenge.

Whatever you say, Rebekah. I'm more interested in seeking out some snacks, and leveling up just enough to get back in the game properly, so I can keep the sponsors interested. Because this? Level grinding and trying to climb back out? This is not super interesting. It's downright boring. Especially since I've already done it once.

I lift my head and survey the prompt again.

Would you like to claim and name this planet?
[YES] [NO]

I reach out and press the glowing Yes on the display in front of me. Immediately, a red light begins flashing, illuminating my cockpit, alarms sounding loudly. I wince and instinctively turn down the volume, but my eyes widen when a new message appears on the display.

Someone is challenging your claim.
Will you contest it?
[YES] [NO]
10...9...8...

"What the…?" I say to myself. I've never seen this before in *Reclaim the Sun*—I didn't even know such a thing was possible in the game. I scramble to start recording whatever it is—Rebekah will definitely kill me if I don't. I want to text her, tell her to turn the stream on or at least check out what's happening, but I'm pretty sure she's in class, and that countdown timer isn't leaving me with many options. Besides, it's not like a lot of people are standing by to potentially tune in. I haven't announced myself or anything. And even if they are, I'm not about to let some trolls come in and ruin this for me.

As my little ship rockets toward the orange planet, I spot another ship coasting a few feet in front of me and off to the side, its colors simple and plain, a silver chassis with no name. Probably a newbie, just getting their feet wet. Then again, I shouldn't make assumptions. From the outside, I probably look like a newb myself.

I debate breaking off and letting them have the planet, because if they are a newb, they could probably use the resources—and if they're a troll, I am in zero condition to battle someone—but I'm just too damn curious about this contested-claim business. I wonder if anyone else has arrived at a planet at the same time yet. With all the trillions of planets in the virtual galaxy, it feels impossible that this is even happening, but it also seems unlikely that I'm the first one to discover this feature.

The sky erupts with a loud *boom* when my ship breaks through the unnamed planet's atmosphere, the other ship right nearby. As the game guides me down toward the surface, the barren landscape comes into focus through the clouds, with long stretches of orange and yellow sand coasting out far and wide, and small dirty beige mountains popping up along the horizon. I catch a few specks of green with what looks like a bit of blue farther out when my ship's landing gear starts to lower, the body of my vessel rumbling as the entire thing slows down and nestles onto the ground with a satisfying *crunch*.

I note that the air is breathable outside, and the cockpit opens with a hiss. A young man steps out of the other ship, and I scramble to do the same, small gusts of wind and dust blowing in my face.

Sand and dirt dance around my visor as I walk swiftly toward him. At first, he seems fixated on something in the distance, but then he looks up and starts spinning about.

"What...what are you doing?" I ask, talking into my headset. I reach down and pull out my blaster, my finger on the trigger.

"Oh!" he exclaims, no longer spinning around. "Damn it." I hear some scuffling, the sharp clap of something falling against a hard surface, then someone giggling and...the sounds of arguing?

He abruptly takes off running toward his ship, and I stare after him, mouth agape. Is he abandoning the challenge for the planet? But no, he keeps running, his body pressing against the side of his ship, legs moving but not going anywhere. The effect is hilarious, and I wonder if his computer is glitching out. Then he stops, turns, and looks at me. He takes out a blaster, his movements slow and awkward. He's got to be playing with a keyboard and mouse.

"Sorry. My little sister jumped on my lap," he explains, his gun aimed at me.

I smile and level my blaster in his direction as well. "Any idea how this works?" I ask, taking a step forward.

"Not a clue," he says cautiously. "I don't suppose I could just let you have this planet, and maybe you'd consider not exploding me and my ride?"

"Perhaps," I venture, but I'm staying ready to fire, just in case he tries anything.

"Or we could split some resources?" I can almost hear the shrug in his voice. "Look, I'm just here to have fun. I'm not really a player versus player kinda guy."

"Yeah, same. Definitely not here for PvP," I agree, though that's far from the truth. I want whatever is on this planet. I want to level up—no, I *need* to level up. I need to get my stream back and running, and I need my player ready to run defense against those assholes, should they come back. And if I'm not streaming, if I'm not engaging with my audience... there are no sponsors. There's no money. And right now, all anyone wants to see is *Reclaim the Sun*, not play-throughs of *Halo* or *Call of Duty* or anything.

And for that, I'm still thinking about shooting him.

He puts away his blaster and raises his arms in surrender. "So...are you going to shoot me, then?" he asks.

I put the gun away.

"Awesome. I'm Aaron."

"Hi," I say.

We stand there, studying each other. He looks like a lot of the other people I've seen up close in the game, save for the fact that he's chosen to make his player's skin brown. He looks a bit like a male version of my player, actually, especially with his dark black hair, but his eyes are a light brown instead of green. There's a thick scar running down his face, from his forehead, across his eye, and down onto his cheek, and I wonder for a moment if he looks the same way in person and what might have happened to him.

"So which way?" he asks, turning around in a circle. I feel the urge to pull out my blaster again at the sight of his back, but shake it off, immediately feeling a bit guilty.

"I saw some green off to the west, I think?" I shrug. "We could get in our ships and hover over there, see what resources are worth scrounging up."

"Great, great," Aaron says. "Why don't you go ahead and claim the planet, and then we'll go see what we can dig up." He chuckles. "Get it, because we're looking for resources—"

"Wow, now you're making me regret NOT shooting you," I say, loading up the menu and typing out a name.

Would you like to claim and name this planet?
[YES][NO]
What would you like to name this planet?
INITIUM NOVUM
Are you sure you want to name this planet
INITIUM NOVUM?
Once a name is chosen it cannot be changed.
[YES] [NO]

A new beginning. I smile and hit enter.

INITIUM NOVUM

Discovered by D1V

I hear Aaron gasp.

"What?" I ask, readying myself, waiting for him to pull out his blaster.

"Your username… Oh. I should have just clicked on you… Oh shit," Aaron stammers, and I whip out my gun, sights right on him. His character takes a few steps back. If he's one of those damn trolls from the Vox Populi, I'm going to blast—

"You said a bad word," I hear a small voice say on the other end of his headset. It must be the little sister he mentioned.

"Sorry, sorry," he murmurs away from his microphone, but I can still hear him. "Don't tell Mom, or she won't let you hang out in here with me."

"Why would you curse—"

"Because we're playing with someone very famous," Aaron whispers.

I shift awkwardly, feeling my cheeks warm beneath my VR headset, though I'm relieved that he doesn't seem to be one of the trolls. I cough slightly, and I hear his microphone rustling as he returns to it.

"Did you, um—" he starts.

"I heard it," I admit, trying not to laugh.

"I, um, I totally watch your stream," Aaron says, and I can hear the nervousness in his voice. It's almost endearing. "None of my friends are going to believe this."

"It's really not that big a deal," I mutter.

"What? Are you kidding?" he says, laughing. "You're a big deal. And I read about what happened, saw those recap videos. I wasn't on that day. Fuck those guys." He grows quiet for a minute, then turns toward his ship. "Look, you can just take the resources. I don't need—"

"No, it's okay," I insist, hurrying after him. "We can split it. Maybe we'll find something good out there. Come on."

I offer up a smile as he turns back around, even though I know he can't see it.

"She sounds nice," the small voice declares from Aaron's side of the headset.

"Shh, oh my God, Mira!" he exclaims, sounding embarrassed.

"Aaron," the voice—Mira—says. She sounds a little farther away, and I squint as I try to listen harder.

"Mira, come on, I'm trying to—"

"Ask her if she's been to Planet Butts."

I can't take it a second longer. I have to mute my mic to hide how hard I'm laughing.

RECLAIM THE SUN: CHAT APPLICATION

AARON: RYAN. RYAN PLEASE BE ONLINE.

AARON: RYAN.

AARON: DUDE.

RYAN: Why are you blowing up the game chat app right now.

RYAN: You have my phone number. You could text me like a human.

RYAN: And no, I'm not online. I'm working on some drawings.

AARON: I AM PLAYING WITH D1V RIGHT NOW.

RYAN: Who is that? And also stop talking in all caps like you're a toddler.

AARON: WHAT?!

RYAN: Stop. Talking. In. All. Caps.

AARON: D1V! The famous Glitch streamer!

RYAN: I don't watch YouTube shows.

AARON: It's not a YouTube show!

AARON: You are killing me right now.

AARON: Okay I gotta go we are exploring the planet.

AARON: I seriously can't believe this is happening.

AARON: I'll tell you all about it later.

RYAN: Please don't.

"Who is that? Who are you talking to?" Mira asks, pointing at the screen as I click the chat window away.

"No one," I say quickly, focusing back on the game.

"And why are you sweating so much?" Mira asks. Face burning, I put my hand over my microphone, like it'll somehow stop D1V from hearing what has clearly already been said.

"I—I'm not sweating," I insist. "It's just a little hot in here."

"No, it isn't. The air conditioner is—"

"Mira, why don't you go play with some of your toys?" I suggest, picking her up off my lap and setting her down next to the computer. She pouts at me. "Please?" I ask desperately. "I just need some unwind time. Aaron time. We'll watch a movie later. Anything you want."

"Yay!" Mira cheers and goes bounding out of the room.

I turn back to the game, and D1V is staring at me. At least her blaster isn't drawn again. A little green icon appears above her head when I move my mouse over her avatar, which means she's using VR. Of course she is. A famous streamer like D1V can totally afford that kind of tech. Hell, sponsors probably give it to her. Maybe one day I'll be lucky enough to find an old headset in a neighbor's trash, but I'm not counting on it.

"Sweating?" she asks, turning around and walking toward the expanse of green in front of us. It only took a few minutes to soar from the place *Reclaim the Sun* had landed us for our supposed challenge, and over to the bit of wilderness we both glimpsed while landing. "Come on now, Aaron."

"Hey, you're a big deal," I say, moving to catch up with her. "You're like, famous!"

"Not that famous, really," D1V says, her voice strangely sad and far away, very different from how she sounds in her streams, all lively and psyched. "So how long have you been playing?"

"All my life," I say, immediately feeling stupid and wishing the ground would open up and devour me. "I mean, er, you mean, *Reclaim the Sun*, this game? Right? Right. Yeah. Um, since the day it came out? I preordered it, got the Day One special edition, even took a day off from school. Just explored all day. Lost a lot of sleep."

"That long?" D1V asks, sounding surprised. "But your ship and your level are—"

"Oh, I get blown up a lot." I laugh. "Upgrading isn't really a priority for me."

"I thought you said you weren't a PvP type of player, though?" D1V continues as we walk, the planet's trees coming into view. They're large, towering green things whose trunks resemble the base of a palm tree, but the canopy and foliage are leafy like a fern. Small leaves and stems, like green feathers.

"I'm not, it's just… Well, me and my friends just aren't terribly serious, I guess?" For someone who's been playing as long as I have, I definitely should have a better ship and accessories and upgrades. I know that. But getting into dogfights in my ship with Ryan, Jason, and Laura is just too tempting, and all too frequent. "I have a few friends I play with a lot, and we tend to just…um, well, blow each other up all the time?"

"Sounds…fun?" D1V says, tone skeptical.

"It is," I press. "It's just a silly game, you know?"

"Ah, sure," she says, and again, there's that sadness in her voice. I feel an odd twinge in my chest, like I should ask what's wrong, why she sounds like she's having a rough time. But I think I already know, what with her public destruction in that Glitch stream and all. It's probably not just a game to her, much like writing the kind of stories I want to write isn't just a game to me.

I wish there was something I could do to help her.

Ryan's advice echoes through my head.

Not everyone needs saving. Or wants it, for that matter.

He's right. It's probably not my place to press. I don't even know her real last name. Where she lives, where she's from. Digging into all that feels like too much. Who am I, after all?

We come to a stop as the strange-looking patch of forest starts to loom overhead, casting D1V, and I suppose myself, in light shadow. She's looking all around, her avatar's head moving this way and that, facing up, glancing side to side, and I can't even imagine what this all looks like in VR. I click away and move with my keyboard as we traverse the landscape. The ground is all littered with patches of green shrub-like plants and a yellow-green moss that crawls over little inclines on the forest floor. Small insects flit by my line of sight, too fast to be seen, and I take a few screenshots to catalog them later and maybe get a better look at what's here. While I might not care about upgrades that much, it's nice to occasionally get them, and keeping track of wildlife in the game is an easy way to get experience points.

The silence between us begins to stretch on a little too long. The ManaPunk crew and I tend to chat up a storm while playing, and the quiet, save for the sound of the breeze and insects in the weird fern forest, is feeling heavy.

"So...what's your life like outside the game?" I venture as D1V steps forward into the woods, her feet crunching against the planet's green surface, the sound crackling in my earpiece. "All I know about you is from the streams, and the articles that are basically *about* the streams, really."

She slows to a halt and seems to hesitate before responding. Did I say something wrong?

"Listen, you seem really nice, Aaron, but..." she starts, then fades off for a moment. "I just don't like to share that kind of information. Please don't be offended," she adds quickly. "It... keeps things a bit safer for me. I mean, you saw."

I think about the videos of those trolls blasting apart her ship and spouting all that hate on social media.

"No, I get it," I tell her, feeling like a jerk for even asking in the first place. "That makes sense."

"Thanks," she says, sounding relieved as she continues walking forward, back to looking around. I hurry to catch up with her, the two of us walking side by side through this uncharted patch of alien forest. "Actually..." D1V stops again. "Speaking of the streams and all, do you mind if I record this?"

"No, go ahead," I say, a bit puzzled. Record?

But...no.

There's no way.

"Good. 'Cause I have been the entire time," she continues, and I can almost hear the smile in her voice as my heart pounds in my chest. Does she mean...for one of her videos?

"You do realize how strange this is, right?" she continues. Something small tumbles through the brush, bits of the
shrubs rustling as it passes, but I can't quite make out what it
is. "Trillions of planets in this place, and you and I find one
at the same time. It'll make for a good video. Especially the
part where it asked us to contest the planet. To fight for it and
whatnot? I wonder if we're the first ones to have that happen.
It feels like something impossible."

I can't wait any longer. I have to ask. I have to know if this
is going where I think it is.

"Wait, I'll get to be in one of your videos?!" I try to hide
my excitement, but epically fail. Just terribly fail. My voice
gets all kinds of high, and I'm sure my face is beet red. I've
never been more grateful for the fact that in-game avatars always keep their cool.

"Yes, and I'll see if I can't cut that excited squeak you just
made from it," D1V says, chuckling. I feel myself blushing
even more.

"Thanks," I say under my breath.

"Maybe the part where you kept running into your ship
can stay, though. Or the part where you were…sweating?"

"Okay, okay, you've made your point," I grumble.

"You picking up anything?" D1V asks, laughter in her
voice, looking around.

"What do you mean?"

"Haven't you been scanning at all?" she asks. "Resources
and all that."

"Oh, er—" I start, and quickly hit a few buttons to load up
my inventory and environment scanner. "Sorry. Like I said,
me and my friends mostly play for fun and get into nonsense.
I took some screenshots to get some points, but yeah. Not a

serious player." I force a laugh, trying not to sound awkward. "In fact, the latest planet I discovered I named—"

"Planet Butts," D1V says deadpan. "I see it in your public profile here. What's Hamtaro?"

"Oh, er, *another* planet my sister named." I can't help but laugh for real this time. I turn to look toward my bedroom door, to see if Mira is lurking over there. She's not. "It's this old cartoon show she likes with hamsters that go on adventures, and it didn't sound like a bad planet name—"

Another one of those unknown creatures rustles by in the green, splitting the foliage as it goes, followed by another and another. I take a few screenshots, hoping to maybe catch up on those experience points.

"That's odd," D1V murmurs, turning to face where the critters are coming from. "Oh. Oh my."

"What—"

I take a few steps forward and follow her gaze.

A large dinosaur-looking monster is lumbering slowly through a small clearing beyond the trees, and whatever the creatures underfoot are, they're definitely hurrying our way from *that* direction. They're running.

You know, because giant monster.

I take some screenshots, imagining something like this will make for a lot of easy points, and D1V moves ahead, clearly captivated by the creature.

"It's amazing," she breathes, and the wonder in her voice genuinely warms my heart. "I know everything in this game is randomly generated, so no one planned that…but isn't that what makes it beautiful? I'm so glad we're capturing this. Rebekah is going to freak."

"Oh yeah, your streaming buddy," I say, watching the monster. It looks like it's trying to eat something, and its body twitches a bit. I'm sure Laura would have some things to say about the coding right now, how the randomly generated parts sometimes lead to creatures that have a hard time moving and all. An odd leg here, some poor coding for an arm there. But listening to D1V's excitement as she talks, I'm glad Laura isn't here to bring us all down with that crushing reality. Getting lost in the magic is nice.

The creature's face resembles that of a mythological dragon, like a beast you might see in *Game of Thrones*, but with a body that's bulky and somewhat elongated. It's low to the ground, with a gait like a rhino, or maybe a hippo—thick and stumpy, but long the way a giant lizard might be. Randomly generated, that's for sure. No way any game designer would ever come up with something as strange as this beast.

"I mean, we're probably the only two people who are ever going to see this particular creature up close," D1V continues. "And here on this planet—"

She takes another step forward.

I hear a branch snap.

The monster's attention immediately fixates on us.

It roars, another randomly generated sound, a bellow that rings out like a mixture of metal being compacted and a dog snarling. It sounds ridiculous coming from the creature, all off pitch, but I don't have time to judge.

I barely have time to blink before it charges at us.

The little creatures in the underbrush catapult into the sky. They're odd, overly plump birdlike things with wings the color of the plants surrounding us. No wonder I couldn't get a good look at them as they fled from the dragon-rhino-snake creature, which I should probably come up with a better name for. They flutter by me, and I pull out my blaster, aiming for the charging beast.

"Don't bother!" D1V shouts. "Run! We need to run!"

"Come on, we can—"

"The one upgrade I have on my blaster shows me the level of monsters. That thing is a thirty-seven!" Her voice is fading as she speaks, and I turn to spot her dashing away.

"So what?" I ask, taking aim.

"We're both level two!"

The creature roars again, and I dash after D1V.

If this was any other gaming session, with Laura or Jason or Ryan, I think we would have stood our ground, firing away at the beast until we were all taken out and had to start over again. Laughing as we got our virtual butts kicked. Part of me still wants to wait and see what happens when that thing attacks. Will I get thrown across the forest? Will it eat me? Will it be funny?

I'm torn between running with D1V and blasting away to my imminent doom, but something about staying on with her feels more fun. Besides, if I lose now and get logged out, I'll probably never be able to find her again. I'm not connected with her on my friends list here in game, and as a celebrity, there's no way she's open to friend requests. And even if she is, it's probably strictly through her clan channels, or her back-log of requests is so big she doesn't even check them anymore.

I should stay.

Maybe I can help.

She needs to level up in this game, for her streaming and videos and all that. Maybe instead of throwing it all away for a good time, I should try to do something. Be her ally. In a way that Ryan would actually approve of.

"Where are we going?!" I shout into my headset. She's a little ahead of me, and I need to make sure she hears me.

"Far away from that thing!" she yells back. "Let's try to make it to the ships. We can—"

Another roar interrupts her, and a beast that looks strikingly like the first lumbers out in front of her, jaws open. The teeth are a weird yellow-orange color, the inside of the mouth blue. It snaps its jaws and snarls, pushing its feet angrily against the ground. D1V stops running and turns in my direction, and I can hear her sigh through the headset. On-screen, she somehow looks crestfallen, even though I know that's impossible.

I finally catch up to her, glancing back to see the beast that was chasing me slow down. It lets loose a roar and glares at us.

"Do you think they'll—" I start.

"Can you record?" she asks quickly.

"Well sure, I think I—" I look down at my keyboard for the correct button combinations.

"Do it. Do it quick. This is going to be awesome." Her tone has shifted, a hint of joy in it now as I tap a few keys. A bit of orange text appears in the bottom corner of my screen, reading *Video Capture*. "Are you recording yet?"

"Yeah, but—"

"Great. You capture that one, I'll capture this one. As great as VR is, recording on it just isn't the same, and I could use whatever you're able to get," she says. I watch as her inventory menu pops up in front of her, and she selects an item I don't quite recognize. A grenade-looking thing materializes in her hand, bright red with bits of yellow striped across it.

I hear her laugh.

"Watch this."

And with that, she throws the grenade at the beast closest to her, a trail of yellow smoke pluming out in its wake. It hits the monster with a soft *pop*, and a cloud of the pale gold mist erupts from the red canister. The monster roars and shakes, taking a few steps back, snorting and stomping its feet toward whatever she just tossed over there.

"Move it, Aaron!" D1V yells, darting off to the side. I follow her, just in time to avoid being trampled by the beast that was chasing us. It rushes forward, its large feet crashing against the earth, lumbering toward the other monster, who is still reeling in the pale yellow smoke.

"What *is* that?!" I shout, trying to make myself heard over the ensuing battle as the two creatures tear into each other.

"It's a Creature Lure," she explains, relief in her voice. "It's a pretty basic item you can buy early in the game. You use it to attract a monster to another monster, or a monster to a ship or person. You should use one while fighting your friends, make something attack them. I bet it would be funny."

I can almost hear the wink in her tone, and I find myself grinning like a fool.

One of the beasts falls, and some of the fern-like trees come tumbling down with it. The remaining monster bites at the fallen one, presumably eating it, but I have no idea. Those animations aren't really as in-depth as everything else, and the movements look more like an improv actor pretending to eat something.

"That…that is awesome," I say.

"Hell yeah, it is." D1V glances at me for a moment, and I wonder if she's smiling off-screen. "Let's get back to looking for resources. You got all that, right? The recording?"

"Oh yeah, definitely," I say, checking quickly to make sure that I do.

"Great." Another menu materializes in front of D1V as she turns to walk away. Her avatar's fingers tap at something in the menu, making little lights blip on and off. It looks like an options screen, the sort you load up when you—

Oh.

No way.

With a soft *bloop*, a message pops up on my screen, pale orange against the background of the actual game.

You have received a Friend Request.
Would you like to add:
D1V
to your friends list?
You can delete a contact whenever you choose.
[YES] [NO]

I can't help myself. I click on D1V to see her profile. Though I've never looked her up or anything before—I'm not a creep—I think it's safe to assume she's private and unsearchable on the game. But now that she's sent me a friend request, I can look.

If anyone loads up my profile, there's a lot of in-game nonsense. Planets I've claimed, people I've explored with, achievements and the like. If you're friends with me, it displays where I'm from, my social media links, and all. It's pretty public, but now, thinking about everything D1V's been through these past few days with the trolls and the attack in the game, I'm wondering if maybe I should shut down that stuff—especially once I see how sparsely populated her profile is.

She's eighteen, so just a year older than me, but that's all I'm getting out of it in terms of personal information. She's got her public social media links to Twitter and her Glitch stream, which I expected, plus her in-game email address—which everyone on here has—deeonevee@reclaimthesun.com.

But beyond that?

Nothing.

It's as if she doesn't exist in real life. But I suppose that's the point.

I click yes, and the dialogue tree disappears. Suddenly I hear D1V laughing on the other end.

"What?" I ask. "What is—"

"Nice profile you got here, Aaron." She chuckles. "Planet Butts. Planet Hamtaro. Planet Ryan Is My Lord and King. Planet I'm Bad at This Game & Should Feel Bad. Is your email address really LauraShouldMarryMe@reclaimthesun.com? Who's Laura?"

"Oh my God, I am going to murder Ryan," I groan, putting my face in my hands. "That's...that's not it. Sometimes we log in to each other's accounts to mess with one another. And by we, I mean mostly Ryan does it." I open my profile and fix it, changing it back to aaron@reclaimthesun.com.

"Wow. Your name as your email address. That's impressive, Mr. Day One. Most people usually have a bunch of numbers or something," she says, and I can hear the smirk in her voice. "Did you get all your precious collectibles with that Day One copy?"

"Don't judge me," I bluster, trying not to think about the pewter spaceship sculptures that came with the special edition, or the rocket-shaped keychain I've got on my keys right now.

"If I was going to judge you, I'd judge you by your location, *Pennsylvania.*"

Again, I can hear the smile in her voice, and I glare at the screen. Where she's from isn't listed, though I get why.

"Hey, after we sign off, can you send me that footage?" D1V asks. "I'll totally credit you in the video and give you a shout-out—"

"Can you mention ManaPunk?" I ask, blurting it out without really thinking. But I might as well take a shot—Jason will love the publicity, and it would look good for me, too.

"What? Why?"

"I work with Jason Pherlin, the founder?" I say, trying to be careful. I'd love a chance to get the game company out there on a major channel, and show that I'm doing work for them, but the last thing I want to do is ruin this new in-game friendship here. "Doing copyediting, some light story writing and stuff. No pressure if you can't. It would just… That would be really amazing."

"Oh okay, that's cool," she says. "I can do that. Aaron from ManaPunk. Done."

I'm grateful that it's not my face on the stream, because I'm smiling way too big right now. My face hurts. I can feel it all the way up in my ears.

"So…what now?" I ask.

"Resources," she reminds me. A blip pops up on my map. Now that we're friends in the game, I can see where she's planning to go.

We're a party. This is awesome.

"Let's head up toward the water, see what we can find. And then I gotta sign off, put the video together."

"Sounds good," I say. "And I'll email you those files right after."

"Perfect," she replies, pausing for a beat. "You um…busy tomorrow?"

"Not really, it's the summer and I—"

"Then let's do this again. Maybe around 8:00?" she suggests, and my heart is beating madly in my chest. This is so cool. "You're a…well, a good partner."

There's another *bloop* noise, and a message pops up on my screen.

You have received an Exploration Request.
Would you like to EXPLORE with D1V at:
8:00 p.m. EST, July 2
[YES] [NO] [RESCHEDULE]

Fighting the urge to dance around in my computer chair, I click Yes.

RECLAIM THE SUN: CHAT APPLICATION

AARON: Hey, are you online?

D1V: I'm always online.

AARON: Oh, cool.

D1V: Hello?

D1V: Aaron? Mr. Day One?

AARON: Hey! Sorry, parents. Are we still doing some exploring?

D1V: Sure. I won't be videoing this one though. Just grinding. No one cares about that.

D1V: ?

D1V: Are you even there?

AARON: Yes! Hey! Sorry, yeah. Parents again. I'm in, obviously.

D1V: What's their deal?

AARON: Parents? Mom's a doctor, dad runs the practice office. Trying desperately to get me to take over.

D1V: Wow. Cliché much?

AARON: Tell me about it. Mom has me running the office for the summer, but I guess... I don't entirely mind it.

D1V: Oh?

AARON: Dad didn't have it easy when he moved to the States. He's in his 40s but he might as well be 60.

D1V: Ah.

AARON: Yeah.

AARON: Heavy stuff for a video game chat, right?

AARON: I promise to be all about resources, crystals, and building materials from now on.

D1V: No, no. It's nice. I don't get out much these days.

AARON: No? I feel like you must be popular, what with the video channel and all.

D1V: Hah! Right. Popular.

D1V: When you spend all your time trying to support your family and save for college...

D1V: Well, the offline world sort of fades away.

AARON: Wow we are GOOD at lighthearted chats.

RECLAIM THE SUN: CHAT APPLICATION

D1V: Up for some grinding?

AARON: Hey! Yeah, I'm around. Are you always up this late?

D1V: It's late?

D1V: It's like 10PM how old are you?

AARON: I'm more of a morning person!

D1V: Why don't you pop on a VR set this time? It's cool when you're with someone in that.

AARON: Ah, sorry, I don't have one.

D1V: Really? I thought with the game development stuff you'd be all over that.

AARON: Eh, it doesn't really pay that much? Not yet, anyway. Maybe one day.

AARON: The only reason I can game on a PC is because I built the thing out of parts I found.

D1V: Found?

AARON: In the garbage. We live in kind of a wealthy area. What about you?

D1V: Not wealthy.

AARON: Are you on the East Coast too?

D1V: Let's talk about something else.

AARON: Oh. Sorry.

D1V: I'm just careful about what I dish out, that's all. You didn't do anything wrong.

D1V: Aaron?

D1V: Still there?

AARON: Yeah sorry, I'm ready! Let's go.

7

DIVYA

I walk down the PATH station stairs, the steps shockingly long and diving deep into the ground, to make my way from Jersey City to Hoboken. The walls are lined with a cream ceramic tile that they somehow manage to keep clean, despite the grit of the train tracks and underground tunnels right at the end of all this. People make their way up and down the escalators, walking, running, even skipping steps, super busy for no real reason. You could just stand there and let it take you, but instead, everyone rushes to save those extra thirty seconds.

I take the stairs to avoid it all.

It's easy to get lost while weaving in and out of the small sea of people—though it's better than the oceans of people that fill the area on the weekends, and during the morning and late-afternoon work rush. I adjust my hoodie as the crowds surround me, as if someone might spot me. But that's just it— no one knows who I am. No one cares, outside of gaming.

Here, I'm safe. I'm not an avatar, a social media profile people can target.

I think about that email from the Vox Populi. The photo of my address. I wonder if whoever sent it actually saw me going home one day, or if they just took a screenshot using Google Maps, figuring out my address the way just about any half-decent hacker can using the Internet. My mind drifts to Aaron, and how unfair it is that he just gets to be *himself* in those public online spaces. He lists his town, his birthday, even his last name on his profile.

Hell, his friends even have his password.

I tug my hoodie a little closer as I hustle through the turnstile and make my way to a waiting train, the door closing with a friendly chime behind me as I enter the air-conditioned space. I grab hold of one of the poles in the train car and hold on tight to the cool metal as the PATH lurches forward, making its weaving way through the New Jersey cities.

My phone buzzes.

RECLAIM THE SUN: CHAT APPLICATION

AARON: Hey, sorry if I made things weird last night.

AARON: I get it, the privacy stuff. I do.

AARON: So basically, my parents aren't super psyched about my life choices? The games?

AARON: I built my computer. Most of it, at least. From things in the trash.

AARON: My family doesn't live too far from universities here in Philadelphia, so I dumpster dive sometimes.

AARON: My pals all call it my Frankenstein computer.

AARON: But it's Frankenstein's monster, actually.

AARON: Please imagine that being said in a very pretentious literary voice.

AARON: Anyhow, that's my story, and you don't have to share yours. I just hope it makes you laugh.

AARON: Or something.

I smile.
It does.
And I almost miss my stop, talking to him.

Rebekah charges at me before I even have a chance to sit down, wrapping her arms around my torso and squeezing the hell out of me. I think I feel my ribs shifting inside my chest.

"I'm...happy to see...you, too..." I groan out, and she lets me go, hopping back into her desk chair, the black seat spinning around a full rotation before she stops and faces me, her eyes totally alight. She runs a finger along the side of her head, fixing a rebellious lock of her mostly short hair, the right side a little longer than the once-buzzed left. The blood orange color is a deeper shade today than it was the last time we were on the stream together, and her small apartment smells faintly of hair dye.

"This. Footage. Divya," she says, a beat between each word.

"I can't even handle it. The amount of people emailing about it... I'm so glad you thought to start recording. Discovering that Easter egg, where people can duel over a planet..." She balls her fists together, shaking them. "Who *cares* about the trolls from the other day? This video is going to be *everywhere*."

Rebekah turns to her screen, clicking away to Google, loading up the news section. "Check it out."

GOOGLE NEWS
"Reclaim the Sun" "contesting planet"

Engadget Games
Glitch streamer D1V discovers planet-contesting duel...

Polygon
Get ready to fight for your planet in *Reclaim the Sun...*

Business Insider
New video footage reveals hidden Easter egg in *Reclaim the Sun...*

See 87 other similar results.

A smile spreads across my face as I scan the list. "Amazing."

"Plus, the video has close to eighty thousand views already," Rebekah says, clicking over to our YouTube channel and Glitch stream site. "We've got some new sponsorship emails, too. By the way, who's the guy?"

"Wait, what?" I ask, and Rebekah crosses her arms, grinning. She leans back in her chair and looks at her nails, then back up at me.

"The guy? From the stream? Who you've been playing with lately? I see you two exploring together when I check my channel." She nods at the computer, like I don't know what she's talking about. "Come on, spill, or we are not going to Quarter Slice Crisis."

I feign a gasp, holding a hand to my heart. "How dare you threaten to take away my terrible pizza!" When Rebekah raises her eyebrows at me, I relent and say, "It's nothing, honestly. We just happened to be landing on the same planet, and he was tolerable enough to hang around with for a little while." It's my turn to cross my arms at her, and she's mirroring the scowl I'm trying to give her. My expression breaks first, and I laugh, no good at this game. "I added him to my friends list—"

"Oh, I know. I saw." Rebekah nods again at the computer. "Come on, you sent me all the recordings. I could even hear your conversations. You're lucky I muted all that, by the way. You might have had a few brokenhearted viewers otherwise."

"Brokenhearted… Listen, you!" I say, pointing a finger at her. "We did some resource runs yesterday and like, two days ago. And we've had some small talk in the chat app. That's it."

"Just…just be careful?" she ventures, looking up at me, her eyes awash with concern. "You know, it's the Internet or whatever. I wouldn't let him get too close. You never know."

"Yeah, I know." The unfairness of it all weighs on me. It's hard to encourage a blossoming friendship with an Internet stranger when there are anonymous misogynistic trolls lurking around my house. "I'm being safe. So…pizza and games?"

"Let me just grab my bag." She hops out of her chair, which goes spinning. I reach out and stop it, the soft leather pressing against my skin. Rebekah's home office isn't much of an office—it's a corner of her one-room studio in Hoboken, which is a quick walk to the PATH train and not too far from where she goes to college. She's got it decorated in a gamer-hipster-chic style that no magazine or Pinterest board could properly represent. Gorgeous furniture that she plucked from rummage sales and street corners on trash day, then sanded down and painted herself. Collectible figurines of her (and consequently my) favorite video game characters, from classics like *Chrono Trigger* and *Final Fantasy III* (the Super Nintendo one, which is actually *Final Fantasy VI* for die-hard fans, and the best one ever made, sorry *Final Fantasy VII* fanboys and -girls). Vintage mirrors paired with long necklaces full of nerdy charms and bookshelves crammed with classic texts and texts on classics—classics being classic games, of course.

I look around the small studio, which feels so perfectly cozy and nerdy, as Rebekah slings her messenger bag over her shoulder. "Space Trash" is embroidered on the side, with patches of logos from the games *Mass Effect* and *Lunar* poorly stitched on. These are new, and look like they're fit to fall off at any moment. I find myself staring at the bag as she walks over, and she quickly pushes it behind her back, glaring at me playfully.

"I stitch together videos and data, not fabric," she says with a smile. "They'll be fine. Let's go. Pizza waits for no woman."

There's something magical about a Hoboken summer, some indefinable air that draws in people from all over—from Jersey City and the nearby suburbs, from Manhattan, Queens, and Brooklyn. Washington Ave—the main downtown strip close to Rebekah's campus—is packed with people browsing the street displays of kitschy boutiques and rummaging through cardboard boxes full of dollar paperbacks outside the used bookstore. The hot pavement and cobblestones are synonymous with the smell of greasy food trucks and the taste of cold brew, and I want to devour it all.

Rebekah and I have always enjoyed making a game out of trying to identify the city dwellers vs. simple bridge-and-tunnel folk, as the New Yorkers like to call us, but I'm not really in the mood to deal with the crush of tourists today.

Apparently Rebekah feels the same way. "Long way passing by the water?" she suggests. I agree, and we take a turn down a side street off Washington, the cobblestones on the ground digging gently into the balls of my feet. It'll steer us away from the bustling shops and crowds, something that my mom frequently laments. She's always going on about how, a little over a decade ago, the area wasn't nearly as booming, and you could wander around on a weekend without dodging folks on the sidewalk.

A handful of what look like college guys are making their way down the same street, and I can see the blue of the Hudson and the dark red and brown bricks of the waterfront just a block or so away. I tense up as the guys walk by, feeling their eyes on me and Rebekah, and she quickly loops an arm through mine.

"Hey," she says gently. "It's alright."

"Thanks." I smile gratefully, leaning my head against hers, even though she's the one who could really use the support. The attack in the game, all those terrible comments… At least that's all online. Not out here in the real world. Rebekah's the one who's lived through it all in person, and I wonder if I'll ever be as strong as her.

My mind wanders back to that photo of my apartment building. Not for the first time, I wonder how the trolls managed to find me. Knowing that they could track me down at any time…it makes every single man who walks by seem like a threat.

Fortunately, I haven't heard anything more from the Vox

Populi since they blew up my ship. I received a few scathing emails from the usual anonymous trolls after posting the video of the discovery I made with Aaron—the contesting capability of the game—but at least there were no photos this time. The threads on social media haven't gotten any better, though.

If I could avoid dudes in real life all summer, that would be fantastic.

The cool breeze coming off the Hudson is a welcome contrast to the heat reverberating off the cobblestone-and-brick-lined streets and sidewalks. I stare across the river toward the island of Manhattan, at the small boats cutting through the water, the drivers and passengers likely carefree and wealthy. Probably the sort of people who try to work "I have a boat" into every conversation. Seeing all that—the New York City skyline, the people of means frolicking in the water below—I feel this awkward urge to pull out my phone and check my bank account balance. What is it about seeing unchecked wealth that makes you so conscious of your own? The rent and utilities have cleared, but the month is barely half over, and I can't bring myself to deal with thinking about fundraising over the next two weeks.

I bet Chad down there, floating on his father's boat, doesn't have to worry about overdrafts.

I look down at my smartwatch, at the steps we've walked so far, and think about selling it in another ten days or so. It's a shame this gadget can't track all the steps I've taken back.

"You pick your classes yet?" Rebekah asks as we get closer to the railing. I lean against it, peering over into the water, the metal hot against my bare arms. You can't exactly see any of the New York City campuses by looking across the river, but I know they're there. NYU, Columbia, Fordham, Pace, SUNY… All of them just waiting for the fall semester, when students will once again be milling about. Students who aren't desperately trying to keep the dreams of their parents alive.

Actually, scratch that, because that's *definitely* happening right now, somewhere, someplace. Parents dreaming that their kids will become lawyers, doctors, teachers, actresses...whatever the case might be. Kinda like Aaron, with his parents and that office he brought up. And those kids are doing it, pushing forward and living dreams for their families, right across the river, in cozy classrooms and giant sprawling lecture halls. Dreams that don't belong to them, but to other people.

In that moment, I feel sad for Aaron.

But chances are, none of *them* are likely paying for their *parents* to do any of that. Though in my mom's defense, it isn't much. She only has a summer semester left of part-time graduate school, and then she'll finally have that master's of library science she's been working so hard to finish.

Her dream seemed so much easier to reach when Dad was still around—four grand a semester felt like nothing. But after he left, that part-time job of hers couldn't quite handle the rent and her tuition and everything else.

Whenever I try to talk to anyone about this—Rebekah, my handful of Internet friends—they always say the same things. Tell her to apply for student loans. Get a scholarship. Tell her to put it off and pick up a job. Which is why I don't talk about it anymore. Like any of those things are such immediate, easy tasks. Like my mom deserves to let go of her dream or work herself to death even more or go into crippling debt because of my asshole father. Like it's easy to get a scholarship or a full student loan when you make just enough to pay for your classes, but not really, because if you pay for those classes, rent and groceries become a fever dream.

Fuck that. I'll struggle so she can soar. I can handle it.

"Div?" Rebekah nudges.

"Hmm? Oh. Classes. Yeah, not yet," I reply. "Still got time to register, still have to pay for them. Actually, I was thinking I might take a gap year."

Rebekah makes a face, her nose crinkled up in doubt.

"Okay, a gap semester."

She makes an even more intense face.

"Stop it with the face!" I exclaim. "I know, I know. But my mom just has these two summer classes left, and I just can't bring myself to leave until things settle down. I really want to give her this summer and some time to find her dream job."

"Sure, but—"

"She deserves it," I insist. "She's sacrificed a lot for me. Hudson County will still be there when I'm ready to go." I look behind me, in the direction of Jersey City, like somehow I'll be able to see the community college in the town next door from here.

"I swear, you're an old soul, Div." Rebekah bumps her shoulder against mine and points away from the water. "Come on. I'm starving."

There's a reason hopping the PATH train into Hoboken is a worthwhile venture, spending time with Rebekah and enjoying the wonderful atmosphere aside. That reason is Quarter Slice Crisis, the ultimate hipster pizza place located not too far from the waterfront downtown. It's squeezed between a Starbucks and a boutique clothing store, both of which are probably none-too-thrilled with the pizzeria-slash-arcade's outward appearance, with its poorly painted illustrations of pizza and video game characters on the enormous plate glass window that is almost always dirty.

Rebekah turns to look at me as someone walks out of the shop, a white paper bag likely filled with food under his arm. "You have quarters?"

"Do I have quarters?" I scoff. "Please."

We walk through the doors of the pizza shop and are immediately blasted by chiptune music screaming from the overhead speakers, the air filled with techno beats. There's always something like this playing in Quarter Slice Crisis, but when I hear vocals singing over the 8-bit beeps and bloops, I turn and look at Rebekah, raising my eyebrows in a silent question. It sounds like an odd mix of Fall Out Boy meets the music of *Sonic the Hedgehog*, and I can't figure out what exactly I'm hearing.

"I Fight Dragons," Rebekah supplies. "Pop punk band, with chiptunes and video game sounds."

I close my eyes and tilt my head up. "This is everything I ever wanted," I say with a contented smile.

We laugh and keep walking in, up toward the register and pizzas displayed on the countertop. Quarter Slice Crisis is one of those places that pays more attention to atmosphere than substance—or in this case, sustenance, as the pies are usually as basic as they come. Cheese. Pepperoni. There's a different type of pizza today, though, labeled with a little Post-it that reads NEW! in big neon letters. I squint at the pie in question, trying to identify the topping.

"Mushroom," the guy behind the counter says. He looks up at me, blinking slowly, incredibly mellow. There's a little red in the whites of his eyes, and I'm convinced he has to be stoned. "Our new vegan option."

I give Rebekah a look, and she shakes her head. Because yes, mushrooms magically make a pizza vegan.

"Just a slice of cheese for me, please," I say, indicating the pizzas on the countertop. "And a large Dr. Pepper." I glance at Rebekah. "Actually, make that two orders."

"What if I wanted to try the vegan pizza?" Rebekah challenges.

"You hate mushrooms," I say dryly. "What? I know you." She smiles. Because I do.

The guy behind the counter slides our slices onto paper plates without warming them up and hands us some cups. He glances at the slices. "They just came out," he mumbles, heading for the back kitchen. "Should be hot enough."

I grab our plates—which should be warm from this supposedly just-out-of-the-oven pizza, but are definitely cold—and we make our way over to the real reason we're here.

The arcade machines.

I know all about the bar arcades here in Hoboken, back home in Jersey City, over in New York. I hear one opened in Philadelphia a few years ago. I know they're spreading all over the place. Quarter Slice Crisis is the answer to that for those of us who are a little too young for sipping whiskey, and way too old to be going to Chuck E. Cheese's. Well, I know there are plenty of people from my senior class who drink, but not me. And I'd rather not go through all the trouble to get a fake ID when I can just game in a place like this, or at home.

I idly wonder if Aaron is the sort who drinks.

While those other places might frequently be packed with drunk adults and screaming children, the only people in QSC today, on a Thursday afternoon, two hours after the lunch rush, are me, Rebekah, and the probably high guy making subpar pizza behind the counter. It was almost always just us and the arcade games, this time of day, this time of year.

Which is perfect. As much as I wanted to come here, I also wanted to avoid seeing anyone in person. Especially anyone from the gaming world.

"There you are," I say, placing my plate of pizza down in between the first-and second-player spots of our favorite game, right above where I'll soon be depositing massive quantities of quarters. I run my hand affectionately over the black steel frame of the arcade machine and pull the light gun out of the holster in front of my screen. Whatever bright orange luster the faux pistol used to have has been long since replaced by a dull melon color, the shade of a traffic cone that's spent too much time outside in the rain.

Rebekah steps up next to me and pulls out the light pink gun.

"I fucking hate this color," she grumbles, aiming it at her screen.

Time Crisis 4.

I drop a few quarters into the machine, listening to the perfect sound of them clinking against the bottom of the bin inside, likely against change I put in there last week, because hardly anyone plays this thing anymore. I know this, because right before the game starts, the high scores flash by, and I see D1V pop up from the top to the bottom, almost nonstop, with a few BEKs here and there, followed by one ASS right at the end. Rebekah claims it wasn't her who put that high score in, but I'm not convinced. No one in this town is better than us at this game.

The intro begins playing, and I wince.

Oof, this game.

The plot is awful, the voice acting is terrible, even the music is completely over-the-top. It's a trademark of any *Time Crisis* game—utterly cheesy and campy as hell.

I love it so much.

The action comes hard and fast, and Rebekah and I are quickly hopping up and down, pressing on the arcade machine's physical pedals by our feet to make our characters hide behind rocks, under cars, around trees…whatever nearby prebuilt obstacle is available to shield us from the barrage of bullets, missiles, grenades, and all the other nonsense the villains throw at us. There are knives and swords sometimes, as ninjas occasionally appear for no reason. People shoot bazookas near one another, because why not. Some characters even throw dynamite now and again, because this is clearly the Wild West.

It's so ridiculous. Yet here I am. Time and time again.

The door to the pizza place chimes, and I glance over quickly, spotting the same dudes we saw walking down the street on our way here. A bloom of panic bursts in my chest, and I push myself to focus on the game. It's just a coincidence. There's no way they followed us.

Right?

Right.

We're about to clear the fourth chapter of the game, already several dollars' worth of quarters in, when Rebekah takes a missile straight in the face. The *Continue?* prompt pops up on screen, the announcer loud and blaring through the speakers. It's almost louder than the rest of the game, and I feel like they must do that on purpose.

"Shit, shit," she growls as the countdown chimes away. The great thing about games like this is that they give you a hell of a lot of time to get more quarters. This isn't a ten-second countdown like playing a fighting game at home, à la *Street*

Fighter V or something. There's a whole minute to kill. Gives you time to find your quarters or steal some from your partner-in-gaming.

I dig through my pockets and come up a few short, and Rebekah is tapped out. "I'll hit the change machine—" I start.

"Don't worry, I got you," a voice says behind me.

My heart hammers, and I turn around to spot one of the guys from earlier. He's wearing a gray T-shirt from Rebekah's college. When he smiles, a dimple appears on his right cheek, and his green eyes light up.

I don't trust him.

He pulls some change out of his massive hoodie pockets and plinks a few quarters into Rebekah's side.

"No, you don't have—" she protests.

"Don't worry about it," he says, his smile widening.

"READY!" shouts the announcer in the game.

"Walt!" one of the guys from his clique calls from across the pizzeria. "Come on, we're gonna do *X-Men*."

I look over my shoulder and see his friends waving him over, three of them huddled around the *X-Men: Children of the Atom* game, a massive arcade machine where four people can play the side-scrolling beat 'em up at once. It's older than I am, and not really my first choice, but people seem to love that cabinet, no matter what arcade I'm in.

"Let me know if you need help with that level," Walt says with a wink before hurrying to join his friends.

I roll my eyes and turn back to the screen. Rebekah smashes the start button and pulls her gun up, staring down the plastic barrel.

"Need help. Fucking men," she grumbles as the game resumes, the momentarily flashed-out screen on her side coming back to life from the missile that got her. I glance over at her quickly and see her eye twitching a little. She's breathing heavily, too, and not in the anxious-because-of-a-video-game-boss-battle sort of way.

"So how's...you know, the sessions and all that?" I ask, ducking behind a cement barrier as a helicopter hovers onto our screen and starts firing at us.

"Really?" Rebekah asks, shooting madly. "Now? You want to ask about that stuff now?"

"Well, I don't know." I shrug, firing again, then quickly looking behind me to the college bros hammering away on the old *X-Men* cabinet. "It's just, those guys here, and—"

"No, no," Rebekah says as she holds her pink gun out to reload. "I get it. It's going...fine. Not the best, but fine."

Last semester, on the way back to her dorm one night, Rebekah was assaulted in an elevator on campus. And as if that wasn't enough, the assholes who attacked her recorded the whole thing, and it quickly leaked. The video went viral, and the guys denied what happened, despite the footage, which only fueled the fire of the story going absolutely everywhere.

Shortly after, Rebekah moved out of the dorms to her hip studio near campus, and the dudes were supposed to be suspended while the investigation was ongoing. But it's still ongoing, and those assholes are still on campus, taking their classes like nothing happened.

Because that's what happens.

She's been taking as many online courses as she can from the comfort of her apartment ever since, even though the college is practically down the block. I know she's been seeing one of the school therapists at the Women's Center on campus as well, but she doesn't talk about their sessions very much.

"You know I'm here for you, right?" I lean across the divide between us and nudge her, just barely making it back to my side in time to dodge an attack. "We can talk about stuff like that, not just games, or computers, and—"

"Div, I know," she says, turning to give me a look full of meaning. "You don't have to ask." She takes aim at the screen. "Just knowing you're there is enough."

"I'll always be there."

We both reload at the same time.

And we fire away.

I wipe at some sweat on my forehead, still holding the *Time Crisis* light gun. It takes about an hour to beat the story. Well, if you're good at the game, that is.

And we are.

"That is awesome," I say, holstering the light gun and crossing my arms.

"A thing of beauty, really," Rebekah agrees, grinning as she pulls out her phone. I take mine out, too, and snap a few photos, our high scores right above one another—a happy accident, unlike our choice in high score names:

TIME CRISIS 4: HIGH SCORES

D1V
D1V
BEK
D1V
BAN
MEN
BEK
ASS

"I really wish that 'ASS' score wasn't still on there, though," Rebekah grumbles.

"You can admit you did that, it's okay." I grin, placing a hand on her shoulder. "I won't judge."

"You're the worst." Rebekah smirks, giving me a side-eye.

"That score is fucking crazy!" a familiar voice exclaims, rocketing me out of our moment. Walt—the guy who gave Rebekah the quarters earlier—is back, along with the dudes he walked in with. They're all dressed pretty much the same, T-shirts and caps with the college's logo on it, except for one guy, a Filipino dude wearing a shirt with some kind of cartoon burger on it, looking like an icon for a smartphone app. "You two are awesome gamers for girls."

Rebekah snorts and looks up at me, smirking. "For girls?" she asks. "Can you guys do any better? I don't recall hearing the final battle for your *X-Men* game over here, and that end scene is pretty damn loud."

Two of the guys in the group look at each other, clearly irritated.

"Eh, we were just playing for fun, anyway," Walt huffs. "Hey, I was wondering, do you want to maybe play games together sometime? Could I get your number?"

The dudes behind him jostle into one another like a group of friends in a sitcom commercial.

My stomach sinks.

"Oh no. Thank you, though, that's nice of you," Rebekah says, casually picking up her bag and slinging it over her shoulder. Her eyes meet mine for a moment, and I get it. I'm ready. It's time to get out of here.

Walt's eyes narrow. "Why not?" he asks, his tone aggressive. "Something wrong with me?"

"Walt, chill, it's no big deal," one of his friends says, and

I notice it's the burger-shirt guy. He grabs at Walt's arm, but Walt promptly shakes him off.

"Fuck off, Brian," Walt snaps, then turns back at us. "Come on, I gave you some quarters for your game. I'm a nice guy, you should want to hang out with me."

"People don't do nice things for one another expecting some kind of reward, asshole," I snap, moving to shuffle Rebekah out of here and away from the group. I put my arm around her and turn to leave, when a hand grabs my shoulder.

The grip is tight.

Angry.

I pull away and glare. Walt is there, looking at me with his eyes narrowed.

And then I see it. That spark of recognition.

My heart begins hammering on all cylinders.

"Yo, Andrew, you were right," Walt says, and I shift to stand in front of Rebekah, who I can feel shaking a little next to me. One of the guys behind Walt—Andrew, I'm guessing—pulls out his phone, and it looks like he's taking pictures. I put my hand up to block his shots.

"Yeah!" Walt exclaims. "She's that streamer girl. You're that girl, aren't—"

Walt moves to seize my arm again, and before I know it, I've slapped him across the face. The crack echoes loud and sharp in the arcade, which is still vacant save for the four guys, me, and Rebekah. I glance over to the counter, where the pizzas are, but the stoner on duty is nowhere to be seen.

Walt glares at me, his eyes narrowed and teeth clenched.

"You fucking bitch, who do you think—" I see his fists ball up as he takes a big step toward me and Rebekah, and I flinch back, covering her, when Walt suddenly tumbles backward.

"Walt, what the fuck man, knock it off!" I look back to

see that Brian guy pulling at Walt, then pushing him away from the two of us.

"Brian, stay the fuck out of this, you—" Walt starts shouting.

But I don't stick around to hear the rest.

I push through the heavy double doors and out of Quarter Slice Crisis, pulling Rebekah with me. The pizzeria-slash-arcade isn't exactly located on a main street, so we bolt off down a side alley. Rebekah picks up speed, taking the lead. She doesn't even have to say anything; I know what she's doing. We're heading toward the waterfront. Toward the public. Toward people.

The side street is dark for a moment, then bursts into light as we reach the more populated areas. Out on the cobblestone streets and brick sidewalks, the cool air breezes off the Hudson and chills my forehead, which I only now realize is drenched in sweat.

Rebekah hurries toward the railing by the water, her face pale, eyes enormous. She throws up, loudly and violently, over the edge, coughing and sputtering. I pat and rub her back, tucking loose strands of red-orange hair behind her ear.

"It's okay," I say, trying to keep the tremor from my voice. "You're safe."

"Fucking assholes," she chokes back.

"They're gone," I continue. "They—"

"Hey!" a breathless male voice shouts, and I spin around to spot Brian, the guy who held that Walt jerk back. He's panting laboriously, bent over, one hand up in the air, the other on his knee. I ball up my fists and look around for someone, anyone. Not just for someone who might be able to help, but someone who might do more harm. His friends, or whoever they are.

"Wait, wait…" he protests, gulping for air. "Don't… I…" He holds something in the air and shakes it.

It's my phone.

He looks up at me, and his face is red, eyes glistening. He's got a horribly busted lip, already purple and pulsing, blood trickling down his chin.

"Sorry," he says, taking a step toward us. I shrink back and look around, searching for an escape. Rebekah is in no condition to run, and for a bizarre moment, I wonder if we can just jump into the water and swim to Manhattan, like we're in an action movie where that's possible.

"Don't...don't bolt," Brian pleads. "Here, just..." He moves closer, and it feels like my heart is crashing against my rib cage, like it's about to jettison out of my chest and into the water. "Here."

He reaches out with my phone, holding it by the very end, like he's trying to give a snack to a dangerous animal in a zoo. I take it from him quickly, snatching it away and burying it in my jacket.

"I'm sorry," he continues, stepping back, hands up. "Walt... His friends... They're all a bunch of assholes. I'm just here checking out the school. Transfer student. Got stuck with them as my like, tour group for the week."

I stare at him.

"Sorry, I'm...talking too much." He clears his throat. "How can I help? I'm Brian—"

"I gathered," I say, clearing my throat and pausing for a beat. "Look, if you want to help, talk to your boy about how to treat women. And don't let him go back there. That's our place."

"Fuck that, not anymore." Rebekah sniffles.

"I'm not letting someone take that place from us," I insist, turning around to face her. But Rebekah's eyes are red and wet, and she looks up at me with a crushed expression that tells me they already have. I wrap an arm around her, feeling my heart break over the loss.

Brian is still standing there, his hands in his pockets, looking incredibly uncomfortable.

"Thanks for getting my phone back," I say, holding my phone up. "Like I said…if you really want to help, educate your friends."

"Yeah, I don't think they're my friends anymore," he says, rubbing at his face, wincing when his hand brushes against his bloody lip.

"Good," I tell him. "You don't need friends like that. No one does."

I pull out my phone, a little crack in the screen, and move to dial.

"Who…who are you calling?" Rebekah asks.

"The cops." I bring the phone up to my ear. "I'm not letting anyone get away with hurting you again."

RECLAIM THE SUN: CHAT APPLICATION

AARON: Hey! Up for some resource grinding tonight?

D1V: Hey, not a good time right now.

AARON: No worries. Is everything okay?

D1V: That's a tough question to answer. I'll go with no for now.

AARON: Do you want to talk about it?

D1V: Not particularly, but thanks.

D1V: Listen I feel like my world is about to go up in flames, so let's talk later.

AARON: Okay. I'm around though if you need a chat.

D1V: K.

It's only a matter of hours before the news about Quarter Slice Crisis is all over the Internet, and the reports online are just awful.

The comments, of course, are even worse.

I glance over at the sign on my desk, in simple black letters on a print I ordered from Etsy.

Don't Read the Comments.

Ah, little sign. If only it were that easy. If only every person who gave that advice, who claimed that they heeded that advice, *actually* took that advice.

Everyone reads the comments.

Every single one.

It's Rebekah's attack all over again. The video, taken by one of the bros at the pizza place, filtering from social media to all the gaming blogs. A thing to be whispered and posted about, by swarms of people that won't hear anything that we have to say about it.

I think the wildest thing about all of this is that nothing is reported in the actual news. Like on television or the major local news outlets. There's no report about two girls being assaulted and threatened in the middle of downtown Hoboken. Nothing about a popular hangout for college kids being unsafe. There's a blip in a hyperlocal news blog, linking to the gaming blogs that are talking about it. But largely, the only people discussing the incident are the video game sites.

And it's there that the comments are worst—from the people in *my* community. Or supposedly my community, at least. There's lots of talk about me "deserving" this or that because of my stream. But how does any of that make sense? How does playing a game and making videos make me deserving of any of this?

I see it too often. People saying how putting myself out there this way, on the Internet, on streaming sites, on social media… Well, what do I expect to happen? That I should anticipate being some kind of victim, for finding joy in something.

How dare you, their voices say, without directly saying it.

I close out all the blogs and my social feeds on my computer just as the doorbell to our apartment rings. I peer out the windows of my bedroom to the street below. There's a black car with dark windows across the way that I've never seen before, and down near the door to our building, a woman in a suit, looking around impatiently. She rings the doorbell again.

I slip on some shoes and hustle down the two floors to the front door, silently wishing we had a fancy intercom system so I could buzz people in from upstairs. I peer through the peephole to get a closer look at the woman and pull back with a gasp as I notice the belt around her waist, the black pistol hanging from it.

She's a police officer. We'd made a statement at the station near campus yesterday right after I got off the phone, but I didn't expect someone to actually show up.

The woman's black hair bounces a little with every movement she makes, and she looks a lot like Misty Knight from the comics and the *Luke Cage* Netflix show—minus the kick-ass robotic arm—which makes me smile and feel way more at ease about her being here. She knocks on the door again, hard, making me step back a bit.

"Hello?" she calls, her voice authoritative. I hear her grumble something else under her breath.

I open the front door a crack, peering at her from behind the fraying screen door.

"Can I help you?" I ask. She squints at me for a moment.

"I'm Detective Nikki Watts," she says, pulling a badge out from inside her jacket. "I'm looking for Divya Sharma—is she here?" She stares at me, as though she's trying to figure out if I'm the person she's looking for.

"That's, um…me," I stammer.

"I got the report from the station about the assault at…" She closes her eyes, like it hurts to say the name of the place. "Quarter Slice Crisis."

"Yeah." I swallow nervously. "We filed that report yesterday. Is everything okay?"

"Save for the exception that I hate puns? Yes. I understand you're friends with Rebekah…" She pulls a notebook out and flips it open quickly, then looks back up at me, her dark brown eyes strangely warm and piercing at the same time. "Rebekah Cole? You do that video game stream together, yes?"

"Oh God, did something happen to her?" I ask, anxiety billowing up in my chest.

"Well, yes and no. I mean, she's fine, your friend is fine," she adds hastily, likely in response to the panicked expression I'm sure is on my face. "Is there somewhere we can sit down and talk about what happened at Quarter…" She shakes her head. "You know what, I'm not even going to say the name of that place. It's so ridiculous. The bad pizza place in Hoboken with the old games. I'm the officer investigating the incident."

A little smile escapes her lips.

"D-1-V," she says, enunciating the letter, number, letter. "My niece really likes your videos, you know."

"No way." I grin. "That's really cool."

"Maybe we can take a selfie after we talk?" she ventures. "Mind if I come in?"

"We're investigating the online harassment that's plaguing a lot of girls in the region," Detective Watts says as I make my way into my kitchen to fetch some water for both of us. I grab a glass, fumbling with it a bit, my nerves jostling about inside me. How does she know my gamer tag? "There's been a serious uptick around the area, at least what's being reported, and we think it's organized. Particularly where you and your friend were yesterday, in Hoboken, and here in Jersey City."

"Hoboken. Do you think it's coming from one of the colleges?" I ask from the kitchen, my voice echoing off the tiles. The idea that some of the harassers might go to the same school as Rebekah is enough to send my heart hammering even more. It's bad enough those guys from the elevator are still floating around campus someplace, without a care in the world.

"Maybe," Detective Watts says as I return to the living room and hand her a glass of water. She moves to sit down on the couch, and consequently sinks into it way too quickly, some of the water splashing onto her jacket.

"Uh, sorry about that," I say, setting down my own glass on a side table and running to grab some paper towels. She mumbles her thanks and dabs at the water spots while I grab the desk chair from my bedroom and wheel it in, feeling weird about the idea of sitting right next to her on the sofa.

I spin the chair around to face her and sit down. "We really need to replace that couch."

Detective Watts looks like she's about to disappear into the pillows. "It's um…cozy." She smiles awkwardly and leans forward. She's weirdly positioned, far down and sunken into the couch, while I'm up high on my desk chair. I fuss with the lever underneath my seat to lower myself a bit, but it doesn't help much.

"I have to be honest here," I say, giving up and crossing my arms. "Why are you investigating this? I've always been under the impression that this sort of stuff… Well, that no one cared. It's just the Internet or whatever. Which, obviously, *I* don't believe, but…that seems to be the general consensus."

Not to mention this is the second damn time Rebekah's been harassed in person, and the outcome of the first time was that she had to move in order to feel even somewhat safe again.

"Yeah." Detective Watts sounds exhausted as she rubs the bridge of her nose. "I know. I'm trying to change that in a big way. We're putting together a new task force with the state police and the colleges in the area—Hoboken, Jersey City, Newark, Union, and all. Trying to loop in New Brunswick. Online harassment is actual harassment. Don't let anyone, any article or blog or nonsense anonymous person on the Internet, tell you otherwise." She stares at me intensely. "Okay?"

I nod. I believe her, of course. But does anyone else? It doesn't feel like it, especially when trolls so often go unpunished.

"So, Divya, why don't you let me start, and you can help me fill in some of the blanks here." She fusses with her notebook again. It's one of those fancy Moleskine notebooks everyone seems to have but never actually uses. By contrast, hers looks worn-out, like it's really seen some things.

"It's my understanding that you and Rebekah have been

dealing with some pretty intense harassment—on social media, in emails and video games," she says. "Just have to search your username to see that these people seem to love posting this stuff afterward. It also seems like some of that harassment might be happening locally. Is this true?"

That email. That photo of my apartment.

I bite my lip and shrug. If I tell her, it might just make things even more complicated for me. I can't let my mom find out—she'll make me stop streaming for sure. And besides, Rebekah was the target yesterday, not me.

"I'm not sure," I venture. "Maybe? The guys at that pizza place definitely knew who I was, and they got that video into the hands of someone who knew where to send it. Though I suppose you can just send something like that to any blog that's talked badly about me. About us."

"Any threats that have been more direct? From what I gathered, that pizza-place incident was more happenstance than planned," Detective Watts says, arching an eyebrow. "Anyone coming here, to your apartment? Any doxing, is basically what I'm asking here. People pushing your address, your personal information, out into public forums?"

The email and the photo of my apartment flash into my mind again, and my heart pounds. The coldness of it all.

Leave. You aren't welcome here.

It would be easy to say "yes." To show her the photo. The anonymous email address it came from, that maybe she and her team could trace.

But that would mean more news articles. More people knowing who I am, and likely finding out where I live. We'd have to move, just when Mom is almost done with her classes. Plus, Rebekah and my few friends are here, even though it's the summer and I'm not really seeing most of them right now. I want to hit reset at the community college, and help my mom start a better life. One without my father. A life that belongs to her for once. To us.

I can't let some anonymous troll on the Internet rip all that away from me. And it's not really doxing yet—is it? It was just a photo. They didn't post it anywhere.

But even as these thoughts run through my mind, as I try to rationalize them in some way, I know I'm just lying to myself. There's this voice telling me to just let it all out, to not be that person who hides and is afraid, but it's hard to be brave when there's so much at stake.

"No," I lie, the word feeling foul and wrong in my mouth. "We get a lot of awful messages on social media, and sometimes through email, but that's really it. I know there are some bloggers writing things and YouTubers making videos, but I avoid them if I can help it. And that guy who recognized me at Quarter Slice, of course."

"Okay, okay," the detective says, writing something down in her little notepad. She looks up at me and back down at the pad, then at me again. "Are you sure there have been no threats made to you here at home? With the incident at the pizza place, and the news articles... I worry that people will have an easier time triangulating where you live."

"I'm sure," I insist, trying to look right at her. Maintain eye contact. Don't dart around the room. I feel my hands getting sweaty against my legs.

"And this is the first time you've been caught on camera, in person?" she presses. "Outside of your videos, I mean."

"Yeah, definitely," I say. "We've never done any events or anything. We were hoping to make an appearance at GamesCon later in the summer, but... I don't know. I guess we'll see."

"GamesCon?" she asks.

"It's like Comic-Con, or those book conventions, but just

for video games. They go on all around the country, and the New York City event is just a few weeks away." I sigh, remembering Rebekah's excitement when she talked about those pins and patches. "We're supposed to set up a table, and I'm gonna do this panel…" I shake my head in frustration.

"Hey." Detective Watts reaches out and puts a hand on my shoulder, her grip strong and sure. "It's going to be okay. We're not going to let them win. You'll be able to do your panel. We'll think of something."

She exhales sharply and stands up, pulling her badge back out, revealing some business cards tucked away inside the folds of the wallet-like flap. "If anything—and I mean *anything*—else happens," she says, handing me a card, "you call me, you hear me? Like I said, a lot of the harassment in this region seems to be coming from the campus and the surrounding area. And those boys at the pizza place, when we find them, are potentially facing criminal charges for what they did to you and Rebekah, if I have my way—"

"Wait," I say, the image of that Brian guy flashing into my mind, with his burger T-shirt. "There was this one guy—"

"Brian?" Detective Watts asks, pulling out her notebook again. "Yes, the precinct told me about him, from your statements. He'll be fine, I suppose."

She shrugs and makes her way toward the door. I follow her down the stairs of my apartment building to the outside, where she stops for a moment and turns around, sliding on a pair of sunglasses like a badass cop in a movie.

"In my opinion, if you associate with trash, you should get thrown out with the rest of the garbage."

RECLAIM THE SUN: CHAT APPLICATION

AARON: Hey! How's it going over there?

AARON: D1V?

AARON: Hey I know things are rough, but I'm around if you want to chat.

AARON: Or blow up some things in the game.

AARON: Or both!

AARON: Just saying.

9
AARON

The calendar in the kitchen feels like it's glaring at me. There, with a Post-it note on today's date, written in my mom's messy doctor handwriting, is a message that seals my fate for the day.

Aaron, Office, Morning–Afternoon.

Today's the day we're supposed to be meeting across town, at that pretentious café Laura picked, to really dig into the illustrations with Jason. I need to be there for Ryan, and my mom *knows* this. She has to—this video game gig is literally the only thing of note that I've been doing this summer, besides playing games with D1V in *Reclaim the Sun*, which I've neglected to mention to my parents. Mom doesn't even get why I want to make games, so she's certainly not going to understand the thrill of playing them with a famous streaming star.

And yet, here we are.

"Goddamn it," I grumble, snatching the Post-it off the calendar. I hustle my way around to the side entrance that leads into the practice and swing the door open, only to catch my dad hurriedly trying to cover something up on the computer.

"Aar–Aaron!" he stammers, making quick work of something on the screen. I walk toward him, trying to get a glimpse of whatever he's fussing with. "I didn't know you were on the schedule."

"Yeah, I was surprised, too…" I trail off, gesturing to the computer. "What's, um, what's going on over there?"

"Oh nothing," he says brightly, shaking the mouse, the screen black. "Trying to get this darn thing to unfreeze." He laughs nervously, in a way that makes him sound decades younger. He manually shuts the computer off. "Maybe that'll do it. Reset the beast. Your mother really needs to replace this thing, am I right?"

"Dad, why are you acting so weird?" I ask, reaching over the desk and turning the PC on again, the old switch making a snapping noise as it clicks back. "Does it have to do with that…that medieval game?"

Speaking of things I've neglected, there's the whole mystery here of my dad and this ancient video game. I've been so invested in everything going on with D1V that I completely forgot about…well, whatever this is.

"What are you talking about?" he asks, his eyes widening.

"The computer was frozen the other day when I was in here," I tell him. "The screen was locked on some old-looking fantasy game. Looked kind of like *Diablo*, only older. Are you…are you *playing* something?"

"Me? What? No," he insists. "Come on, this thing can barely *run* Microsoft Word, never mind a video game. Maybe *Solitaire*."

"Hmm." I eye him suspiciously, totally not believing him. I make a mental note to check the computer later, maybe when I get back from the ManaPunk meeting. If he's playing something, I want to know what it is. And why he'd hide it.

"Where's Mom?" I ask.

"Seeing a patient." He glances back toward the exam rooms and catches sight of the Post-it in my hand. "When does she have you on for?"

"Ugh," I groan. "Morning through the afternoon. I'm supposed to—"

"I'll cover for you. I've got this," he interrupts before I can launch into what the ManaPunk meeting is about today.

I blink in surprise. "Are you sure? Mom might get mad."

"She won't. I'll talk to her."

A grin spreads across my face. "Thanks, Dad."

"Anytime." He smiles back, but his eyes keep flitting to the computer. "You can go. It's okay."

"Alright, alright, I'm going." I try not to laugh as I walk back into the house. It's got to be that old game, but why hide it? Especially from me? Seriously, I don't see the point. I wonder if Mom knows he's playing some archaic RPG on the office computer, and the thought of her reaction makes me chuckle.

As I make my way back upstairs to grab my pack and laptop, my phone starts buzzing. It's Ryan calling, which is odd—he usually just texts me.

I answer it. "Hey," Ryan says, hanging on the vowel. "You coming to the meeting?"

"Yeah, of course, just getting ready to leave now."

"Did you, um…read the blogs at all today?"

"No, why?" I ask curiously. "What's up?"

"You might want to get caught up on the way here."

"It's all so terrible," Ryan says, staring at his phone.

"Have you ever been to Quarter Slice Crisis?" I ask, looking down at mine. I find that I'm straining to hear him over the morning rush at Autofocus Café. I still can't believe Laura picked this damn place—the line to order is so long that I'm convinced the meeting will be over before we can get any caffeine.

"A few times. The pizza there is garbage." Ryan sticks his tongue out and makes a disgusted noise. "Alberto took me there on a date once, when we hopped a BoltBus out of town for the day. 'He likes video games, he'll like this!' So sweet."

The news article I'm reading on *Kotaku* is like something out of a nightmare, and so is the piece Ryan found on *Giant Bomb*, both complete with a video that I can't believe *anyone* would think is a good idea to share. There's D1V, the first time I've seen her in an actual, physical space and not just on a stream or as a thumbnail on social media. It's also the first time I've realized that her profile photos are super photoshopped, in a way that would make it hard to recognize her, though I suppose if you watch her videos, it doesn't really matter. This is her, in real life. Moving and talking and being a person.

And it's devastating.

It's her and Rebekah, the girl who does the live streams with her, trying to get away from some guy by an arcade machine. The guy grabs D1V, she slaps him, and then she bolts out the door with Rebekah. The dudes pursue, the person holding the camera running down the street behind the guys, the footage jostling about, like something out of one of those found-footage horror movies. But it's so much worse than watching a movie like *Cloverfield* or *Chronicle*. Because it's real.

There's a bit more in the article about the campus police getting involved, at some college in Hoboken, and how Rebekah had been the subject of an assault a year ago, with a ton of links branching out to other stories. Stories about the boys on campus still being there, Rebekah moving away, lawsuits that are pending. I open a few and then quickly shut them, feeling like I'm invading her privacy. I only know Rebekah from the Internet—as an avatar on social media, barely recognizable. It feels wrong to know so much about her personal life in just a few clicks, with the big takeaway being the lack of consequences for those involved.

Like I said, a nightmare.

I tap away from the news on my phone and load up the game's chat app, checking out my friends list to see if D1V is signed on. She's there, currently exploring in *Reclaim the Sun.*

"Should I message her?" I ask Ryan, staring at my phone. "She...hasn't been answering me lately."

"Can you blame her? Come on, man, she probably needs space," he says. I glance at him, and he's staring down at my phone, a quizzical look on his face. We take a few steps forward in the line, the cashier looming. "I mean, what are you going to say?" He looks up at me. "What can you even do right now?"

"Try to be a friend, you know?" I shrug. "If something awful like that happened to me, I'd want to hear from people who care about me. I think?"

"Sooo, you care about her?" Ryan asks, raising his eyebrows.

"Well, I mean, we've gamed together a few times now. Chatted a bit," I say, feeling a little heat flush to my cheeks. "I like to think we're becoming friends."

"Alright," he says. "Just...just don't do that thing."

"What thing?" I ask.

"That *thing*," he presses. "The whole 'I'm going to be the nice guy who swoops in and saves the day, maybe then she'll like me later!' thing."

"Oh, come on, you know me better than that!" I exclaim. "That's exactly what happened at that arcade. That guy gave her a quarter and then expected her to go out with him or something. That's not my style."

"Okay, okay," Ryan says, raising his hands in surrender. "I just had to make sure."

My eyes drift back to my friends list, to her icon there in the app, the green dot telling me that she's online.

"Now what's on your mind?" Ryan asks, nudging my shoulder.

"It's…nothing." I shake my head.

"You can't do that. You can't tease that you're gonna say something and then not say it. Hurry up and spit it out, before Jason and Laura get here."

"It's just…that video. And this interview…" I feel the words forming in my head and in my mouth, and I feel like a jerk before they even come out. "I keep thinking about how if she was at Quarter Slice Crisis, that means she might be from around there, right? Plus, her streaming partner goes to college in that area. I mean, there aren't any conventions going on. So chances are she probably lives in—"

"I'm going to stop you right there," Ryan says.

"But it's not that far," I continue. "Philadelphia to Hoboken, or even New York, if that's where she is? I could take a BoltBus. Or the SEPTA to the NJ Transit, even though it's hell. We could maybe be in-real-life friends—"

"Dude. Don't say that. Don't like, think about how you could find a way to meet her. That makes you—"

"That's the other point," I interject. "I also can't help but think of those trolls that have been attacking her and saying all that shit on social media. I mean, she doesn't have her location listed in her profile, on purpose, to keep people from harassing her. In the game, on the chat application, on any of her social media stuff…nowhere." I exhale, shaking my head. "Someone else is bound to figure it out, right?"

Ryan gives me a look.

"I'll message her."

He stares at me harder.

"But I won't be that guy?" I add.

"You're exhausting. But you might be right," Ryan admits as we reach the front of the line. He points toward the seating area. "I'll get the drinks. Go grab a table for everyone."

RECLAIM THE SUN: CHAT APPLICATION

ME: Hey, ridiculous question, considering everything that happened.

ME: But is everything okay?

ME: I know you didn't want to talk about it before, but I saw the news and now I know.

ME: And I can't pretend that someone I'm starting to become friends with isn't hurting.

ME: Just, you know, checking.

D1V: Hey. Not ridiculous. But no. Everything is a dumpster on fire.

ME: I saw some of those articles. I'm so sorry.

D1V: Thanks.

Ryan pulls a seat out, the hard polished wooden chair squeaking against the stone floor of the café. A large steaming cup of hot chocolate plunks down next to me, and I grab the cardboard sleeve around the white cup. It's dark and bitter, and I must make a face, because Ryan laughs.

"Sorry, it's some pure cocoa thing. Might want some sugar for that."

"You think?" I grab a bunch of raw sugar packets off our table and stir them in, and the result is all kinds of perfect. For a moment, I actually don't mind that Laura has dragged us clear across town to meet at this place.

"Man, that was fast," I say, exhaling in post-chocolate-sip bliss.

"The wait is never that bad when you just get regular drinks," Ryan notes, stirring some sugar into his tea. It's so strong I can smell the spices. "It's when you're in a Starbucks and people show up asking for that Butterbeer drink from *Harry Potter* or whatever the latest unicorn-flavored nonsense is that they take forever."

I smile at him and glance down at my phone again. At that "thanks" from D1V.

Do I say anything more? Suggest we load up a game of *Reclaim the Sun* and go exploring together after this meeting? Ask how her friend is doing? This weird sinking feeling of dread creeps over me, and I have absolutely no idea what to say.

"Did she respond—" Ryan starts, but then my phone chimes. I look back at my screen.

RECLAIM THE SUN: CHAT APPLICATION

D1V: Whenever someone asks me this, I want to set them on fire, so do excuse how this sounds.

D1V: But can you send me a photo of yourself right now?

D1V: A series of them, so I know you didn't just grab one off a friend's Facebook or something.

D1V: I legit hate myself for this so please don't make fun of me.

A picture of me? A series of them? I stare at the screen for a moment, until I feel Ryan peering over my shoulder.

"Are you waiting for something?" he asks, pointing at the phone.

"No, I—"

The app beeps again.

D1V: After the pizza place, those people following me. Coming after Rebekah.

D1V: I need to see who you are. I need to know that you aren't one of them.

D1V: Even though I know you aren't. It might not make sense to you, but that doesn't matter.

D1V: It's not about you. It's about me feeling safe.

My heart quickens, and my stomach twists itself up. Not for a second had I considered D1V might feel…unsafe, chatting and gaming with me. That never registered in my brain, not for a minute. When I think about myself, I envision the most unthreatening person imaginable…but that's me. That's my perception. And now that I know this is what she's feeling, I want to help change that as quickly as possible.

I immediately flip to my phone's camera and take a few selfies. It's the first time I've ever taken photos for someone with no regard to how I look in the picture. This morning was rushed, as I was hurrying out the door to hustle across town, so my wavy black hair is a mess and there's some stubble peeking through on my cheeks. The hair in between my eyebrows—which are technically just a single solid eyebrow that I meticulously try to maintain as two—is starting to grow back. Also I'm pretty sure I wore this T-shirt yesterday.

Snap. Snap. Snap.

"I could take those for you, you know," Ryan offers.

"Better yet…" I hold the phone farther away from me, getting Ryan in the shot and switching to video.

"Hey, D1V!" I exclaim, awkwardly waving. "This is Ryan, one of the guys I make video games with. He also doubles as my best friend."

"Hi," Ryan says. "Those guys were assholes. I hope you feel… I don't know, better? Safer? Safe. That's what's important here." He sends me an exasperated look. "You could have given me time to prepare something, dude." He turns back to the camera. "Please don't put this on your channel or whatever it is. I'm not a YouTube person."

"It's not YouTu—" I start to say, then stop, shaking my head ruefully. "Never mind. Not important. Let's game later!" I say, ending the recording with a smile.

"That was…oddly sweet," Ryan comments. "I better not end up in a stream, though. I'm not into all that social media stuff."

"We're not interesting enough, anyway," I say with a shrug. "And you should watch those gaming streams. It's who you're illustrating for, who we make games for."

I send the photos to D1V through the game's chat app and start uploading the video to her just as someone drags a couple more chairs over to our table.

Laura has arrived.

"Welcome to my home turf," she says, grinning. She gestures around the coffee shop, as though we're being given a rare glimpse inside a sprawling kingdom, then frowns at our lack of enthusiasm. "Hey, this place is magic, okay? This table? It's repurposed from a bowling alley."

"This tea tastes like it was repurposed from a bowling ball," Ryan says, smirking.

Laura glares at him.

"Fine, it's delicious," Ryan admits, taking a sip of the strong tea in question.

"Damn right it is. You guys good?" She eyes our cups.

"All full," Ryan says, holding his cup up. "No worries."

Laura unloads her backpack and places her incredibly large laptop on the dark wood table with a *thunk*. The base of the thing is as thick as four laptops stacked together—or, to be more specific, about the size of a laptop circa 1999. I'd found one like that in the trash near a neighbor's house once back in junior high, and the best it could do was run Windows 95. It's still under my bed, packed full of Super Nintendo ROMs and other downloaded emulators for video game consoles long since retired.

I bet the old desktop in the practice could run some ROMs. I wonder if that's what my dad has been playing.

I catch Ryan smirking at it, the machine we all affectionally refer to as The Butcher's Block.

"Don't start," Laura says, pointing at me and Ryan, scowling. "I don't mock the pretentious Moleskine notebooks you use for all your doodles, so stop making fun of the tools of my trade. I like having the laptop dock attached. It feels powerful."

Ryan's forehead wrinkles up. "Last time we hung out you made fun of my notebook!"

"Okay, fine, I do it all the time," Laura admits, grinning. "But that's only because I love you." She walks off toward the counter and the line weaving up to it.

"I wonder where Jason is," I muse, turning to Ryan. "Feels like he and Laura are attached at the hip these days."

"Dude," Ryan says, "you need to stop obsessing over this."

"I'm not obsessing over it. I'm just stating a fact!" I protest. "And for the record, again, I'm not into Laura. I'm just worried about her with Jason."

"Oh no, I can tell, because of how smitten you are with the YouTuber."

"That's not what she does—"

"Not denying the feelings, I see?"

"Oh my God, would you stop—"

"And for the record, *again*, it's not your place to interject yourself into her relationship," he says, crossing his arms. "You're not Mario, and Jason isn't Bowser. She's not a princess who needs or wants your saving."

"I get it," I grumble. "I'm trying."

"How'd you get out of doctor training today, anyway?" Ryan asks, settling on one notebook and placing the rest in his bag. "I didn't think we were gonna see you today."

"You know, it was weird," I start, thinking back to this morning. "My dad was a total mess, in the office, hiding something on the computer."

"Porn?" Ryan grins.

"Gross, bro." I wince. "No, some kind of game, I think? The screen was frozen the other day on this old game and... Oh!" It hits me—the photos I took. "I took a picture. Hold on." I flip through my photos, and there it is, all grainy with lines running through it and off-color from taking a picture of a screen, but clear enough. "What do you think?"

Ryan squints at the screen, his eyebrows furrowed.

"Your dad is playing that?" he asks as I pull the phone back.

"Maybe?" I shrug. "I couldn't tell if that's what he was doing this morning. Why, what is it?"

"I think it's one of the *Ultima* games?" He glances back at my phone before the screen shuts off. "It's an old RPG adventure game. There was even an online version."

"Huh." I shake my head. "I just can't imagine why he'd hide that."

"Maybe you should ask him?" Ryan shrugs. "That tends to be the way to solve mysteries the quickest, you know."

I nudge against his shoulder.

"You have your illustrations with you?" I flick my hand at his sketchbook.

"Yes, but I already know how you feel about my illustrations."

"That they are as brilliant and flawless as the creator?" I ask.

"You are correct in your assessment." He smiles, opening the sketchbook. He flips toward the end, and as each page flickers by, the interior goes from sketches in shades of grey pencil, or hard pen-and-ink-style drawings, to stunning full-color illustrations. He settles on one close to the end of the sketchbook, and I can't stop myself from smiling.

I know those characters.

The Mage. The Rogue. The Elf. Characters from the story I've been writing for ManaPunk, for Jason's first venture into role-playing games. Our first venture. The three of them are standing on the precipice of a cliff, overlooking a lush green valley. The Mage's cape is billowing in the wind, a staff in hand, a purple glow bursting from an orb on top. The Rogue and the Elf are there next to the Mage, the Rogue's arms crossed, the Elf with hands on hips. You can't see their faces, but I can see them in my mind. Strong. Triumphant. Completely sure of what they want and how they are going to get it.

A vision ahead of them. An adventure. A mission. A goal.

I know you're not supposed to project wish fulfillment for yourself into your own writing. Every piece of writing advice I've ever read has hammered that home. But sometimes

I can't help but see myself in these fantasy characters—that is, the way I wish I was. The way they approach their life in the game, with more certainty and fewer questions. It's how I want to tackle things. With that steadfast sureness.

I think these characters would demand their paychecks.

Sigh.

They kinda look like the characters I saw on the frozen screen in the office. And for a minute, I'm wondering if me and my dad have something real in common. It's not like we're wildly different or something, one of those estranged father-son relationships where all the communication happens over the course of a few head nods and handshakes. We talk all the time—about school, home, whatever nonsense we're both watching on Netflix together.

But this. This is something we've never talked about, for some odd reason. And I can't quite figure out why that would be. We'd stopped talking about video games and playing them together when I was younger, so the idea that he's still at it surprises me—and leaves me feeling a little sad.

Laura makes her way back over to the table, two cups of coffee in her hand, just as Jason bounds through the café entrance, pure energy and smiles. He waves to a few people, who he probably doesn't even know, and makes his way over to us. He pulls out a seat next to Laura and kisses her on the cheek a little too long, while Ryan kicks me under the table, a reminder to "stay out of it," no doubt.

Jason rubs his hands together.

"Alright, you guys." He nudges his chair closer to the table. "I have some news. I've entered *Thundertail* into the GamesCon Indie Game Showcase. They started accepting submissions just two days ago, and I presented some of the concept art and the basic story in the proposal last night. Had a great screen-share call with them."

Laura grabs Jason's hand, smiling at him, and then gives us an equally excited smile.

Ryan glances over at me, worry washing over his face.

Screen-share? What could he even *show* them?

"Jason, the game isn't done yet," Ryan says, his tone stern and concerned. "How can you submit an unfinished game to the showcase? What assets can you share with an unfinished game? Also, you haven't paid for any of—"

"It's not a big deal." Jason waves him off. "All we needed to show them were some bits and pieces of what we produced already, like the art, which you've been working on, and some loose concept of the story—that's you, Aaron—and a tiny bit of gameplay." He glances at Laura and then back at us. "The two of us have been coding all week and created some early concept dungeon-crawl levels."

"What!" I exclaim, trying to hold in the excitement washing over me, which is at war with the slight feeling of irritation at him showcasing our work this early without telling or paying us. "It…you… We can play our game?"

"With *my* characters and designs?" Ryan asks, his tone still sharp.

"Technically, yes." Jason shrugs, grinning. "It's just a very, very rough demo. The purpose of the showcase at the convention is to ideally get an investor. Someone who will jump on board, fund the game, and take a share of the profits. Maybe even a publisher bigger than…well, me. Someone bigger than ManaPunk."

"Oh," I say, all that excitement fading away. "What happened to—"

"Doing it ourselves? Being indie? Making it our own? Getting *paid* for *our* work?!" Ryan interrupts, glaring at Jason and closing his notebooks. "You want to go with a publisher, with a bigger company, who owns all this? Someone other than me who can put a trademark on my art, Jason? Other than us?" He points at his closed-up drawings, and I see worry flicker over Jason's generally carefree face. "I didn't sink days and weeks and months of my life into all of this only to have some asshole be able to make action figures or crappy *Candy Crush*–style games using my work down the line. Especially with no contract or paycheck on the horizon. Furthermore—"

"That…that's not what's happening here, Ryan," Jason says calmly. He glances at Laura.

"Tell them," she urges.

"Tell us what?" Ryan demands.

My phone chimes, and I flick it to vibrate, but not before seeing it's another message from D1V, sent to me through the game's chat app. A bit of tension seizes up in my chest as I reluctantly put the phone down on the table.

Jason sighs.

"Look, I know I'm late on your checks. I know. But the thing is, ManaPunk isn't doing so hot," he says hesitantly. "Mobile games…well, even when sales seem amazing—and they *are* pretty good—sometimes it's only just enough to keep me afloat. Never mind the freelance publicist and marketing team we have on board to support the earlier games, or the tech support I source out to keep them updated every time the iOS or Android systems roll out another update. There are a lot of working gears in the machine that none of you have to deal with, and I'm running out of oil to keep them going smoothly."

"Running out of *money*," Ryan says, and I can feel the glare in his voice. "That's what you mean. Say it like it is. Money for us."

"Yeah…but…finding a publisher, that's the best way to wriggle out of this." Jason reaches out and puts his hand on one of Ryan's notebooks, and Ryan grabs it, holding firm. There's an awkward silence in the air between the two of them, as Ryan stares down Jason, and Jason continues to look at Ryan like he's his only hope in all this. Like maybe the both of us are, at this point.

And it strikes me that maybe he is. We are.

Which is terrifying.

I glance down at my phone. Three more messages. I bite my lip.

"I'll need to see contracts," Ryan says firmly, breaking the silence. "Contracts that I'm going to run by my family and my father's lawyer."

"Of course," Jason says, the words escaping with a breath.

"I need to know where my art is going, how it's being used," he presses. "Every single step of the way. The second you try to convince me to port it over to some match 3 game bullshit—"

"Ryan, come on, man," Jason says, his hand still on the notebook.

"I know my worth," Ryan says sternly. "You best know it, too." He exhales and finally lets go of his notebook.

Jason starts flipping through it and quickly reaches the end, the finished illustrations. Full color and glorious. I can practically see his eyes lighting up from across the table, a beaming smile on his face. He looks up at Ryan.

"This," he says, closing the notebook and shaking it at Ryan and me. "These finished illustrations. And with your story, Aaron? This is going to save me." He clears his throat and quickly adds, "Save us."

I try not to smile too hard at this, hearing him say my story will save the company. I think that's the first positive reaction I've had from him about it.

"Contracts," Ryan reminds him, plucking the notebook out of Jason's hands. "Or no art."

"You got it," Jason says, smiling. "Now!" He slaps his hands on the table. "Let's see those awful games and apps, and then we can start talking about next steps. I'm thinking posters and wallpapers and giveaways for the convention and on the website. My mind is just swimming with the possibilities."

"I love how you follow my demands to see no crappy games or action figures with proclamations of posters and giveaways." Ryan scowls. "If I see a coaster or a beer cozy, I am coming for you."

My phone vibrates as the two of them start bickering again. I try not to look at it, but I can't keep my eyes from darting down toward the screen.

"Alright, Mr. Famous," grumbles Jason, pointing at the phone. "I know you're a big deal now, thanks to your guest appearance in that video."

It buzzes again, vibrating against the table. Eight messages. Eight little notifications taunting me as I glance down at the screen. It takes me a moment to realize Jason is talking about D1V's stream, and that he actually watched it. Or at least, he read the email with me telling him about it. I'll take whatever props I can.

"To be fair, I did get ManaPunk a shout-out on that stream," I say, looking down at the phone.

"Yeah, I know. I don't get you guys and those streaming videos, though." He snorts. "Games are meant to be played. What's the point of watching someone else play it, when you could actually play it yourself?"

"Why watch football or basketball or golf when you could play those things?" Laura asks.

"That's not... No, that's not the same thing," Jason counters.

"Kinda is." Laura shrugs. "Just because you don't get it,

doesn't mean there isn't worth there. Same goes for not lik-ing sports. People are allowed to like things."

"Point goes to Laura." Ryan grins, snapping his fingers.

"Hey, are we even going over story stuff today?" I ask, the words tumbling out of my mouth before I can fully think them through. "'Cause if we aren't, I can forfeit my turn with our app game and get going."

Jason glares at me and the phone, shaking his head in dis-gust.

"It's not just this," I insist. "I have to…handle the office back home."

I glance over at Ryan, who subtly raises his eyebrows in a silent question. I know he won't blow up my spot, but I'll definitely be hearing about this from him later, that's for sure.

"I can get some writing done there, too," I offer.

"Fine, fine," Jason concedes. "We're definitely going over story elements next week, though. I need that opening and introduction perfect if we're gonna sell this based on a con-cept. In fact, email it to me when you get a second." He turns to Ryan. "And I could really use some of the illustrated con-cept art scanned in."

"Contracts," Ryan says with a shrug.

"Yeah, yeah," Jason snaps. "I'll have them. But I need *some-thing* in advance for the showcase." He glances at me again. "Story."

"You got it, great," I say, knowing full well I'm going to get home and load up *Reclaim the Sun* as quickly as I can, story be damned. I studiously avoid looking my phone as I pack up my laptop and peer over at Ryan instead. He flashes me a sly grin and shakes his head. It's all I need to know he approves of my nonsense.

I subtly open the game's chat app as I make my way to the

café entrance. Once I reach the door, I glance down to see the video transfer finished and D1V's new messages.

D1V: Oh my God

D1V: You sent a video.

D1V: You're ridiculous.

D1V HAS SENT YOU A PARTY REQUEST.

D1V: Oh, that's right, you're not actually at your computer, but in a coffee shop.

D1V: Well when you get back home, accept my party request.

D1V: I'll be on all night.

D1V: Oh, and hey. Thank you.

I practically sprint out of the coffee shop and wave down a cab rounding the corner.

RECLAIM THE SUN: CHAT APPLICATION

AARON: On my way home now.

D1V: Wait what? Now?

D1V: Aren't you with your video game designer pals or something? Making the next Flappy Bird?

AARON: Oh, sooooo funny.

D1V: Or are you more of an Angry Birds fan?

AARON: You are about to get blocked.

D1V: You wouldn't.

AARON: I wouldn't. And no, they can wait. They don't need me today.

D1V: If you're about to say something sappy about me needing you, I will light my phone on fire.

AARON: What is with you and lighting things on fire?

AARON: Also, they literally don't need me. It's an art day. They don't need my stories.

D1V: Oh.

AARON: I mean.

AARON: You could use a friend though, right?

D1V: THERE IT IS.

D1V: I KNEW IT.

D1V: (takes out lighter, holds up phone).

D1V: Goodbye, dear phone.

AARON: Okay you couldn't type on your phone while setting it on fire.

AARON: Also it's not like that. Just saying.

D1V: I'm just busting your chops.

AARON: Can we talk using the like, speakers in the game and whatnot later?

AARON: Your sarcasm is very lost in here, and you are the queen of it.

D1V: Hah, sure.

10
DIVYA

"He sent you a video," Rebekah says deadpan. She's staring at me from the little screen in the corner of my monitor, her mouth in a thin line.

"Yeah, it was actually kinda funny?" I dig for my phone.

"I don't want to see it." She rolls her eyes.

"Whatever, he's a good one." I slide the phone onto my desk. "He makes me laugh. We did some resource runs and talked a lot."

"What do you even talk about?"

"Oh, nothing important, really," I say. "*Reclaim the Sun.* The game he's working on, which sounds pretty neat. What streaming is like. Bad movies. Nothing terribly... I don't know, real?"

"Okay. That's fine, just—"

"—be careful," I finish, turning back to her little screen. "I know, Beks. Don't worry. Speaking of, have you heard anything else from Detective Watts?"

"Man, she is so cool," Rebekah croons.

"I know." I grin. "I'm glad we have someone like her in our corner."

"Same. But no, nothing new. You okay?"

"Yeah. You?"

"Yeah." There's a short pause while Rebekah fusses over something on her keyboard and fiddles with her phone. She exhales and looks back at me, smiling. I know that smile. The soft, pained one that hides so much behind it. I know she isn't okay. How could she be? It's only been a week since Quarter Slice Crisis, and every single mention of the incident online seems to link back to the articles about Rebecca's assault last year, rubbing salt into a wound that isn't even close to healed yet.

I don't know what to say to her half the time. So I try my best to be there to listen, on the rare moments she wants to say anything about it.

"So…you think I'll like this guy," Rebekah says, her eyes narrowing.

"I do. He's—"

"Wait, is he male?"

"Well, yeah, he—"

"Then nope."

I laugh and look back at the *Reclaim the Sun* start menu, flipping through my small friends list. A few members of the Angst Armada are online, the ones I've grown to trust, and of course there's Rebekah and a handful of old acquaintances from high school, but no sign of Aaron yet. I wonder if I'll meet any people I can game with once I start classes at the community college.

"How long are we going to wait for your *boyfriend*?" Rebekah asks, putting extra emphasis where it is certainly not needed.

"I am going to blow up your ship the second we get into the game if you say that word again," I growl, playfully scowling at her. She's right, though. It's not like we have all night. Well, I kind of do, but Rebekah doesn't—she has class tomorrow morning and can't be streaming nonstop like me.

"Alright, alright," Rebekah says, holding up her hands in surrender. "But seriously, if we're going to do a bit of surprise streaming, we should really get on with it." When I continue to hesitate, she adds, "Look, *he* can always join us later."

"I know, but..." I trail off, looking at my friends list and the in-game messenger again. I pick up my phone to see if he's sent me a text, then remember he doesn't actually have my phone number. Even though he seems like a great guy, there's no way I'm giving that out. Not yet, anyway.

I let out a sigh. "Okay. Let's post on social and dive in."

"You sure you're ready?" Rebekah asks, not for the first time tonight. "For another public stream and co-op? I just... I worry."

"Yeah, I'm ready. Fuck those guys." I glance down at her screen. "Are you?"

"Probably not," Rebekah says, her tone defeated. I wish I could reach through the screen and hug her. These trolls, their threats, the attack... I can't even imagine what it's like for her, how triggering it all is. But since it's way too late to hop the PATH to Hoboken for a visit and some fried snacks, I decide I'll do the next best thing.

Wreak havoc across the universe in her name.

"I got you," I tell her, trying to project as much confidence as possible. "Let's go."

In less than a minute, we've alerted Twitter, our small but loyal Facebook group, and our Glitch stream subscribers. And in the minutes that follow, numerous blips appear in our multiplayer party channel. Familiar usernames from past excursions. My beloved Angst Armada, returning to the fold once more.

I wonder, if things go sideways, will they have my back this time? Will they leave me on the ground, to fall into the icy depths of an unknown planet, again? I get that they didn't want to lose their ships and their experience points and all that...but it didn't feel great, watching them leave.

Oh well.

As the people pop in, they burst into the party chat window quickly, but like popcorn in the microwave, the growing numbers start to peter down, from multiple bursts to just one or two every few seconds. With a little more time, alerting the streaming community that we'd be doing this or that on a given date or time, we'd probably have hundreds more.

But after everything that's happened here, in the online space and whatever is going on outside, keeping it a little lower key feels right. I'm in no rush to have someone log on and kick my ass during my comeback.

"Looks like this is it," I say to Rebekah in a private channel.

"It'll make for a good video. D1V's return!" Rebekah exclaims, though I still hear hints of heartbreak in her voice. The exclamation isn't fooling me.

"Beks, we don't have to—" I start.

"Nope," she says, shaking her head in that little video window, and I think I catch her wiping at her eyes with her sleeve, but it happens too quickly for me to be sure. "Nope, we're doing this. Recording in three...two...one..."

With a click, I can suddenly hear the entire channel. An array of voices, cheering and shouting. My people. My Armada.

"Why, hello, my dears," I say into the microphone, summoning up all the energy I can. I flick on the streaming cam, and a live video of myself pops up in the corner of the screen, recording my every reaction as we play through the game. "I'm back. Did you all miss me?"

More cheering, louder and louder, and then suddenly several alerts and pings start popping up on my screen. Sounds and alerts I haven't seen before.

I squint at the text, and it takes a while before I realize what's happening.

You have a fund transfer from
THE NERDY NARWHAL
in the amount of 10,000 credits.
Do you wish to accept?
[YES] [NO]

My jaw drops as more and more pop up on the screen. 500 credits. 1,000 credits. 20,000 credits. 25 credits.

Transfers from users in the Armada.

My heart is hammering in my chest, and I can't believe what's happening right now, or that I ever doubted them.

"For you, our captain!" shouts one girl.

Another cheer: "'O Captain! My Captain!'"

"We've been planning this!" I hear another young girl shout.

And so on.

It's like that scene from *Dead Poets Society*, only in space. And instead of desks and chairs, we have planets and starships.

And it is beautiful.

My credits account in *Reclaim the Sun* keeps going up and up as I accept each incoming…donation? Pledge? I'm not even sure what to call them. I turn to look at Rebekah's window, and she is jumping up and down in her seat, the sound muted, but I can tell she is just *screaming*.

When the alerts finally start to slow down, there are over 100,000 credits in my account, an amount that would easily customize the hell out of my ship and get me the best upgrades possible. It's an amount that in actual physical money would be close to $1,000 and would take an exorbitant amount of time to gather on one's own. I'd managed to wrangle up about 2,000 credits over the weeks since the troll incident, doing little runs on planets and resource gathering on my own and sometimes with Aaron or Rebekah. Just barely enough to upgrade my weapons and ship a little.

Nothing like this.

And just like that, I'm crying.

I can't help it.

"My Armada!" I exclaim, pressing my hands to my heart. "I love you!"

"You deserve it!" someone shouts.

"Fuck those guys!" another exclaims, to an array of cheers.

"Thank you," I say with a watery chuckle. "Alright, everyone, let's get going! I can upgrade later. I want to spend this time with you. With every single one of you." I reach out and grab my VR headset, glancing over at Rebekah's little screen. She looks up at me, her eyes glistening, and nods. I won't be able to see her small window while in VR, but she gets it. I know she does.

This crew, this bundle of fans and gamers... I want to be as immersed in this moment as I possibly can. Feel as close to them as possible.

For some weird reason, my mind drifts to thoughts of Aaron, and my heart wrenches a bit at his absence. He'd love being here to see all this. And... I'd like him here with me.

I try to shake my wistfulness away, but it lingers there in my head, wedged in the back. He's been a good friend lately, checking in the way he has.

I put the headset on, and my bedroom disappears, the visor
snug against my head. I blink a few times to get used to the
lenses, and as the headset finishes syncing to the computer,
there it is. The dashboard of my ship, with the heads-up display showcasing hundreds of thousands of credits. I grip the
VR controls, the sticks in my hands, fingers on the triggers,
as I look left, then right. Out the windows, to the ships floating near me.

Everything about this moment is awesome.

With a quick flick of my wrist with one of the controllers,
I open up the player list for our channel, taking stock of everyone who's here and keeping an eye out for Aaron's name.
There's a mix of familiar usernames and some new folks. I
spend what feels like a significant amount of time studying
those new names, trying to see something, anything, that
might be hiding behind them. Another troll, someone who
might have infiltrated my ranks and Armada. Anyone who
might turn on me once we take off.

But there's no way to know, and no time to vet every single
player. There are over a hundred people in here.

"Let's go!" I shout, pressing forward on my ship's controls.
The character list screen sweeps away, replaced by the black
emptiness of space. My little ship, the *Cedere Nescio*, floats list-
lessly with the rest of the Armada. Unlike most of my fleet,
I'm nowhere near fully upgraded—though now I definitely
have all I need to build myself up again. I hope they're feeling patient for now, though, because jumping definitely isn't
going to be as fast as it used to be.

While my ship's scanners survey the nearby star systems,
I look out my vessel's cockpit window. Sometimes just staring out at the stars reveals little secrets. A glimmering speck
that shines a shade lighter or darker than the rest, an off-color
white or a pale yellow or a deep red can mean more than just

a star. It could be a sun. A large moon. A planet. A place ripe for exploration and discovery.

"If anyone spots anything, just send me a message!" I say into the headset, worried that this could take a while. "My scanners aren't that great yet."

"Just go upgrade!" someone shouts.

"We'll wait!" More cheers erupt.

"It's okay," I say with laugh. "I've got all the time in the world to do that. I want this moment with all of you."

After a few more minutes of what is going to be utterly boring footage, I lift up my headset for a minute, blinking against the natural light as it floods my eyes. I glance over at Rebekah in her little screen. Her arms are crossed, her feet up on the desk, and she looks about as bored as I imagine the rest of the Armada must be.

Something beeps in my headset, and I watch Rebekah jostle up to read something. I put my headset back on, and as my eyes adjust to the digital world again, I see a text alert floating in front of me.

INCOMING TRANSMISSION

MAGGS: Hey D1V! I've got some heavy upgrades on my ship, and there's a Class 3 planet over here. I'll send the coordinates. It doesn't say anything about it being discovered yet.
My gift to you and the Armada!
SPACE MAP LOCATION: 52.7 / 62.5 / 31.6

I load up the channel list and find Maggs's profile, which opens up to show a geeky gal with bright red hair and bold blue-rimmed glasses.

I grin. Definitely one of us.

I move my controller so I can reply to her message, and a little microphone symbol blips up. As I talk, the chat window writes out what I dictate.

TRANSMISSION FOLDER

ME: Maggs, you are a queen. I accept your gift and dub you a lieutenant in the Armada. Shoot me an email, I'll send you a patch when we finish getting them made. Or a pin. I think we're doing both.

I send the message, and her reply is almost immediate.

INCOMING TRANSMISSION

MAGGS: Oh my God that's amzinfg
YOU"RE AMAZINGEGG!

I laugh. She must be on a keyboard-and-mouse setup, because that's clearly not something you can dictate out loud. I speak the coordinates for the ship, and the screens alert me to it being an unknown quadrant, but I opt to trust Maggs. My scanners can't detect that far out—apparently hers can, though.

I close out her window and open up a chat with the entire channel, their voices flooding my headset.

"Listen up, Armada!" I announce, and they quiet down. "Maggs has found a Class 3 planet in the far-off reaches of space, and it's ours for the taking. Tag my ship, or hers, and follow us to adventure!"

My ship's dashboard alerts me to several locked-on vessels. They beep in one after another, dozens upon dozens of them.

"Um, apologies in advance if this takes a minute. I've got a lot of work to do on this ship, but can get to that soon, thanks to all of you. Ready in three…two…"

Then my chat window chimes, displaying a little orange screen, and my heart does this weird, unexpected fluttering thing that catches me completely off guard.

It's Aaron.

INCOMING TRANSMISSION

AARON: Room for one more in the Armada?
Sorry I'm late is that D1V tell her I said hi
and she's very pretty oh my God Mira
stop it get out of here.

I have to cover my mouth so I don't explode with laughter into the channel. I close out the group chat and reply quickly to him. And Mira.

TRANSMISSION FOLDER

ME: About to take off, hurry up and lock on!
Let's dance.

I send the message and hear his ship lock on to mine.

INCOMING TRANSMISSION

AARON: ARE YOU GOING TO PROM WITH HER—

Oh my God, I can't with Aaron's little sister. They seem so cute together, so sweet. I wink at the screen, only to realize it's not like he can actually see me doing any of that. Or that anyone can see me doing that. Oh well.

I open the group channel back up, the chattering of voices filling my ears again.

"Technical hiccup, sorry!" I exclaim into the mic. "Had a few stragglers. Let's do this thing! Three...two...one...jump!"

My little ship rockets into the black. A few bright blurs speed by me, either stars or passing ships, I can't be sure. The colors move and swirl, and I turn from side to side, looking at them as they zip by, all curious and strangely beautiful and no doubt gorgeous in the video stream that Rebekah is recording on her side of things.

In less than a minute, thankfully, my ship slows to a stop, and a large planet appears. It's impossibly bright blue, the shimmering hue of a winter sky, complete with white wisps swirling over it.

The stats load up in front of me:

CLASS THREE PLANET [ESTIMATED]
Status: Uncharted, Undiscovered
Life Support Capability: Positive
Detectable Resources: Gas, Ore
Would you like to claim and name this planet?
[YES] [NO]

A quick wave of anxiousness sweeps over me as I read the description, thinking about what happened the last time. But there aren't any red flags on this one. It hasn't been charted yet or claimed. It's empty. It's mine.

It's mine?

I load up the channel window and select Maggs. There's a voice chat option, to talk to her live, instead of just sending a message.

I tap it.

"Oh my God," a young girl's voice breathes, and in that

moment, I realize I'm probably older than this girl. Maybe way older. She sounds like she's twelve or thirteen. "H-hi? Hello? Is this a mistake? I think you chatted me."

"It's no mistake," I say cheerfully, and then I press the broadcast button so the entire Armada can hear us. "My Armada! Meet Maggs. She's the one who discovered this blue planet and shared it with me. With us! So it seems only fitting that she should lay claim to it."

"Oh my God," I hear her whisper again, barely a squeak.

"Go ahead, Maggs!" I tell her, a grin spreading across my face. I hear her typing through the headset, and after a few more keystrokes, the planet's name pops up on the screen. A cheer erupts from the Armada at the sight.

PLANET OMGWHATISMYLIFE

Discovered by MAGGS

"Descend, Armada!" I exclaim, trying to mask the laughter in my voice. "Go explore, and thank you, Maggs!"

I push forward on the flight stick, and my ship speeds toward the planet's surface, the bright blue glistening as it grows closer. I break through the atmosphere, the approaching clouds exploding around me, ships in the Armada at all sides, and I gasp at the immensity of the ocean. My eyes dart to the small plots of land that seem to dot the water like freckles. Seemingly tiny islands, but as we get closer, I realize they're massive. Almost the entire Armada could fit on one with room to spare.

And the islands are everywhere.

I pick an arbitrary one out of the endless number of them and bring my ship in to land, settling on the soft soil. A few other ships follow me, two of which are Rebekah's and Aaron's. I wait as they both hop out and walk over to me, the sound of their footsteps, the roar of ships flying overhead, and the cooling of thrusters competing for my attention in my headset.

I mute my microphone from the rest of the Armada, setting us up in a private party as they get closer.

Rebekah hums next to Aaron. If she could look him up and down, I feel like she would. "He's definitely not as cute as he is in the video."

"Hey, I don't look like my avatar. Wait, you showed her the video?!" Aaron exclaims.

"Um, I show her everything," I tell him, feeling my cheeks flush a bit.

"Everything?!" Aaron asks, a hitch in his voice.

"Well, not our messages and stuff," I say quickly.

I hear Aaron audibly exhale.

"I mean, you *could* show me those messages," Rebekah says after a beat, chuckling. "They sound *very* interesting."

"No way," I say with a laugh. "So what happened, Aaron? Why so late?"

"Parents," Aaron replies, sounding exasperated. "I actually don't have much time. I need to help in the office a bit more, make things easier for my dad in the morning."

"What's he do?" Rebekah asks.

"He helps my mom run her practice. She's a doctor," Aaron explains, his tone sad. "They want me to take over someday. They keep trying to steal this summer away from me, I swear. 'If we're paying for college, you're going to be a doctor!' My mom loves to guilt me with—"

"Oh wow, what a horrible problem to have," Rebekah faux cries. "My student loans give me panic attacks at night, Dr. Aaron."

"I'm sorry. I know I'm luckier than most. It's just… I really

don't want to be a doctor. I want to write, play video games..."
Aaron trails off, and I hear Rebekah groan again. "What?"

"Oh nothing," she says. "I'm just already exhausted by your privilege."

"Hey, you don't know anything about me or my fam—"
Aaron starts to dig in.

"Alright, alright!" I interrupt before they start *really* fighting. "Let's cool it with all that and do some exploring."

The two of them grumble a bit more, but grow quiet as we walk over the terrain. The ground is some sort of weird soil-and-sand mixture that makes my feet slide a bit with each step. There are a few hardy-looking small green plants here and there, and a handful of treelike bits of green, but nothing towering or impressive. In fact, it's easy to see right across to the far side of the island, and over to the other islands nearby, each of those with their own ships and crews exploring them.

"Hmm." I wave my hand, and a display opens up with data about what we're walking on. The resources seem meager around us. Not a lot of wood or food, but apparently limitless water.

Over the sounds of the game, I hear the familiar loud whine of the apartment door opening.

"Divya?" My mom's back early. "Are you home?"

I mute the channel and call to her. "Streaming in my room, Mom. Just a second."

"I need..." She trails off, and I unmute the channel. Sounds like someone brought home groceries.

"Hey streamers, I'll be right back." I remove my headset and shut off the VR, the stream routing back to my computer's camera, the sound thundering back through my speakers. I wink and point at the camera. I get up to head out of my bedroom, ready to smile at my mom, show her what I'm working on, when the door swings open and she barrels in.

"Oh shit!" Rebekah shouts. "Turn it off! Turn off the video!"

I dart over and flick at the switch on my little HD camera, pulling it off the monitor just in case, and run over to my mom, who stumbles over to sit on my bed, her shoulders heaving with sobs. Her normally lustrous hair is a matted mess, caked with something that leaves a yellow tint in some places, clear in others. I wrap my arms around her while looking through her hair and at her clothes, finding bits of white everywhere.

"What happened?!" I ask, holding her tightly. "What is all this?"

She cries into my shoulder for several moments, then shudders and pulls away. The black eyeshadow and mascara that she likes to apply in thick lines is dripping down her cheeks, coloring in the wrinkle lines under her eyes and around her mouth.

"These…these boys," she stammers. "They were waiting outside the library."

I pluck a piece of the white something off her outfit.

It's a shell.

An eggshell.

Some fucking assholes egged my mother.

"They just came after me, throwing the eggs." She wipes at the mascara and the tears on her face. "I tried to run, but I slipped and fell by the library gardens, and…and they just kept throwing them, laughing, until they ran out and took off."

"Oh my God, Mom, that's awful!" I feel this heat bursting in my chest, this rage. It had to be some of those trolls. It just had to be. The ones who sent me that damn picture in the email.

"I couldn't get a cab. My phone broke when I fell, and then the bus—" she sniffles "—they wouldn't let me on looking like this. I had to walk all the way back. Everyone kept staring at me."

Something chimes over by my desk, and she looks up at my computer, her eyes wide, horrified.

"Divya, darling…is your game still on? Is that…recording?"

I look back to the computer and see Rebekah in her little window, waving about frantically, her mouth open and shouting at me. My phone starts buzzing on my desk. A ton of chat requests and messages are pinging up on my screen, and I spot my little webcam.

It's on my desk, on an awkward angle, pointing at us.

And it's still on.

I see us on the screen, in the upper left corner. We're off to the side somewhat, but still clear as day.

"Fuck!" I march over to the computer, bend down, and pull the plug out completely, the screen and tower going black quickly. I fight the rising urge to pick up the entire gaming rig and throw it out my window just to watch the machine shatter on the pavement below.

Instead, I pick up my phone. There are a bunch of chat messages from Aaron and Rebekah, but I flick them away and open the call screen.

"What…what are you doing?" my mom asks, leaning over to look at the phone.

"Making a call I should have made a while ago," I say, shaking my head, thinking about that damn email, the trolls with my address, who clearly went out of their way to find out that my mom works at the library. Did they follow her? Have they been following me?

I search my room for Detective Watts's business card and find it on my desk, right in the middle of all my hastily pushed aside stuff. I dial her number. My mind reels as I take a few deep breaths, trying to stay calm. Just how much did that camera capture—of my mom, of that discussion, of what happened? Did it make it to the stream? And if they figured out where my mom works, do they know where she's going to school, too? I suppose once they knew where I lived, it couldn't be that hard... But why target my mom instead of me? Why?

My phone chimes, and I pull it away from my ear to look at the screen. It's a text from Rebekah, a screenshot of an email. There's no subject, but the email has a single sentence inside.

Hi Rebekah. The Vox Populi send their regards.

"Detective Watts," a voice on the other end says, all professional. I fumble with my phone and bring it back up to my ear.

"Hi. Detective?" I exhale, a sob lurking in my throat, and it's taking everything in me to keep talking through it. "It's Divya. Divya Sharma. My mother was attacked. They came after my family."

I think about that email and the photo.

"And I need to show you something."

RECLAIM THE SUN: CHAT APPLICATION

AARON: Oh my God D1V.

AARON: Are you okay? What happened?

D1V: Can't get into it right now.

D1V: At the police station.

D1V: Trolls figured out where my mom works, harassed her in person.

AARON: Fuck.

AARON: I'm so so sorry.

D1V: Not your fault.

AARON: I wish there was something I could do.

AARON: You let me know if you need anything, okay? Anything.

D1V: I took a screenshot of that.

D1V: I'll save it for when I want to buy a car or a new gaming rig.

AARON: Can it be a remote-control car?

D1V: Sure.

AARON: And as for the gaming rig, will an old Game Boy Advance suffice?

D1V: That would be excellent.

AARON: Perfect.

D1V: Aaron?

AARON: Yes?

D1V: Don't stop talking to me. Tell me a story. Tell me something good.

D1V: I hate being here. I hate the questions.

AARON: When I was a kid, my dad was playing this video game with me.

AARON: One of those games that took a photo of you and pasted your face on the body of your character.

AARON: One day I played the game by myself, used his character. And the character died.

AARON: I thought I killed him. Like the real him. I was in tears. He still makes fun of me.

D1V: That is really sad and really hilarious. Tell me more.

11

AARON

"Thank you, Aaron. Your father could really use a day off."

My mom is talking to me—I hear her, the words are there floating in the air, but I can't bring myself to grab them. I'm behind the computer in the reception area, ignoring the patient records that desperately need updating while my eyes are fixated on the countless news articles that seem to be pouring out about D1V. I go back and forth from that over to the chat application on my phone I've been using to talk to her.

"Aaron?" my mom presses.

"Yeah, yeah," I say. "I got it."

"I'll be in the back if you need anything," she says and turns to walk into her office. The sound of her heels against the floor abruptly stop, and I glance up to see her fiddling with her ID badge, the door to her personal office still closed.

"Mom?" I venture.

"How's the…" She looks up at me and clears her throat. "How's the writing going?"

She smiles, and I can't help but wonder if this is a trap.

"It's okay," I offer hesitantly. "Ryan likes everything I'm

working on, but Jason…" I shrug. "He's just difficult, is all. Doesn't see the vision. Doesn't—"

"Pay you guys?" she asks, stepping back toward the desk.

"He's going to," I tell her firmly, though I wish I felt as confident about this as I sound. He still hasn't sent over those contracts for me and Ryan. "He will. He's gearing up to present the game at a conference, and we'll be set."

"Aaron," she continues, clearing her throat again. "I know I give you a hard time, about your games, this…" She gestures at the computer, her eyebrows furrowed. "This world of yours that I don't really understand. I just worry about Jason taking advantage of you. And of Ryan, too. I mean, he's a bit tougher—"

"Yeah, he is." I can't help but laugh, remembering how assertive he was at our meeting the other day.

"But…when your father was working at all those restaurants, in the kitchens, even when he was managing a place, I would see it." She shakes her head. "The long hours he wasn't paid enough to work, the overtime he didn't get… God, and when he ran deliveries, and people wouldn't tip…" She sighs. "I just can't bear watching you go through that. And neither can he, even if he won't say it."

"I thought…" I'm not even sure what to say right now. She's said before that she didn't want Jason to take advantage of me, but I always thought that was just an excuse. I thought she hated the games because it got in the way of her dream for me, this doctor stuff, not because of what Dad had been through. "Sorry, I didn't think of it like that."

"I just worry." She fiddles with her ID tag again.

"If he doesn't pay me, he can't use the work for the game," I explain. "I won't let him do that. Ryan wouldn't, that's for sure. He even asked Jason to draw up contracts for us."

"That was good thinking on his part." She smiles. "I know you two will be careful. I love you."

"Love you, too."

She heads into the back, leaving me alone up front with my thoughts. Thankfully, the waiting area is empty, and the appointment schedule is light, because now my head is swimming. With the presumptions I've made, and with everything going on with D1V.

The schedule might be light, but my heart feels all kinds of heavy.

Every blog seems to be listing the same stuff, with screenshots of social media updates from D1V that she's long since deleted but are still being shared around.

About her mother getting egged by some trolls who found out where she lived.

About the video capturing the moment her mom came home.

About those same monsters recording the livestream of it all and spreading it like wildfire in the darkest corners of the Internet, hailing it as some kind of "victory." It seems like every time a video gets taken down off YouTube, another one pops up in its place, posted by another anonymous, nameless profile.

The way these people are so organized, so determined, so calculated…

It makes me want to throw up.

I need to find a way to help her.

If these monsters can figure out where D1V lives, where her mom works…all of these personal things about her just using… I don't know, Google searches or whatever, then why can't we find *them*? The people harassing *her*? The police who are trying to help, the support people who run the actual game where this is taking place—why are their searches coming up empty?

All these people, who are hiding behind their fake avatar pictures on social media and posting under faux names in comments sections, spewing vile hate virtually and spawning that into real-life horror—why do they seem to get a free pass?

There's still an hour until Mom's first patient is due to arrive, so I open the browser on the aging desktop computer and start searching. It's ridiculous. I know. The best minds are supposedly looking into it already, so what the hell can I possibly do?

Still. It feels good to try.

I go to all the blogs covering what happened and scour through the comments sections, which are just a collection of human garbage. Usernames that are one word followed by a bundle of numbers, with no other posts beyond the one here or there. No profile photos. No information about who they are. Some of the comments are labeled as "marked for deletion" or "pending" on a few of the outlets, and when I click to see their full contents, I feel sick to my stomach. They're either full of the vilest of the comments section or have photos of D1V. Some are screenshots of her and her mom, or animated GIFs from the Quarter Slice Crisis incident. The worst are photoshopped images of her doing unspeakable things, or having horrible things done to her.

It's mind-boggling. Where does this hate even come from? And who has the time to create these kinds of intricate animated pictures and photoshops?

Link-sharing sites don't provide much else, either. I scour through Reddit, looking at the forums sharing the posts about D1V. There's a subforum encouraging people to keep pressing her, a place that looks like it's made just for trolls, but even here, where these people congregate, I'm finding nothing. Profiles that post a ton of stuff but are anonymous, focused on one spot, one place.

The organization of it all is terrifying.

I feel this awful wave of helplessness, followed by another wave of guilt. Because this fleeting feeling is nothing compared to what D1V must be going through every minute of every day. I wonder why she keeps doing it. *How* she keeps doing it. Where does that strength come from? There's no way I could deal with that.

My phone buzzes, and I see there's a message from D1V in the *Reclaim the Sun* chat client. I look around the office quickly to make sure no one is here, a movement that's really more instinctive than necessary, especially considering the chat my mom just had with me.

I open the app.

RECLAIM THE SUN: CHAT APPLICATION

D1V: Hey.

D1V: Rebekah has class and all my social media feeds are locked down.

D1V: So...hi, you're my silver medal.

AARON: Hahah, wow.

D1V: Kidding. At the office?

AARON: Yeah, giving my dad the day off.

AARON: My mom had this talk with me about how she's into my gaming dreams, kinda?

AARON: Just worried about me not getting paid.

D1V: Not getting paid?

AARON: Yeah, the ManaPunk team still owes me and Ryan for our freelance work on the last title.

D1V: Eek.

AARON: Yeah.

AARON: How are you feeling?

D1V: Let's not get into that. Tell me more about your family. Your dad. What's the deal with that?

AARON: Ah. Well, he moved here when he was about our age. He doesn't talk about it much.

AARON: Worked a lot of rough jobs, eventually worked his way up at a restaurant.

AARON: Met my mom when he was the manager.

D1V: That part is sweet.

AARON: Yeah. I just feel bad. My mom is always trying to get him to relax, but he hates that.

AARON: He doesn't want to be taken care of.

AARON: He just wants to take care of us, and other people. Like his family back home.

D1V: Sounds like someone I know. Always trying to be the savior type.

AARON: Oh hah hah. Now you really need to meet Ryan.

AARON: Anyway. I'm glad to get him away from the desk. He needs a break, even if he won't admit it.

D1V: Well, you know what they say.

D1V: It's hard to change your stars.

AARON: Did you just reference A Knight's Tale?

D1V: ☺

AARON: You're awesome.

The string of messages has me grinning like a fool, but our conversation is interrupted when my phone rings, the name and number taking over the screen. It's Jason. I stare at the ringing number for a moment, utterly perplexed. He's not the sort to use his phone like a phone, so it's either incredibly important or, far more likely, he left his phone in his pocket and is accidentally butt-dialing me—something you'd think would have died in the age of the smartphone, but he still figures out a way to do it.

God, maybe he finally has a paycheck for me. That'll definitely help ease my mom's worries. And Ryan's. And mine.

I pick it up.

"Hello?" I ask carefully, expecting to hear the rustling of pants or the inside of a backpack. "Jason? You never use the pho—"

"Aaron. What's the deal with you and that D1V girl?" he asks. The tone of his voice, the one that's normally jovial and playful, is replaced with a harsh edge I seldom ever hear from him. The one that only surfaces when we pester him about paychecks. "The streamer, the one getting trolled and all?"

"The...deal? I'm not even sure what you're asking." I look around the office again and keep talking. "We chat sometimes. Online friends, I guess. Why?"

Though something inside me twinges a little bit as I say that. There's something more between us, in the chat rooms, that feels like more than an "I guess." But the edge in Jason's voice makes me want to hide.

He exhales, and there's a long pause.

"Jason?" I venture. "What's up?"

"Aaron, I have to let you and Ryan go from the project. From ManaPunk."

It feels like my heart just explodes in my chest.

"What?!" I shout into the phone. "What are you talking about? Why?"

"I'm bringing the game to publishers at the indie showcase in New York, and with all the attention your...*friend* has been getting on social media and in the news..." He sighs. "When she mentioned you and ManaPunk in that first video, sure, it was a great bump for us attentionwise, but now people think we're sympathizers with what's going on. That we're supporting her."

"Aren't we?!" I demand. "Don't you see what those people are doing to her? It's not just on the Internet—it's in real life. They egged her *mom*, Jason. They attacked her. Those people—"

"*Those people*, Aaron…" Jason exhales again, and it's starting to drive me crazy. "I can't believe I have to say this out loud, but those people are our audience. They buy our games. The publicity and marketing team that handles ManaPunk's social feeds are seeing people calling for a boycott on our current and future games."

"So what?!" I yell. "To hell with those people. We don't need their money."

"Yeah, I do, though," Jason says, his tone full of finality.

There's a long pause.

"So…that's it?" I ask coldly. "What about Ryan's artwork? What about my story? What about *our* money?"

"I already talked to Ryan, and he's fine with it," Jason says calmly. "We'll still be using his concept art, and we'll still use your story. A paycheck is coming, and you'll still get a portion of the game sales, don't worry. I just…" He pauses. "There's a nondisclosure agreement I need you both to sign, and I won't be able to credit you as a writer in the game."

"Fuck that," I spit. "I worked too hard. I gave up my weekends and my nights this entire year. I dealt with your harsh, needless criticism, and so did Ryan."

"He's already agreed to it," Jason says.

"I'll believe that when I see it," I snap.

"Look, the showcase is in another two weeks," he says, and I can hear the exhaustion in his voice. "I'd really appreciate it if you could sign the contract and the NDA and move on from all this. It's not about this girl, it's about your career. Just because you aren't credited doesn't mean you can't put it on a resume. Or a college application. And think about the money. If you don't sign… Well, I'll just have to fire you without giving you a share, instead of letting you leave of your own volition and still get an uncredited stake in the title."

"You sound like a lawyer."

"That's because I have one," Jason says. "I had to get one."

"Who even are you right now?" I ask. "After everything we've done for the company? You're really going to do this to us?"

But it's like he doesn't even hear me. "Choose wisely, Aaron," he advises. "I really don't want to be the enemy here. We're friends, you and me. Remember, the money from this game, it'll help you go to whatever college you want. Or start your own studio. That's what you want, right? You can get away from your doctor parents and—"

"You keep talking about money, but you haven't even paid me yet! Or Ryan! And friends?! You're trying to use that against me? Fuck off, Jason," I tell him, but I feel my voice cracking. There's a sob in the back of my throat, and I'm not about to let it out. I refuse to give him the satisfaction.

My lip quivers as I hang up the phone, tossing it onto the desk. I lean back in the office chair and stare at the computer, and then around at the waiting area. At my future. The hard, inevitable future of this place, the fluorescent lights and angry patients and years of medical school that I don't want to go through. I feel the tears, hot and heavy, streaming down my face, and I hurry to wipe them away. All those nights, all that time spent working on that damn story, and all last year, fussing over that puzzle game Jason released, copyediting shitty menu text and tutorials.

And now there's nothing.

Well, I guess that's not entirely true.

There's either nothing, an NDA, or there's a lawyer and some sort of legal battle to keep my name on the game and the story. Except I don't see my mom being down to bankroll a lawyer and court case.

I look over at the door to her office, still closed. I'm surprised she hasn't come out, with all the shouting I was doing. I glance at my phone, upside down against a corkboard full of to-dos and business cards, and wonder how Ryan is taking the news. His parents will certainly take it better than mine; even if things go entirely south, it's not like he has to prove himself the way I feel like I have to. He'll probably get a scholarship to art school and be just fine next year, anyway.

The scholarship for people who want to write video game narratives doesn't quite exist yet, at least as far as I know.

I move to grab the phone when something catches my eye on the desktop: a folder squeezed all the way into the corner of the screen, as though somehow that would prevent someone from seeing it. I select it, the tiny edge of the pixelated folder barely large enough to get the mouse cursor over, and drag it over where I can actually see the full folder.

Dad's Files.

I stare at the folder and wonder if this is where he stores that game he's been trying to hide. I click it open and feel my eyes go wide.

There's an icon for a game called *Ultima Online*—just like Ryan had suspected when he saw the photo I took—as well as what looks like hundreds of Word documents. Their file names all have long strings of numbers and letters, all nonsensical, with dates that stretch back... God, years. Over a decade. I scroll down, down, down... They just keep going.

There are Word files in here older than Mira.

I glance away from the computer and peek around the office, as though my father might walk in while I'm here thumbing around. The waiting room is still empty, the only sound the hum of the old PC and the soft voice of my mother talking in the back. She must be on the phone, since I haven't seen a patient come in yet.

I open one of the Word docs, my eyes flitting back and forth from the screen to the waiting room as the old computer opens Microsoft Word, the hard drive whirring angrily. It's as though the computer is trying as hard as it can to do what I've asked, the ancient beast making actual sounds. It's something newer computers rarely do, unless there's something wrong with them.

When it finally blips up on the screen, I squint at it, not entirely sure what I'm looking at.

It's a letter.

My Dearest,

How many days has it been? Or has it been weeks? Without you, time has no meaning in this place, where I'm surrounded by strangers. I walk through this world, listless, and find no joy in the treasures that surround me. For what is the point of any kind of riches, whether they are found in wealth or in friends and family, when I cannot share them with you?

Soon I will see you again.

I will return to you, my queen, my love.

Yours, as ever.

My stomach drops, and I feel as though I have to force myself to breathe, inhaling and exhaling. I grip the soft foam-rubber armrests of the office chair and slide myself back, staring at the computer in horror.

My dad.

He's…having an affair?

Suddenly, the door to one of the patient rooms swings open, and my mom walks out with an older woman, the two of them chatting about...something... I don't know. Every-thing feels like a blur.

When did a patient walk in? How did I miss that?

Their words are floating through the air and landing on my ears unheard. There's a laugh, and I see someone wave. My mom? The patient? I turn my attention back to the of-fice PC, hurriedly closing all the windows and hiding Dad's secret folder down in the corner again.

His secret folder.

His secret life.

Am I really hiding this for him? Why?

Some of those Word files are over a decade old. How old was the one I opened? What else is in there? What other se-crets are in these letters? Has this person been in the picture before Mira? Is there more than one? Was he talking to this woman while Mom was pregnant?

My heart plummets down into my body, past where my stomach maybe was, and everything inside me feels hollow. Empty. It blends intensely with an awful swell of anxiety, an urge to open that folder again, to find out more.

"Aaron?"

I blink and look up to see my mom standing at the desk, an inquisitive look on her face.

"You okay?" she asks, crossing her arms. "You don't look so great. Are you...are you crying, sweetie?"

"No. Yes," I mutter, and wipe at my eyes. I didn't realize that was still happening. I shake my head as my mom leans on the desk, and I feel myself digging for anything else to talk about. In the span of ten minutes, I lost my summer job and all the plans I'd laid out for myself, then stumbled upon this... thing...with my dad...

I clear my throat. "Jason, the ManaPunk guy... He has to let me go. Because of the Internet stuff."

"What Internet stuff?" my mom asks, giving me a confused look.

"There's..." I exhale. My heart starts pounding again as I realize I've never explained any of this to my mom, to anyone in the family, really, and that if I don't dig into it properly, she'll likely unplug me from everything. And right now, I'm not sure who I need to protect more—myself and these dreams I'm barely able to cling to, or my mom from all this nonsense tucked away on the computer here.

"There's this girl I've been talking to. She's sort of famous in the video game world." I stammer the words out, still reeling over what I found out about Dad, but I have to talk about something else. *Anything.* "She's being targeted by a bunch of trolls online. They've been harassing her on social media and in the games she plays."

"That's awful!" my mom exclaims. "Why?"

"That's the big question, isn't it? 'Cause she's a girl. 'Cause she's brown like us. 'Cause people are garbage. 'Cause you can't trust anyone anymore." I feel myself getting heated and try to dial it back. "It gets worse, though. They sent her emails, pictures of her apartment building. They harassed her mom where she works." I watch as my mom's face goes from surprise to abject horror. "And since I'm associated with her, Jason said he has to sever ties with me, since his game company is getting all this attention now from those trolls, and that's supposedly our audience."

"And how long have you been hanging out with this girl?" my mom asks. It feels like she's asking the wrong question here.

"We haven't. We just talk online, game sometimes."

My mom fiddles with her ID badge, and her eyes search the room.

"Aaron, I'm not sure you should be—"

"Please don't tell me not to talk to her anymore," I plead, standing up. "Jason is already pushing me away."

"How's it going to look on college applications with your name in the news and—"

"Mom, I'm already in the news! On the blogs! And I'm not going to be a doctor!" I shout. I grab my phone off the desk and charge by her. "Who the fuck cares?"

"Aaron, don't use that language with me," she says sternly. I can feel myself breathing heavily now, my chest tight, and I know the rage isn't just about D1V and my mom's disapproval and what she wants for my career, but I don't care.

"You're going to medical school, or we aren't paying for college—"

"Will you stop hanging that over me already?!" I roar, almost to the door. "I'll take out student loans! I'll go into horrible debt! I'll work shitty jobs like…like *Dad* did for years, if that means I can get away from all this and you and live the life I want. It's bad enough you keep Dad locked up in here. You can't keep pushing me to do the same thing."

"Aaron." My mom suddenly starts tearing up. "Is that what you really think of me? Of this family? I don't put your dad here and make him do anything. He's here because I love him, and he loves me. He likes being an active part of his family."

I'm balling my fists, trying so, so hard not to say something that will shatter this entire family right now. It would be so easy. They're just words. And then D1V flashes through my mind, reminding me of the way words hurt. The gaping wounds they leave behind. Even words from strangers. Forget them being from family.

Mom takes a step forward, her eyes wet, her mouth trembling in a way I don't think I've ever seen before.

"You ask your dad what it was like for him back home. Ask him," she says, pointing at me. "You ask him about his old jobs before we got together. The restaurants. The manual labor. All that stuff he hated. I don't want that for you. And I know he doesn't want that for you, either. That's…that's all parents want. Something better for their children."

My phone buzzes in my hand, and I hold it up.

"I'm not going to stop talking to her," I say.

"And I'm not going to stop pushing you toward a better career," my mom fires back, a watery little smile starting to trickle in at the edge of her mouth.

"I'm not going to stop telling you I won't do it, though," I counter. "It's not what I want for my life."

"That's fine." She shrugs. "You've still got your senior year to figure out, and for me to keep convincing you."

I glance back over at the desk and huff. The PC, all of Dad's secrets, barely hidden there, a tiny corner of a folder on the desktop. Mom could easily find that, if she wasn't so busy. Catch the odd pixel out of place down there. A secret agent hiding secrets my dad is not.

The door into the office from the house swings open, and my dad peeks in, as if he's been summoned by my thoughts. His eyes dart between the two of us, his face awash in concern. I have to struggle to not glare at him as I glance back at the computer, filled with evidence.

I need to read those other letters. I need to find out who he's talking to. Or has been talking to, all this time.

He steps in and closes the door.

"Mira and I can hear you all way across the house," he says

quietly. "Everything okay? Need me to come back and fill in? I can—"

"You shouldn't have to—" my mom starts.

"I want to," my dad insists. "It's okay." He turns to me, a small smile on his face. "There's only a couple patients on the schedule. Go. Enjoy your summer."

I lower my head, forcing myself to unclench my jaw. He keeps smiling back, oblivious to what I've found. A number of emotions swirl around inside me—relief that I can escape all of this, but so furious at what I've discovered.

I have to turn away, back to my mom. I give her a hug.

"I'm… I'm sorry," I say. I've been so hard on her, and she doesn't deserve any of this.

"It's okay," she says. "Get going."

And I'm out the door. I don't look back.

12
DIVYA

There's a package on my doorstep.

It's day three…maybe four? Whatever the case, it's been a minute since I've actually ventured outside, or turned on my computer, or bothered with anything. And now, there's this.

It's ridiculous. This shouldn't be the place I'm in right now, in my life. Glaring at packages like they're something out of a New Jersey Transit public service announcement poster about mysterious, unmarked bags in a train car.

But here we are.

Whatever it is, it's upside down. I look down the street from my apartment building, one way, and then the other, and then across for any odd cars. No one with tinted windows. No one sitting by and waiting to see the results.

"Ah, fuck it," I huff, and kick the box over.

My name and address are written on the front, in neat, lovely handwriting. And the return address… I squint for a moment, then squat down to read it. I don't recognize the address—it's from out in California someplace—but the last name…

Siddiqui. I know that name, but I can't quite place it.

I scoop the box up and head inside. Once I'm back in my living room, I carefully open it, peeling away the brown paper wrapped around the box. After the second or third tear, I gasp, realizing what's inside, and shred the rest of the paper off it. I hold the box up, staring at the packaging, the photos depicting what's inside.

It's the latest VR headset from Oculus, which is being released after the giant GamesCon convention. They're supposed to be doing some presentations with these there, but it's not supposed to hit actual retailers for another month or so.

And it's here. In my living room.

I flip the box over and see a little card attached to the back. Not a folder, though, or some hurriedly folded bundle of press releases stuffed by a frustrated intern. A personal note in a small light blue envelope.

I open it and pull out a card. There's a pattern of pixels on the front of it, forming something not quite recognizable, something artsy. Inside, though, written quickly and in the same neat, elegant handwriting…

Log on. Fight back.
H. Siddiqui
Oculus, PR

…and now I recognize the name. The publicist over at Oculus who sent me my first headset, the one I've been using to explore in *Reclaim the Sun*. She'd reached out a while ago, and her email is sitting in my inbox unanswered. I strangle back a sob and inhale sharply, trying not to cry.

She doesn't have to say anything else. I know she understands.

I grab the headset and the card and race into my room. My desk is still a wreck from the other day, from what happened to Mom. I see my beat-up webcam, dangling haphazardly from the desk, and wince. I realign my computer on the desk, positioning the monitor flush with the straight line of the edge, and scoop my keyboard and mouse off the floor.

My other Oculus headset is also sitting on the floor, upside down, tossed aside carelessly, just like the keyboard, webcam, and everything else was. I grab it, inspecting the sides. It looks fine, and when I glance over at my new one, an idea bubbles up in my mind. I know I could sell the old one, head to the used-gadgets place downtown. I could maybe get $400, without a doubt.

But...

I place the old headset on my bed and grab the new one, fussing with the plastic bags holding the new HDMI cords and the like, to get it all hooked up to my computer.

And then I see it. My little slogan, on my desk.

I stare at the Don't Read the Comments sign, then back at the note from Oculus. Without a moment's hesitation, I fold the note in half and place it over my old motto, the notecard covering the frame like a tent. The PR representative's note stares back at me.

I turn my computer on. The PC hums to life, the sound encouraging.

Log on. Fight back.

That's exactly what I'm going to do.

13
AARON

Ryan lives just a few blocks away, and since we've been inseparable since forever, I know, I just *know*, that if he got the news around the same time I did, he'll be out on his front porch waiting for me. It's that best friend ESP you get after over a decade of hanging out with the same person almost every day.

My phone buzzes while I'm walking toward his house, and I load up the chat client.

RECLAIM THE SUN: CHAT APPLICATION

D1V: Hey so, bit of an odd question for you here.

D1V: But your mom's practice, it's the one on 9th and Pine, right? In Philadelphia?

D1V: Don't be weirded out.

I stop walking and stare at my phone for a beat, then turn back to my house, hurriedly hustling down the sidewalk. I peer around the corner, as if D1V is going to be right there, sitting on my doorstep or something. A ridiculous romantic comedyesque moment flashes through my head, her waiting on my step, the two of us running toward each other in slow motion—

I groan, feeling foolish. Of course she's not there.

I shake my head and continue toward Ryan's.

AARON: Hey! Um. Yes? Why? How do you know that?

D1V: Well, I mean, Aaron.

D1V: You aren't exactly a case study in how to prevent someone from looking you up.

D1V: Your last name is in your profile, and so is the city you live in.

D1V: Also, you told me your mom is a doctor, and there's only one Dr. Jericho in Philly.

AARON: Ah.

D1V: You even said you didn't want to be the "next Dr. Jericho" once.

AARON: So, I should be a little more careful, is what you're saying.

D1V: Maybe. You're a dude. You have it easier on the Internet.

AARON: Hey, I don't know about all that.

D1V: How many people have come after you, while gaming with me and being in those articles?

I don't even have to think, really. The whole thing with Jason and ManaPunk—that's different. It's not someone threatening my life, my safety, my family. It's someone worried about... I don't know, potential consequences? Not upset at me for just, you know, existing.

AARON: You're right, I see what you're saying. I'm sorry.

D1V: It's fine, just, pointing that out, is all.

D1V: I'm um... I'm sending you something.

AARON: What?

AARON: Like, in the mail?

D1V: No by drone YES IN THE MAIL. I hope you like it, and that it um.

D1V: Uh.

D1V: Brings us closer.

D1V: Or something.

D1V: OKAY I FEEL AWKWARD NOW BYYYYYE.

Closer? I feel like I'm sweating, and I stop walking and sit down on the curb, my feet on the cobblestone streets that line Ryan's and my neighborhood. I have no idea what to say, and I just stare at the phone for a beat, the chat client window open. It buzzes again, and I refocus, shaking the haze away from staring too long.

D1V: Everything okay over there?

AARON: Yeah, yeah. It's fine, I'm just...flustered.

D1V: Good kind, or bad kind?

AARON: Can it be both?

D1V: Oh.

AARON: Oh God, not because of you. Good kind because of you. Always good.

AARON: Bad because of my summer job. Mana-Punk let me go.

AARON: Apparently I'm too controversial.

D1V: Oh shit.

D1V: Aaron, I'm sorry. That's my fault, isn't it?

AARON: Nope, not your fault. Those guys who keep harassing you. Them. Never you.

D1V: Still.

AARON: Still nothing.

I stare at the little message box and can feel myself breathing heavily. I know what I want to say here. I think over the sentence in my head. The benefit of talking to someone via text and online, I suppose. Though if we were to ever meet up in person, I worry that I'll never find the right words.

AARON: I'd pick you over that summer job, any day, any time.

D1V: ♥

AARON: You didn't do anything wrong, okay? It's not your fault. I'll find something else.

D1V: That's just it though, isn't it?

D1V: I'm not doing anything, and I'm still somehow hurting the people I care about.

D1V: Rebekah. My mom. You.

I exhale and stand up again, heading in the direction of Ryan's once more. It normally takes me about five minutes to walk over there, but D1V's chats are slowing me down. I'm not the best text-and-walker even under the best of circumstances, but seeing the word "care" so close to D1V saying "you" adds to the whirlwind of emotions swirling inside my chest. That, plus the heart emoji, her mailing me something...

AARON: I'll be fine. Really. You should focus on yourself.

D1V: That's not something I'm good at.

D1V: Hell, I only do the streaming to help my mom. I'm using what I make to help pay for her school.

D1V: Heh, and the rent. And the groceries.

AARON: Oh wow. I didn't know it was that intense. I'm sorry.

AARON: You can make that much streaming though? That's kind of amazing.

D1V: Some people can. I don't. I mean, some of it is from that, but most of it is sponsorships.

D1V: Mentioning this or that. And then sometimes I sell stuff that I get sent.

D1V: I usually make more from that than anything else.

AARON: This is blowing my mind. It sounds so hard though.

AARON: I'm sorry that something that's such a big part of your life makes you so sad.

D1V: It's okay, she only has a few summer classes left.

D1V: And after all this, I might be done. I'm not sure yet.

AARON: Yeah, I can understand that.

"Aaron!" I hear Ryan shout. I look up from my phone and realize I'm two houses away from his. As in, past his. I walked right by him, staring at my phone and talking to D1V. I spin around, and he's sitting on the stoop of his porch, waving at me, a sketchbook in his hands. I start walking back, and he shakes his head, his shoulders bouncing in a chuckle as he returns to his drawing.

"Hey." I lift my chin at him and sit down on the old wood steps. His parents' house has this quirky shabby-chic look that Ryan's mom says is on purpose, but Ryan swears is just his parents being lazy. The painted brick siding is peeling, an off-white color. And then there's the door, an eye-popping bright red against the dull paint everywhere else. The little window boxes that dot the front two windows are meticulously maintained, though, and it does make the home look like something out of an old postcard. His house pops up on Instagram all the time.

Still, when paint chips fall in your drinks every summer, the charm starts to fade as quickly as the color.

"You're gonna get yourself run over by a car or something," Ryan says, nodding at my phone. "He called you, too, huh?"

"Yeah." I look down at my hands. "I'm sorry he let you go. Sucks to be my friend."

"It sure does, but not for that reason." He nudges his shoulder against mine, so I know he's joking. "I seriously don't care. I'm not mentioned in any of those articles, just you. Why not also fire Laura? Anyone associated with you? It makes no sense, so fuck him and his contracts and stuff."

"Wait, you didn't sign it?" I ask. "He said you were going to—"

"Hell, no," Ryan fumes, closing his notebook. "I'm not going to give him my art with the promise of *maybe* I'll get paid. 'Oh, but what about all the exposure?' People *die* from exposure. Don't try using that line on me. Let him stew over how he'll get a working demo of his game out in the next two weeks without any art and without a story. All because he's afraid of some jerks on the Internet? Fuck that."

I want to hug Ryan.

So I do.

"Come on, man," Ryan groans, squirming away. "How's your *girlfriend*?" He smirks. "You know, the one ruining your career, my career, and sending everything in our little world into a tailspin?"

"Hey, none of this is her fault—"

"Dude, I'm kidding," he says, pulling out his sketch pad again. "She okay? Any updates?"

"Nothing really," I say. "Not since…well, everything. I just feel so bad. Her mom. Those people. And it's not like I can track them down or anything. The police can't even figure it out. They all use anonymous names, and it's all just… very soul-crushing."

"I think if you're going to be a monster, you should at least have the courage to tell the world that you are one," Ryan comments, scratching away at something with a pencil. I look over his arm and notice that he's working on some kind of dragon-type creature. "If you're so proud to have twisted views that you go out and act on them in public, against people, you should show your face."

"Agreed."

"Or at least have your face shown to people." Ryan makes a disgusted noise. "Sorry you couldn't find anything."

"Yeah, me, too."

"Is it weird that I'm having like, anxiety attacks over the fact that I don't know what I'll do for the rest of my summer?" He lets out a short laugh. "I kinda had all this—" he slaps his sketchbook "—planned out. Do art for the game.

Build my portfolio. Have something truly kickass to show-case for colleges."

"I'm sorry."

"Not your fault, again." Ryan gives me a quick look. "Maybe I'll get a part-time job at the art store at the end of Market Street. Down in Old City? Get some discount supplies for the summer. Or start doing art commissions on Tumblr. That could be fun." He smiles at me, and I smile back. End-lessly positive, that Ryan. "What are you going to do?"

"Not sure. Play more games, scour the Internet for intern-ships? Write short stories?"

"Good plans." His expression turns sly. "You could always go meet your girlfriend."

"Damn it, Ryan." I shove him lightly. He laughs, and then laughs even harder when my phone buzzes again. "Shut up."

RECLAIM THE SUN: CHAT APPLICATION

D1V: What are your plans today, anyway?

D1V: We could explore a little or something.

AARON: Sure, that'd be great. I could use a day in a virtual world to forget the one I live in.

D1V: Same, except I need that virtual world to live in my current one, which still kinda sucks.

AARON: I don't even know what to say.

D1V: Seriously, the sarcasm does not land in here. Or with you. You do not do well with jokes.

AARON: You are correct. Talk to you online in a bit. Ryan says hi.

"One, I didn't say hi." I look up to find Ryan peering over my shoulder. "And two, you are not going to sit on my stoop and text and not talk to me." He scoots up two steps and then starts pushing me off the stairs with his feet against my back.

I laugh and stand up, brushing away whatever dirt he got on my back.

"Go on, get outta here," he says, waving me off with his sketch pad.

RECLAIM THE SUN: CHAT APPLICATION

D1V: Is it there yet?

D1V: Is it?

D1V: Did you check your mail?

AARON: Hahah, oh my God it's only been a day. What did you even send me?

D1V: You'll see.

D1V: Also, I sent it overnight.

D1V: ...is it there now?

AARON: Fine, I'll go check.

AARON: Oh.

AARON: I really don't have the words right now.

D1V: Try!

AARON: I mean. I might be crying.

AARON: I can't even get my parents to support this passion of mine like this.

AARON: This is.

AARON: What do I say? What do I do?

D1V: Here's what you do. Ready?

AARON: Yeah.

D1V: You put it on.

D1V: See you soon.

AARON: ♥

D1V: ♥

14
AARON

I put my phone down and stare at the open box on my bed.

It's an Oculus.

Not some old one, either, like one I'd maybe find in a neighbor's trash can or on Craigslist in a few years. And even then, I can't imagine someone tossing one, though I suppose people thought the same thing about computers before they became as accessible as they are.

Nope, it's the model that came out just this past fall. I remember seeing the ads everywhere over the holidays, promoting it as the season's hottest gift.

Well, hottest gift that cost like $600.

The commercials were like those ads where a loving partner surprises their spouse or boyfriend or girlfriend with a Mercedes-Benz with that red bow on top. I see them every single year. No one can ever name a single person who could afford to do something like that, and you immediately hate the people in the ad. Same with the Oculus. No way were my parents dropping that kind of cash on a gift, even though they certainly have it. Not when it might encourage my unfortunate "hobby."

But now I have one.

Here's what you do. Ready?

You put it on.

See you soon.

D1V's latest messages to me float into my head, and I feel myself get flushed. And the hearts in the chat.

People send hearts all the time, though; it doesn't mean anything. Right?

Right.

I take the Oculus over to my PC and pull out the cables, then breathe in sharply. I stare at my monster of a desktop and then look back down at the VR headset.

"If I turn you around," I say, glaring at the tower, "and you don't have the ports to hook this up, we are going to have a problem."

I reach over the back of the desktop and pull it around.

"Don't screw this up for us," I urge the machine.

By some miracle, my tower has the right port for the VR headset. Whether or not it'll be fast enough, powerful enough, to run the software and showcase the graphics inside...that's another story altogether. I already have to reduce *Reclaim the Sun*'s graphic settings in order for it to play smoothly, and things like shadows and other small particle effects are off.

I'll be lucky if I can even take a few steps in this thing.

But I'm gonna try.

It takes a solid half hour for the software to load up on my desktop, and another half hour for the software update to download for *Reclaim the Sun* so I can actually use the VR headset with it.

But I'm finally ready.

I take a deep breath, sit down at my computer with the headset on, and enter the game.

The world of *Reclaim the Sun* warps into view on the headset, big and sprawling, the open universe in front of me, swallowing me up. It takes me a second to realize I'm in my ship, and I have to look down to see my controls. I can also see my hands on the screen, and as I move the VR controls in my actual hands, I watch the virtual ones move in front of me.

This is awesome.

I'm fussing around with the hand controls, getting an idea of how to navigate everything, like the menus and inventory, when a transmission window pops up. It looks the same way it usually does on the monitor, only it's floating in front of me, and I feel as though I could maybe reach out and grab it.

So I do, pressing the open button.

INCOMING TRANSMISSION

D1V: Meet me here.

D1V HAS SENT COORDINATES TO ALPHA 3.8, PLANET KERRIGAN, IN THE QUADRANT SETI ALPHA-EIGHT. DO YOU WISH TO JUMP? [YES] [NO]

I move to fix my hair, and then laugh at myself, because what the hell am I doing? One, I can't really do anything to it with this headset on. And two, I'm not actually going to see her in person.

I hit yes, and gasp as stars and planets go rocketing by me, the cinematic in place for warping an absolutely stunning thing to watch while wearing VR. The colors blast by in streaks along the edges of my ship's cockpit, like multicolored crashes of lightning. After a few moments, it slows down, the wild lines and colors fading until blackness once again swallows the screen, and a small blue planet comes into focus.

There's a little ship floating nearby.

I move to click on it to see if it's D1V and feel my mouse go clattering off my desk before I remember I've got this headset on and VR controllers strapped to my hands. This is going to take some getting used to. I raise my hand up and reach out, the virtual version of me pointing a finger at D1V's ship, selecting it.

The *Cedere Nescio*.

It's her.

INCOMING TRANSMISSION

D1V: Hey, turn your headset on.

D1V HAS SENT YOU A CHANNEL INVITE.
DO YOU WISH TO ACCEPT?
[YES] [NO]

I hit yes and navigate my way over to the menu, turning on my headset so I can actually hear her talking.

"Hello? Helloooooooooo," I hear D1V's voice say in my ear, and I smile. I've heard her speak so many times in her videos and in the chats in game, but now, in stereo in this amazing device, it feels different somehow. It's the same, but... I can't explain it. She's closer, in some strange way.

"Hi. Yes, I'm here," I say.

"Finally!" she exclaims.

"What uh, is this place?" I ask, peering at the planet below.

"Just one of the many places me and the Armada have discovered," she says, and I can almost hear the shrug in her voice.

"We've got some supply drops here we like to keep stocked up, but there aren't any resources worth mining here. Nothing that can help with upgrades, at least. Place to hang out mostly, it's sort of our big chatroom planet. No one in the Armada tells anyone outside about it."

"A safe haven?"

"Pretty much!" she says. "Let's—"

"Hey, wait, D1V, this headset, I have to thank—"

"*Go!*" she shouts, interrupting any attempt to thank her, something I suspect she does on purpose. Her little ship takes off toward the surface, and I push mine along after hers.

RECLAIM THE SUN: CHAT APPLICATION

D1V: Hey, you around? Me and Aaron are exploring a bit.

D1V: I sent him that old headset, it'll probably be funny watching him flail around.

BEKS: Hey.

BEKS: Can't today, busy.

D1V: Okay! Maybe we can do a stream tomorrow, you and me.

BEKS: Yeah maybe.

D1V: You okay?

D1V: Beks?

BEKS: Yeah, no, it's fine. Sorry, school stuff.

D1V: Gotcha.

Aaron's ship comes into view and starts its landing sequence. Staring up at it from the planet's surface, I can tell he's had it painted since we last explored together—black and silver. The upgrades are still there, and for some reason this pulls a smile out of me. He isn't running and gunning around anymore with his pals, but instead, he's making the effort to take care of what he has.

Seems like I'm a good influence.

I can't help but feel like Rebekah would approve. She's always so good at reeling me in when it comes to recording. Keeping me on a schedule, making sure I'm putting my everything into each stream.

She should be here right now.

Exploring with us.

I'm having a hard time reaching her lately, both in and out of the game. After everything that happened, she's been pulling back more and more. Going quiet, not answering messages, never around online.

I don't know what else to do, so here I am, pouring myself into a virtual world that's supposed to be less complicated than the real one. But when I look up at this boy's spaceship...

I realize it isn't.

I fight the scowl on my face, at the fact that a landing ship in a digital landscape is currently tugging at my heartstrings. There's a flutter in my stomach as Aaron nears the ground. He has a VR headset on. That I sent him. Things are different now; I've changed the dynamic of...whatever this is, and now we can see each other. Kinda. At least, the representations we show of one another, these digital facsimiles of who we really are.

But there's clearly so much of him, right here, on his virtual sleeve. He just puts it all out there.

"What are your plans now?" I ask. "Now that they've fired you and all that."

"It's not so much the fact that they fired me, as it is *he* did. I thought we were friends," Aaron returns. His ship nestles down on the ground, letting out a soft *hiss*. The cockpit opens up and he hops out, and I have to stifle a laugh. His avatar is staring around everywhere. His head looks up to the sky, he spins around in a circle, clearly taking it all in. And I get it. Rocking a VR headset in a game like this—there's just so much to check out.

I clear my throat and he stops, spinning toward me.

"Oh. Hey," he says with a little laugh. He walks in my direction, his movements still a little wonky, likely having a hard time getting the hang of the joysticks. "Whatever, though. I'm bummed I wasted so much time, but I'd rather not work with someone who'd rather align themselves with all this trolling nonsense, just to make money."

"It's just a win-win all around. I stop streaming, they win. Video game companies stay silent, they win. Sucks."

"Yeah," Aaron agrees.

There's a quiet beat between us, and my heart flutters. I'm almost mad at myself for it, because…well, I'm staring at a generic video game avatar of someone. This isn't him.

But at the same time, it is.

"Hey, D1V, look," he starts, taking a few more steps toward me. His shoulders and head take up the frame now in my headset, and he tilts his head, looking at me, the headset responding to whatever he's doing on that side. It doesn't respond to every little movement—like, he can't hug me, the world isn't quite to the level of *Ready Player One* just yet—but tiny gestures like head movements and lifting your arms and waving your hands? That stuff registers.

"I can't thank you enough," he says. "For this."

"It's no problem," I say, feeling my cheeks heat.

"No, but really. This means something to me. My family… They aren't the most supportive of this. My love of this." He gestures at the whole of what's around him. "And then…my dad…" He's stammering, and I hear him take a loud breath.

"What is it?"

"Well, he's been hiding this game on the desktop in the office. In my mom's practice. I don't know why—it's just some old game, it's not like I'd judge him for it or something." He clears his throat. "Though maybe my mom would. Maybe that's the problem, why it's happening."

"Why what's—" I start.

"He's cheating on her," Aaron says, his voice a bit softer now. His tone makes my breath catch in my throat. He sounds so…wounded. "I think. I found this letter. A whole folder full of documents that I haven't gotten to peek at yet. But that one letter? It's him confessing his feelings for someone else." His avatar shakes his head. "I don't know what to do."

"Oh God, Aaron," I breathe. "I'm so, so sorry. I've…been

there. With my dad, and all that. When he left. I know it's not easy."

"Yeah." His voice sounds so dejected, and I'm not sure what else to say. Out of the corner of my eye, I spot a sprawling lake, not too far from where we've landed. Maybe a little exploring will help take his mind off things.

"Come on," I say, heading toward the lake.

Kerrigan is a gorgeous little planet, one of the first ones I claimed with my Armada. The resources here aren't really worth anything, and what is here—things like wood, water, stone—everyone mostly leaves alone, so we can have this lovely landscape to just hang out in and wander. A home base. I named it after the iconic Zerg-Terran badass that is Kerrigan in the *StarCraft* series, her rage unforgiving and her love unrelenting. I've been telling Rebekah that I hope Christie Golden is at GamesCon this year, so I can gush about my love of her *StarCraft* novelizations.

When we reach the water, I glance over at Aaron, his gaze focused out across the horizon.

"Alright, I have a silly question," I start, studying his avatar's face.

"Okay?"

"What's with the scar there?"

He laughs. "Oh. I, um, I got really into *Lost* one summer?" I hear the grin in his voice as he talks. "The entire series was on Netflix, and I had this really awful case of food poisoning from some takeout my mom had brought home, and playing games was just giving me a headache, so…"

"Netflix and ill?" I ask, immediately hating myself for the pun.

"Exactly." His avatar looks out at the water and then back at me again. "My dad watched almost every episode with me, even though him and my mom had already watched it when it first aired. He'd seen it all, and still hung out. The scar on my avatar is just me being John Locke in my own little way."

"I'm, um, not totally sure who that is." I suck air through my teeth. "Sorry."

"It's okay. You ever listen to Moneen? Or like, emo or punk at all?"

"Um." I think about it for a minute. I feel like these are things we skipped, in whatever this is that's happening between us. The quirky get-to-know-you questions, like what kind of music do you like or what you binge-watched last on Netflix. Where do you want to go to college, or favorite colors, movies, foods. All replaced with wandering virtual planets and cataloging alien life for points.

Yet whatever I'm wrestling with in my chest here—it feels real enough, even without all the details.

Maybe we can learn those later.

God, what is happening?

"No, I... I don't think so?" I say at last. "I'm more of a pop person, I guess?"

"They have this song," he continues. "'Don't Ever Tell Locke What He Can't Do.' It's kind of like a personal anthem for me."

"I don't think I've ever heard—"

"'You trying to say we can't?!'" he sings, loudly, terribly off key. "'Yes I caaaaaaan! You can't have all that you want? YES I CAAAAAAAAN!'"

I bust out laughing and can't stop.

"What? You don't like my singing?" he asks. "Are you... trying to say I can't sing?"

"No!" I manage through the laughter. "I'd never—"

"Because 'YES I CAAAAAAAAAN!'" he belts out again, prompting another fit of giggles. Once I've composed myself again, he adds, "Maybe I can take you record shopping someday."

I feel my heartbeat go mad.

"Their album *The Red Tree* is so good," he gushes. "And that song—whenever I hear it, I feel like I can do anything. With or without the support from my family, from the game company... Hey, wait, I have an idea!" I hear him fussing with something in the background, and his avatar goes a little bonkers, moving around this way and that, I'm guessing from him putting down the headset and the controllers. The sound of roaring guitars and an intense drumbeat suddenly rings through my ears, in the headset, and I see his character straighten back out again.

Record shopping.

In real life.

"I figure we can listen to them together while we're exploring. Maybe after a song, you can put on something you like, and—"

"I don't know if I'm ready to meet up." I feel the words rushing out of me, even as I try to hold them back. He's sharing all this...personal stuff. He just keeps going. Way more personal than what we've dug into before in chats.

He wants to go record shopping. In person. I think about the used-record stores around Jersey City and Hoboken, their bins large and full of eager vinyl folders peeking over the top, primed for rummaging. I imagine our hands, making quick work of flipping through records together...and I have to shake the image away.

"I don't know if I'll ever be," I whisper.

The song stops.

There's a beat, a pause in the air. I can hear the water lapping on the giant lake, the sounds of randomly generated creatures in the distance. The digital wind. I've ruined whatever moment this is—this *was*. But I'm just not ready yet.

Because none of this is real.

But maybe I want it to be.

Because some part of this, whatever is happening between us, is real.

And maybe I want it to be.

"That's okay," Aaron says, taking a step forward.

"Are you sure?" I ask, staring at him.

"I don't need to see you, to *see* you," he says, standing right in front of me. "I see you. I see all of you. With or without a headset."

For a moment, I wish there wasn't this digital space between us. An entire state. That I could reach out through the cables and data and code and grab the hands I see right there. The hands of this strange, quirky boy from a chat room and a video game. Who sings for me, even though I'd really rather he not.

But I can't.

There's a stinging in my eyes and the back of my throat, and it's not just some wave of sadness. There's this anger mixed with it, for the fear that's been pressed into me. From the Vox Populi, the trolls, the people who harassed Rebekah and attacked my mom. I want to push past it, but it's part of me. Like Rebekah said, I'll carry it forever now, even though I don't want to.

I choke back what feels like a sob, and barely eke out my suggestion. "Let's…go exploring."

We round the side of the massive lake, and the conversation starts to die out. For a while, we walk in silence, and Aaron switches off his music in favor of something a little softer, with pianos and a sad, gentle voice that feels as though it fits the natural surroundings. The Fray, maybe.

I glance over at Aaron, who turns his head to look at me.

The late-afternoon digital sun is low in the sky, just enough to silhouette his profile against the water, and if this was a real walk outside, I'd probably stop and try to take his photo. Golden hour for Instagram and all that.

"You alright?" he asks, slowing to a stop.

I wish this walk was alongside some actual water. Maybe here, in Jersey City, wandering downtown. We could rummage for records, like he said, or drink coffee in Word, my favorite bookstore. I could catch him during golden hour, framed perfectly for a photo in the setting of the sun, in a dog park surrounded by corgis and Yorkies and Boston terriers, the signature small pups of the town.

But I can't.

At least, not yet.

"Yeah," I say, lying. "Yeah, I'm fine."

16
AARON

"Look, I'm happy for you," Ryan says, an annoying grin on his face. "But perhaps we should take a moment to define just what a 'date' actually is. Have you ever googled the term?"

I let out a frustrated groan. He's been busting my chops for the past ten minutes, and I'm not sure how much more I can take. It's a summer Saturday in Philadelphia, which means the flea markets are open across Center City. And as great as rummaging for discarded computers in the nearby university dumpsters at the end of the semester is, the flea markets are an untapped gold mine of parts and accessories.

Most people come here to scrounge for vintage antiques and jewelry and rare coins...stuff like that. At least, that's what it seems like.

Me? Give me all your old electronics, thank you very much.

The gaming mouse I use? It's worth a hundred dollars brand-new, and I totally found it at one of these for five bucks. It's a bit older, sure, but works just fine. I've retired it for now, though, in favor of the VR headset D1V gave me. It's been amazing the past few days, exploring with that thing.

"Tell me Alberto is almost here," I plead. "Please." I peek under the folding table that Ryan is currently digging around on top of, but there are just closed plastic bins under there. This is not the right stop for me.

"You say that like he's going to go easier on you or something." Ryan laughs and examines a small brass piece of something, before dropping it back in a thin cardboard container about the size of a shoebox lid. The stand we've stopped at is filled with baubles and trinkets, like a steampunk fan's ultimate fantasy. Glue a couple of these onto a hat, and you are golden for Comic-Con.

I look beyond the table, toward the end of the block, where the flea market stretches all the way down. The markets in Center City aren't set up in a parking lot or something, but instead span full city blocks, lining sidewalks. This one takes over South Street and Lombard, all the way along Ninth and Seventh. The crowd is an interesting bunch of people—a mix of tourists who look baffled, as we're really close to South Street, and others who, like me and Ryan, are clearly scouring for treasures.

I squint and make out a table about half a block down that appears to be loaded with gadgets. "Any idea where he's meeting us?" I ask. I hate meeting up at things like flea markets or festivals or anything where a bunch of people are milling about. It's impossible to find one another, and you end up spending half the time trying to keep an eye on whoever you're supposed to be there with.

"Not sure," Ryan says. He weaves in and out of the crowd with me as we make our way to the gadget-filled table. There are a bundle of battered computer parts strewn about, some old digital cameras, and a handful of ancient handheld video games. I pick up an old Tiger game, one of those LCD toys from the late '80s, with the colorful still-screen backdrops that tried to make up for the lackluster black-and-white graphics, and pop open the back. A pair of AA batteries have burst, and the acid is all over, crystallized and definitely dangerous.

I look up at the vendor, holding the device in my hands, and he shrugs.

"A quarter," he offers. I put it down and glance up just in time to see Alberto nudge past someone, working his way over to me and Ryan.

"There he is." Ryan smiles, and Alberto gives him a quick kiss.

"Sorry I'm late," he says, reaching over to me for a one-armed hug. "The El took forever." Alberto and his family live over in Northern Liberties, a hip section of Philadelphia, in a house that looks as if it's been carved out of marble. It's really like something out of a movie.

"You didn't miss much," Ryan tells him. "Except the recap of this one's date."

"Oh?" Alberto asks, turning to me. He crosses his arms and grins. "The video game girl?"

"I hate you so much," I growl at Ryan, who raises his hands innocently. "It wasn't a date—I regret saying that—just a good gaming session. She sent me an Oculus VR headset, so we could—"

Alberto yawns loudly.

"Oh my God, seriously?" I laugh, shoving him.

As we continue along the stretch of tables, Ryan stops to scope out some bits of art and Alberto fusses over some vintage jeans. Another display nearby catches my attention. Looks like some tech pieces on top, but also maybe some movies.

I think about the headset, and those movies give me an idea.

"Be right back, you guys," I call, but they both just wave me off.

I make my way around some people to the table, where a

bundle of broken-looking electronics line the top, as well as some still-sealed PlayStation 2 and Xbox 360 games. Nothing all that impressive. The blue cases next to them—the thin plastic cases that hint at Blu-rays—catch my eye, though. I pluck out a few, all marked at just two dollars, and open the cases.

And I find exactly what I'm looking for.

I totally understand why D1V isn't ready to meet up in person. I'm still angry at myself for even suggesting it, getting all amped up while talking about music and using the headset and…just getting caught in the swirl of the emotions. And Ryan might laugh at my sad, loose definition of date, but this…this is better than nothing.

I pull out my phone and open the chat.

RECLAIM THE SUN: CHAT APPLICATION

AARON: Hey, busy later?

D1V: Oh, hello you.

D1V: No, why? Up to try that headset out a bit more?

AARON: Kinda, yeah. I have an idea.

AARON: I'll message you when I get home.

AARON: This afternoon, maybe?

D1V: Sure?

AARON: It's a date.

D1V: Date.

D1V: I'm making a face at you right now.

AARON: I'm sure you are.

Someone slams into me, muttering a quick apology as they continue through the crowd, and it pulls me away from my phone. Ryan and Alberto are walking over, a pair of jeans slung over Alberto's shoulder. As they approach, Ryan looks down at the movies in my hand and scowls.

"Those are *terrible* movies," he says with a disdainful sniff, as though I'm holding out trash.

"They are not!" I exclaim, wrestling my wallet out of my pocket.

Alberto plucks one out of my hands and examines it.

"You can't be serious," he says, looking up at me, a smirk on his face.

"I like that movie!" I snatch it back and turn to the man behind the table, a thick beard and long locks of curly hair framing his face.

"One...two..." he mumbles, counting the movies. "Alright, six movies, that'll be twelve dollars... Let's just call it ten, sound good?"

I hand him two crinkled five-dollar bills from my wallet and turn back to Alberto and Ryan, who are both staring at me, arms crossed, shaking their heads.

"Look, you don't get it. I'm going to—"

"Oh, I figured it out," Ryan says dryly.

"You could have at least picked something better," Alberto adds, smirking.

"You guys are the worst," I complain. "I'm skipping pizza and heading home."

I move to brush by them, but Alberto holds out a hand, blocking my way. He flashes me a grin. He knows I'm not going to bail on our usual trip to Lorenzo's, not when we're this close to the place, with its monstrous two-dollar slices that are bigger than my head.

"Goddamn it. Fine, let's go," I grumble. "But then I'm heading home."

I have a date to prep for.

I'm sweating like someone playing a round of competitive *StarCraft II* as I get myself situated in my room. Running around in the summer heat on the streets of Center City, Philadelphia, the pavement unforgiving, sending waves of warmth against you...it doesn't make for an attractive look at the end of it all. I pull my T-shirt off and use the still-damp fabric to wipe at my forehead, then give up, hustling into the bathroom to wash my face.

I look in the mirror, my brown skin flushed, bits of red in my eyes from the stinging of sweat and salt...

And I laugh.

It doesn't matter. None of it matters. I'll have a headset on— we can't see each other. Yet there's still this...this *something*, that makes me want to look nice. Bits of stubble are starting to pop up along my jaw again, even though I just shaved a few days ago, and I tilt my head, still fussing with myself in the mirror.

I towel my face off and take a few deep breaths. "Here we go," I announce to the mirror.

I hurry back to my room, but not before stopping in the hallway to listen for noise downstairs. All is silent—Mom is probably in the practice, and Dad...he's probably on the computer, doing...

Whatever the hell he's doing.

I shake my head. It doesn't matter. I've got some popcorn on my bed, a can of soda on the nightstand, a bag of Sour Patch Kids next to that. And, most important, I've got movies. It's now or never.

RECLAIM THE SUN: CHAT APPLICATION

AARON: Hi!

D1V: Well.

D1V: If it isn't Mr. Date.

AARON: You know, I really wish you could have gone flea marketing with me and the guys.

AARON: They love busting my chops too.

D1V: Heh. Maybe someday.

D1V: Not yet though.

AARON: I know.

AARON: So, look, I um...have this idea.

AARON: XPOE-8231-FK93-AALW-MP3Q

DIV: What's that?

AARON: A download code.

D1V: For...what?

AARON: Claim it in MoviesEverywhere, and then load up the Ocutime app.

D1V: Ooookay.

D1V: What.

D1V: Hahah, Aaron what is this?

AARON: So we can watch movies together! In the headset! In VR!

AARON: Like, that's the date.

AARON: Was this uh, not a good idea?

AARON: I made popcorn and everything.

D1V: No, no. This is...this is cute.

D1V: It's just, this movie...

AARON: It's old, I know.

D1V: I'll humor you, but then after this, we're watching one of my movies.

D1V: Say Anything, Aaron? You're such a cliché.

D1V: I like you though.

AARON: ♥

In the VR headset, the movie looks huge and massive, as though it's on a gigantic movie screen right in front of me. Like I'm sitting in the front row of the theater, or at least super close to it.

"Hey," D1V says, her voice in my ear.

I turn to the side, but she isn't there, of course. Just rows of faux seats.

The smell of the buttered popcorn I made in the downstairs microwave keeps me planted in the virtual reality I've chosen, this digital place. "What do you think?" I ask.

"It's cute," she says, and I can hear the smile in her voice. "The movie and…this."

My hand twitches, and the fact that she isn't here, in a seat next to me, weighs on me a little. The warmth in her voice, the fact that she's here, but not. The urge to reach out and hold her hand in this movie theater feels so real, so present, and I have to push myself to keep staring straight ahead. At the screen. At John Cusack as he bumbles around, a romantic mess.

I look over at the empty seats in the VR and reach my hand out anyway.

And I wonder.

If she's doing the same.

RECLAIM THE SUN: CHAT APPLICATION

D1V: Hey you!

D1V: What's going on, it's been a minute.

D1V: Beks? I see you online. Come on.

BEKS: Hey, sorry.

BEKS: Didn't realize I was signed on.

D1V: What? What is happening?

BEKS: Div, I don't think we should do GamesCon.

D1V: Why?

D1V: Okay, I mean I know why, but aren't we fighting back?

BEKS: We should cancel.

BEKS: You should email them and cancel.

D1V: Beks, what's going on?

BEKS: I gotta go.

17
DIVYA

Damn it.

All…this. It wasn't supposed to happen. Getting close to somebody out there. But here we are. It's only been a little over a week, and I can't bring myself to tell my mom that the smile on my face lately is coming from the place that's brought our little family so much pain.

I glance at the time—it's getting late, and about time for a streaming session. I message Aaron to see if he's around and check my email. I've successfully managed to avoid it all day, but if I want to keep the sponsors happy and the gadgets rolling in, I have to stay in the loop.

Det. Nikki Watts	Chatter, open ASAP	4:44 p.m.
Polygon Digest	GamesCon Preview: What to Expect	3:15 p.m.
Twitter Notifications	Direct Msg from Maggs	3:01 p.m.
H. Siddiqui	RE: RE: Sponsoring a new VR set?	2:37 p.m.
Desi Geek Girls	Scheduling a podcast interview?	1:42 p.m.

While my heart soars at the prospect of being on *Desi Geek Girls*, my favorite podcast, I squint at the most recent email. It's from the detective. Do...do detectives and police officers send emails?

I leave a star on the podcast email and the message from Hannah at Oculus, then open Detective Watts's message.

[INBOX]
(4:44 p.m.)

Chatter, open ASAP
Detective Nikki Watts <dwatts@jcgov.org]]

to me

Good afternoon Divya.
With GamesCon approaching there's been an uptick in discussions on social media and various Internet forums.
 I would seriously reconsider appearing there and update all your passwords across your various digital platforms.
 Please be careful, and don't hesitate to reach out.
Sincerely,
Detective Nikki Watts

Emotions are running through me like Cortana in *Halo*. They're rampant.

It's a mix of being terrified and furious at all of this. Afraid for what will happen to me and to my mom if I don't do something, but pissed off at the idea that these trolls are winning just by making me feel that way. By making me feel *anything*.

And the idea of canceling... I can't. Not after all this. I deserve to be there.

I close out of my email and debate texting Rebekah again,

to see if she wants to gear up for the stream and get our accounts locked down. Update passwords and all that. She responds back with a quick "class" response, but even with that one word, her tone is still so distant and cold. I can't figure out what's going on with her.

I send Aaron a quick message in the *Reclaim the Sun* messenger app to see if he's around, and instead of responding, his gamertag blips up on my screen, and he messages me a wink. I smile and turn on the voice client with a click of my mouse, opening up a channel to Aaron.

"Hey," I say, feeling this warmth in my chest.

"Hey yourself," he responds, and there's a beat of silence. "You sound different. Are you not in VR?"

"Not tonight," I say. "I want to get a stream in and record." I reach up and adjust my webcam. "You're welcome to join in the fun, of course."

"Sure, why not? Is Rebekah around?"

"At class." It feels like ever since the incident with my mom, she's practically disappeared, and then the distance here, too... It hurts. I mean, I *get* it—a lot of people on her campus know who she is and recognize her. Combine that with everything that went down at Quarter Slice Crisis, plus her past experiences... I understand. I'd be a monster not to.

But it still hurts.

She's even pushing for us to cancel our GamesCon appearance, our first convention ever, but there's no way in hell I'm going to let that happen. I know I wasn't terribly hyped about it initially, even in talking with Rebekah, but now? Not even Detective Watts's warnings are gonna keep me from it—trolls or not, I *earned* this. My audience. The opportunity to speak out about harassment. To fight back. And even the chance to sell a little bit of merch. The enamel pins and stitched patches that Rebekah had designed are on their way, and they're way too cute not to put into the hands of our fans. I'll go by myself if I have to, to keep Rebekah feeling safe.

Fuck the trolls.

I open the public channel and put a call out to the Armada, and a handful of ships warp in almost instantly, cheers echoing in my headset.

Ah, my people.

With about two dozen or so ships floating next to me and Aaron, I punch in the coordinates for a greenish-looking speck in the distance, the planet popping up on my long-range scanners.

CLASS THREE PLANET [CONFIRMED]
Status: Uncharted, Undiscovered
Life Support Capability: Positive
Population: Small creatures, plant life,
no sentient evidence available.
Detectable Resources: Timber, Water, Minerals
Would you like to claim and name this planet?
[YES] [NO]

Thanks to the upgrades, numerous other details about the planet appear on the screen, making the choice all the easier to go forth and discover. Tons of resources and some small creatures to photograph and catalog for extra experience and points? Yes, please, sign me up. And if we all go in as a group, extra points all around.

This is perfect.

"Alright, Armada, lock on to me. I'm picking up lots of resources and...well, it just looks great." I grin into the webcam. "We deserve this one. I'm going to go ahead and turn the stream on and start recording in three...two...one..."

I hit Record, and the stream is live. I'm hoping against all hope that no one in the small bunch of ships is a troll in disguise.

"Let's go!" I exclaim, pressing down on the jump. My ship and all the others rocket forward. After just a few seconds, the green planet comes into focus. It almost looks like a floating ball of moss. Bits of blue pop up among the green, but also some splashes of yellow.

"Weird," I hear Aaron say in my headset.

"The fact that it's almost all land, or those little yellow splotches?" I ask, flicking to a private chat.

"Both," he says with a chuckle.

"If we encounter any trouble, do your best to escape," I advise the Armada, going public again. "Save yourselves. We spend too much time on these ships to have them ruined."

With that, I push the throttle forward and my ship speeds toward the surface. I squint at all the greenery, trying to find a safe landing spot, when it strikes me that all of it is likely safe. It's a planet of moss, or at least, whatever alien moss this is. My landing gear comes down quickly with a soft *click*, and my ship sinks in a little as it touches the ground, like placing something on a large, soft blanket.

I pop open the cockpit and hop out, surveying my surroundings. The fields push out far, way past the horizon, but nearby, there is a bubbling lake of something yellow. I walk toward it, the sounds of the other Armada ships echoing around me—landing gear lowering, cockpits opening, feet hurrying along the soft, springy surface.

Aaron appears at my side. "What do you think that is?" he asks, gesturing at the yellow pool.

Just steps away now, I see that the yellow is a bit darker than I originally thought. I squint at the screen and load up one of the mineral analyzing tools. It takes up most of my view, but after a quick scan, it comes back with an answer that sends my heart racing.

"It's a lake of *gold*," I whisper.

I turn around, looking past Aaron and back toward the Armada that made the trip with me. Minerals and resources are a key part of *Reclaim the Sun*, and they're randomly generated planet to planet. But lakes of molten gold? I haven't heard of anyone finding *anything* like that in game yet.

I turn back to it, making sure I get some long, hard looks at the surface, walking around the edge of it all. I need this for the recording. Absolutely need it. Rebekah will lose it if I don't capture every single moment, and it's killing me that she's not here for this.

"I can't even fathom how many in-game credits all this is worth," Aaron says, his voice far and distant. I look up and see he's nearing the other side of the lake. "Do you think we can swim in it?"

"Um, no," I reply. "You'll probably die immediately and have to start over."

"I gotta try," he says, taking a step toward the lake.

"Aaron, come on, you did all this leveling up," I protest. "Don't waste it."

He steps back again. "You're right, you're right," he says and makes his way over toward me.

"Man, Rebekah is going to lose her—" I start.

A concussive blast nearly knocks me off my feet. In the distance, a ship bursts into flames as blaster fire erupts all over the ground, peppering the surface, leaving a trail of fire in the green moss wherever it hits. The channel lights up with screams and loud exclamations from the Armada, and their ships hover into view above where most us have landed.

I immediately recognize the logos on the sides of the ships. The Vox Populi.

The damn trolls are here.

"Get back to your ship!" I shout at Aaron, who immediately takes off running. I sprint alongside him before breaking off toward my own vessel. The Vox Populi circle overhead in their ships all the while, occasionally taking out a member of the Armada, but for the most part, they wait silently.

And then it hits me.

They aren't just here to fight.

They're waiting for us to leave.

They couldn't have tried taking the planet at the same time as us, so we could have dueled, the way Aaron and I almost did when we first met. No, instead, they sat waiting, following us, ready to attack. And now, instead of fighting fair, they're straight-up camping here, ready to steal what *we* found.

I climb into the *Cedere Nescio* and take to the skies, the planet of green and gold flashing by beneath me, shimmering and bright.

Aaron thunders in over my headset as I turn my ship to face those of the Vox Populi. "What are you doing?!" he demands.

"We can't let them take the planet!" I shout, broadcasting to the entire Armada.

"What?" he shouts back. "Why? Fuck this, no way, D1V. You and the Armada should—"

I cut him off. "Think about how much those gold lakes are worth in credits. They'll be funded for life, Aaron. That's why they're just sitting there. They'll never stop. This game will be ruined for *everyone*. Their ships will always be faster. Their upgrades will always be better."

I feel a bloom of heat in my chest as the Populi ships come into firing range. While a handful of the Armada have fled like I told them to, a number have stuck behind, their vessels floating up behind me, flanking me, and a few hovering in front of me, all close together. They're forming a shield, and the gesture is not lost on me.

The sounds of them chuckling and talking to one another erupt into my headset.

I grit my teeth.

Log on.

Fight back.

Alright. Let's do this.

"Oh, look who it is." The computerized deep voice I heard the last time I saw them in game speaks up, and one of the ships jets forward ever so slightly. "It's amazing what a little pressure can do, even to the strongest friendship."

"Excuse me?" I nudge my ship farther ahead, past the others trying to protect me. Friendship? What is he saying?

"D1V, don't do it," someone in my Armada speaks up.

"Stop!" I think it's Aaron.

"Stay behind us," another person says through the channel.

"What are you even talking about?" I press, looking back and forth from his ship to the blast panel in mine. His ship looks heavy, upgraded as much as it can be, and so do the rest of his friends. I've gone all out on mine, too, but if his entire fleet descends on me, that's it. Game over, start again, all those credits I fought for, all the belief my Armada put in me, everything they pledged to help restore my ship…gone.

This planet. All these resources. It'll belong to them.

"Your *commander*," the voice says mockingly. "Your little streaming friend, Rebekah." I hear him laugh, and the sound of a few more boys chuckling. "One little letter sent to her apartment, and it all came falling down."

My heart stops in my chest.

That's why she's been so closed off.

That's why she's been so distant.

I turn away from my computer and reach for my phone. There, all over it, are scores of texts from Rebekah. The silence broken at last.

REBEKAH: I'm sorry. I'm sorry I've been so quiet.

REBEKAH: I'm watching the stream.

REBEKAH: They found my address.

REBEKAH: They threatened to send photoshopped nude photos of me to my school.

REBEKAH: They said they hacked my phone and email.

REBEKAH: Div please don't hate me.

REBEKAH: I was afraid.

I want to scream and throttle the world. How dare they. How fucking *dare* they.

Rebekah.

My best friend.

The one person in this world who has seen me through everything.

My parents' divorce, my mom and I having to move to this shitty apartment. Watching things get taken away from us, piece by piece, bit by bit. Who helped me start this thing, even as she wrestled with her own trauma. That elevator. The black eye. The cracked rib. The trip to the ER and the long talks with the cops. The new studio she can barely afford. The articles and the rumors and the women's center meetings, and all the shit talk she didn't deserve.

The only safe place for either of us has been online. In these games. With beautiful strangers that make the world worth living.

And now I am going to set this world on fire.

I turn back to the game. "This is where you fucked up," I say coldly into the microphone. "You think I'm going to be mad at her? Turn on her? Over a damn video game? It's just a *game*!"

As their laughter echoes through my headset, I load up my missiles, preparing to fire.

"What you're doing out there isn't a game!" I shout at them. "It's real life. Those are real people—"

"Take her down," the deep voice says.

And the battle begins.

Several of my Armada's ships fly hard and fast, hurtling themselves in front of mine. The Vox Populi's missiles and blasters make quick work of them, smashing their small ships into pieces, their names quickly disappearing from my channel list. I hear them as they sign off, pressing for me to run. Get into deep space. Jump. Log out once I'm far away. Crackling voices interlaced with explosions and cursing.

But I can't.

I just can't let them get away with this.

The urge to put my VR headset on is so great. I want to watch them burn in real time, as close up and in my face as possible, but there's no time for it. Delaying by even a second could cost us everything, and the headset takes way too long to connect.

I fly down toward the green earth, the moss all aflame, burning in straight lines like razor cuts in the ground. Aaron and several other ships follow suit. I select my missiles and stare at the glowing lakes of gold that litter the planet.

If the trolls get their hands on such vast resources, it won't just ruin the game for everyone else. They can take the in-game credits and sell them for real-life currency, something people do notoriously on message boards and on eBay. This planet is probably worth millions of credits. Maybe tens of thousands of actual dollars. They could use that money for anything they want. Nefarious or not.

They don't deserve it.

For a moment, I dream of everything I could do with that kind of money. College at County, paid for. No having to explain a gap year to anyone. Mom's summer classes, done. Rent, secured. Dad can fuck right off. No asking for anyone to help me out ever again.

I can almost feel the throttle shaking in my hands, even though my hands are firmly resting on a keyboard and mouse. Another explosion rattles my ship, followed by a second and a third in quick succession. The channel shows more of my Armada disappearing, but a couple are still with me per the onboard sonar.

Fuck it.

You. Get. Nothing.

I let my missiles loose, targeting the gold lakes. They twist and turn through the air, high-powered and upgraded to all hell, and explode over the gold, setting the liquid surface ablaze. I watch as the resource meter on the planet ticks away, moving down, the virtual currency being destroyed and burned.

Shouts of rage and loud cursing fill my ears, and I grin.

Sure, gold doesn't burn in real life.

But this is a video game. Randomly generated nonsense.

I'm not about to file a complaint to argue about the physics of the world, especially if it allows me to keep these resources out of the hands of those trolls. Save that for the monsters who come after me. The ones who have nothing better to do than write think pieces and hot takes on that kind of stuff.

"Blast her! She's taking out all the gold!" the Populi leader bellows, his computerized voice blinking out for just a second, revealing a deep, real voice. For some reason, it makes me laugh, the idea that he's someone older. It makes him that much more pathetic, somehow. Some grown man, waging war on me and Rebekah.

Rebekah. The rage surges through me again. She wasn't being cold or pushing me away out of anger or something I'd done wrong. She was afraid. She was trying to protect me from *this*.

I catch sight of Aaron's ship pushing ahead of mine. He dips down, blasting some of the lakes himself. The remaining vessels behind me quickly follow suit, and many of them are taken out in the process, the ships exploding into balls of flame, tumbling down into the green, leaving trails of blackened waste in their wake.

Blip. Blip. Blip.

Ten ships left.

Seven.

Four.

Two.

"It's time to get out of here, D1V," I hear Aaron say over the sound of blaster fire and explosions echoing through my cockpit. "I'm out of missiles."

"Go ahead," I tell him. "I'm not leaving until I've destroyed the planet."

I hear Aaron sigh loudly. "Well, the upgrades were nice while they lasted," he says.

"Aaron, what are you—"

I watch his ship take a nosedive toward the ground. An explosion thunders in my headset, combined with the sound of Aaron cursing as his ship hits one of the lakes of gold and erupts in a ball of fire, lighting up the shimmering pool of liquid credits with it.

Blip.

One.

I wince. All that work he put into that ship of his. That patience. All that time we spent exploring and leveling up together. Wasted. Gone.

But then I smile. At least he spent it doing something stupidly heroic in a virtual world.

I kind of adore him for that.

Now I'm all that's left.

I can still see some pools of gold glimmering in the distance, but it's a fraction, a sliver of what they would have had before we literally set the world on fire. This beautiful randomly generated world. For a moment, my heart breaks a little for it. There will never be another like it in this game, and we had to destroy it, so someone else couldn't claim it.

I yank on the throttle of my ship, a blinking orange screen warning that I might stall out after ascending straight up too quickly. I let go, and the ship dips back, flipping around until I'm facing the remainder of the Populi fleet. There's at least a dozen of them left.

I load up my remaining missiles as they hover there. They target my ship in response, alarms blaring in my ears, rattling my skull.

"Wait," the computerized voice says, and the warning sirens fade away as the targeting systems in their ships let me off the hook. "Let's see if it works."

"Let's see if what—" I start.

And just like that, I'm logged out of the game.

"The hell?" I grumble as the title screen comes up. I type my password in. I get an error message. I do it again. The same.

My heart races. There's no way they could have… Could they?

I move to reset my password and head over to my email to await the new one.

But I can't get into my email. My password isn't working there, either.

I request a new one. They're supposed to send a text to my phone, to let me know the new log-in code. I wait a few agonizing seconds, but when my phone finally buzzes, it's a number I don't recognize.

555-324-6456: Nope.

I sink back in my chair, dread coursing through me. Slowly, I load up my social media channels, terrified of what I might find. My Twitter, personal Facebook, Glitch stream, every-thing…it's all been hacked. My Twitter feed is blasting out a steady array of hate messages, my Facebook is posting adver-tisements for sunglasses, shoes, and other various products.

But the worst is my Glitch channel.

All my videos.

My revenue streams. The platform I built to get me these sponsors.

Gone. All gone.

I've been erased.

They couldn't beat me, so they deleted me.

They won.

I move to delete the text from the troll and stop. There's a number there. It could help. Maybe someone could trace it, though my experience with law enforcement is limited to what I've seen on *Law & Order: SVU* marathons and discussions with Detective Watts.

Maybe she could do something with it.

I move to open the game's chat application, to talk to Aaron, but it boots me out immediately. Wrong password. Right. It's all gone.

Aaron.

Aaron is gone.

It's almost strange, the sinking feeling in my stomach. No social media, no email, the chat app… All my resources for reaching out and talking to him ripped from me. I never even got his phone number.

I rack my brain. There's got to be a way.

But maybe…maybe he's better off. Away from all this.

I can figure it out later. For now, I close out of everything and open Rebekah's actual texts to my phone, not the chat client. They might have hacked my recovery info for my social feeds, but at least my phone is still mine, even if they do have the number now. There are a bunch of messages from Rebekah following the earlier ones, each more upset than the last.

I pluck Detective Watts's business card out of my wallet and look from her number to Rebekah's texts.

Rebekah first, then Watts. She needs to know everything is okay. She needs to know I don't blame her for any of this.

As I start typing out a response, a light flickers across my phone screen—some kind of reflection. I glance around my room and eventually find the source, a flashing coming from my VR headset on the bed.

I reach over to pick it up and peek into the headset. The lenses aren't reflecting what's on my monitor, mirroring the game's menu or login or anything like it should. Instead, it's just flashing, white and black and white and black and white and—

It's a damn strobe.

They sent me a seizure-inducing video.

Seizures aren't something I live with—I've never had something like that happen to me from flashing lights or a video game or anything. But the reality doesn't matter to them.

It's the possibility.

The potential.

I could have fallen out of my chair. The headset's cable could have pulled my computer down on top of me.

They could have *killed* me. If the possibility was even remotely there, they took it.

My phone rings, and I jump, my heart racing. I place the headset back on the bed and gingerly pick up the phone to answer.

"Div?" It's Rebekah, and her voice chokes back a sob.

That's it. Me. My best friend. My mother.

My life.

After my appearance at GamesCon, I'm done.

RECLAIM THE SUN: CHAT APPLICATION

AARON: D1V?

AARON: Are you there? What happened?

AARON: All your feeds are down, and I can't find you.

AARON: I'll email you.

AARON: Are you okay?

D1V: LOOOOOOOL.

D1V: D1V'S NOT HERE MAN.

AARON: What?

AARON: Who is this?

D1V: THESE CHAT LOGS ARE HILARIOUS.

D1V: YOU THINK SHE REALLY CARES ABOUT YOU.

D1V: LOL.

AARON: Whoever this is, you better log out.

D1V: OR WHAT.

D1V: LOL.

D1V: BYE.

18

AARON

"What do you mean, gone?" Ryan asks, leaning against the reception desk in my mom's practice. "We live in the age of social media and the Internet, my friend. You can't just disappear."

He plucks one of the terrible doctor's office lollipops out of the giant jar near the sign-in sheet, unwraps it, and quickly pops it in his mouth. Then he makes a face and takes it out, rewrapping it with exaggerated care.

"Don't," I say, giving him a look.

He drops the lollipop back in the jar, grinning.

"Dude!" I move to grab the jar, but he snatches it away, pulling his lollipop out again.

"Come on, I was joking." Ryan smiles and grabs a different lollipop, this one apparently good, as he doesn't toss it back in. "Now explain."

"It's like what I've been texting you!" I say, exasperated. "I don't know how they did it, but I've spent the past few days trying to find something, *anything*, and she's just... She's not there anymore."

I pull out my phone. Since D1V signed off a few days ago, all her social media accounts vanished. Her Glitch channel lost all its content and immediately went to private. And when I tried to reach her in the game's mobile chat client...

Well, let's just say I know it's not her texting me all these... sexually explicit instructions.

"Have you tried messaging her friend?" Ryan asks, his speech a little broken up with the giant lollipop rattling against his teeth. "Rebekah? She's in those streams, too."

I shake my head. "I've emailed a few times, but she isn't responding. I think maybe she got hacked, too, I don't know." I rotate the monitor on the office PC around, so Ryan can see. "All of her social accounts are locked down. Not deleted. But definitely private and shut away."

I move to spin the monitor back to me when Ryan grabs it. "Wait, wait," he says, squinting at the screen. He points at an icon on the desktop. "What is that? Is that... Is that it?"

My shoulders slump. "Yeah, that's it." With a quick click of the mouse, my dad's folder is open on the desktop, the massive list of Word documents ready to be explored, that little icon of *Ultima Online* the only contrasting blip of color among them.

"That's...that's a lot," Ryan says, his tone defeated.

I close the folder containing my dad's secret and navigate back to the newsfeeds. They're full of what I already know, what I've been reading again and again over the past few days. Massive hacking attack on D1V. Social media accounts broken into. Glitch channel deleted. Game profile gone and reregistered. A laundry list of things, all at once. A collaborative effort.

A news alert pings in the corner of the screen, and it opens up to an article on *Polygon*—again, about D1V. This one mentions my name in the list of gamers who were playing.

"I'm not sure how they get away with just calling it trolling," I say. "It's like terrorism at this point. And look at all this attention. Her name is everywhere."

"So is yours." Ryan indicates the screen.

I shrug. My own notoriety doesn't matter. It's D1V who's at the center of all this. She's the one hurting.

"I need to see her," I say resolutely.

"Riiiiight," Ryan drawls, taking the lollipop out of his mouth and twirling it about. "Because that's a good idea. Go surprise the girl who's been stalked online to the point that they've deleted her digital life and harassed her and her family. In person."

"But it isn't like that—"

"No, no," he says, holding his hands up. "You're right. It's very romantic."

"Damn it." I groan and stand up. "What am I supposed to do, then?" I glance over at the appointment schedule tacked on the desk's wall. "I can't just sit here and not do anything. We care about each other. We…we have something."

"Give her time to get all of her life back together, man," Ryan suggests, perching on the desk. "If it was that bad, I bet she would have reached out somehow. Well, it *is* that bad, but if she really needed you. You know?"

My heart sinks a little.

"Sorry, I'm fucking this up." He bites down on the lollipop. "Look, I don't want to bring you down here. I'm just saying. Probably not the best idea to go running in thinking you're some gallant knight or something. You kept wanting to do that for Laura, thinking Jason is an asshole—"

"Jason *is* an asshole," I remind him. "He still hasn't paid us."

"That may be," Ryan admits. "But still, not your place. She's happy."

"Yeah… Yeah, you're right." I groan. "I should have just asked for her phone number at some point." I sit back down and run my hands through my hair. "You know? Such an easy question. But nope. Only talked through a chat application linked to the game that she's banned from. All her social networks are gone. I don't have her normal email. Her in-game email is dead. Her best friend is on lockdown." The futility of it all is exhausting. "How did people even find each other before technology?"

"Give her time," Ryan says. "In the meantime, let's go hit Gamezone or something. Get your mind off all this."

I give him a look.

"Hey, I know video games got you into this mess, but you love them," he says, pointing at me with the white stem that remains of his lollipop. "At least, I think you do, Mr. Didn't Know What *Ultima Online* Is. We'll get some mindless ten-dollar shooting game, like an old *Halo* or something, and blow each other up for a few hours, and you'll feel fine. Plus, this isn't just all about you. What about my day? What about my life? I have needs, too."

"Wait…did something happen?" I feel flush all over, having prattled about my problems all afternoon as opposed to talking with my best friend.

"Everything is fine. I'm messing with you." Ryan grins and pops the white stick back in his mouth, moving it back and forth. "Should this be my new look?" he asks. "Maybe get a toothpick? Be one of those people?"

"No," I say. "Absolutely not."

The Gamezone isn't terribly far away. While our homes might feel like they aren't in the city, as Philadelphia is really great at providing the illusion of suburban life in an actual city, it only takes a fifteen-minute stroll in any direction to start seeing signs of city life. Proper downtown areas, and all that. Stores, high-rises, condos with downstairs shops, all just a quick powerwalk away on the busier streets, all mostly named after trees. Chestnut. Walnut. No matter how many cute row houses are nearby, you can almost always look up and spot skyscrapers in the distance.

Tucked between a comic book shop and a nail salon sits the local Gamezone. It's a lot like those popular Gamestop stores, which you can find in just about every mall and city everywhere, and even goes so far as to rip off the logo and color scheme. It's an indie game shop, so everything is a bit more expensive, but they throw some decent gaming events, which makes up for it. Community and all.

I push open the front door, Ryan following me inside. A large cardboard cutout of the Master Chief from *Halo* stands near the entrance, advertising the next game in the neverending series. I jerk my elbow at it in silent question, but Ryan shakes his head, pointing over at the old PlayStation titles across the way, and a very tempting five-dollar bin that mostly looks full of aging *Call of Duty* titles.

I follow him over, my eyes scanning the used games for something that'll keep us busy, and I wince at the big advertisement for *Reclaim the Sun*. The game's logo, accompanied by the critical reviews and scores from different video game sites, is big and bold, hanging next to the newer games.

"I feel you," a Gamezone employee says, sauntering over. He's a little taller than me, and maybe a year or two older, if that. A college-aged guy is working in the shop as well, fussing with the computer behind the counter. "It's not even that great a game." He tips his head at the *Reclaim the Sun* ad and shrugs. "But you know, people buy into the hype."

"Yeah, that and all the drama," the other employee says, not even looking up from the register. "I'm telling you, they engineer that shit just to get publicity."

"Oh my God, Chad, not again with this," the younger employee says, turning away from me and Ryan.

"What?" Chad humphs. "I bet it is. That streamer chick isn't even that hot."

That streamer chick? I glance at Ryan, feeling a flare of rage building up. He's talking about D1V. It can't possibly be anyone else.

"Here's how it works. They get some model to pretend they care about a video game, give her a bunch of fake subscribers, and then get these so-called trolls to attack her." Chad makes a dismissive noise. "There's no way any of that is real."

"Explain the GamesCon appearance then, huh?" the younger guy says, crossing his arms. "There would be a huge lawsuit if that was all fake."

"Why do you think she disappeared?" Chad asks, holding his arms out. "All staged. And now that panel at GamesCon is going to be massive. All this attention. Just you watch. People will write about it, game sales will spike, all because it's a big machine. Bunch of fake geek girls and all that."

"She's…" I step toward the counter, anger and hope warring inside me. "She's still doing that panel? Even after everything that happened?"

"Supposedly," the non-Chad employee says, handing me a flyer. "I heard rumors that GamesCon is going to be her first and last public appearance. That other girl on the stream with her said it in some interview I read this morning."

"Rebekah?" I venture.

"Yeah, you watch that stream? You a Glitcher?" He smiles, crossing his arms. "I'm super into it."

"I do," I say, trying to avoid looking at Chad, who's rolling his eyes behind the register. "Not much of a live-streaming gamer myself, but I check it out sometimes."

"Rebekah." Chad inclines his head, a smug smile spreading across his face. "Now, I hope *she's* the real deal. I'd sure love to get a piece of that."

Before I realize what I'm doing, I'm stalking toward Chad, my fists balled up. Ryan runs up and grabs me from behind, pulling me back, and a flare of heat blooms inside my chest.

"Shut the fuck up!" I shout at Chad. Chad. Fucking Chad. Of course, his goddamn name is Chad. "You don't get to talk about her that way!"

"Whoa-ho-ho!" Chad says, grinning broadly. He strolls around the counter slowly, tauntingly. "Looks like we got us a mega fan here." He stops in front of me and leans down to whisper menacingly, "You know what? If any of that nonsense that happened was real... I think those chicks deserve it."

I scream at him, wrestling against Ryan.

"Chad, come on," protests the other employee.

"Dude, knock it off," Ryan grunts as I keep trying to lunge away from him. He's dragging me back toward the door, and I'm baffled by how strong he is.

"It's true!" Chad calls as we get closer to the exit. "If it's real, GamesCon is going to be really interesting. I heard the Populi are gonna put on quite the show."

The door closes behind us, and I spin around to glare at Ryan.

"What?" he says. "What were you going to do, punch that guy?"

"Maybe!" I exclaim.

"Yeah, that would have ended well. 'Sorry, Officer, he was defending his online friend that he's never met and why are you handcuffing him why is he in jail now what's assault—"

"Okay, okay," I say, waving him off. "I get it. Let's just go buy a digital game. Fuck those guys." I look back at the store and notice the GamesCon flyer hanging on the front door. I storm over and tear it off, and the two of us head back toward our neighborhood.

I study the flyer as we walk. There's a large *Reclaim the Sun* logo next to GamesCon's, with some details about D1V's panel, "Harassment in Video Game Culture & Women: A Conversation." There are a few other streamers on the panel with her, and it's in the morning on the Friday of the convention. I can't help but scowl at the list of panelists, considering it's supposed to be a discussion about women in games and it looks like D1V is the only woman on the thing.

I glance back at the store, still simmering over that obnoxious employee and his glee at D1V's downfall, his doubt over whether she's even a real person or not. Which is part of the damn problem—people assume that those behind a screen, or masked with an avatar, aren't real people. Then there was all that stuff about how he thinks the convention will be really interesting. And he mentioned the Populi...

It's not the possibility that I might be able to meet her that sends my heart racing and my feet flying back home in a hurry, Ryan half jogging next to me, complaining that I need to slow down. No. It's the fact that she'll be there. At that event in New York City. With someone like that, like Chad, someone unwelcoming, waiting for her. And that something is supposed to happen at the convention.

Really interesting... The Populi are gonna put on quite the show.

I have to find a way to stop them.

19
DIVYA

"I don't care," I say flatly, closing my laptop. "I'm going."

As I meet Rebekah's eyes, I struggle to hide the rising emotions I'm feeling after reading all the comments online. After being forced to ignore my golden rule. The little sign in my room. Don't Read the Comments.

This time, I read all of them. Every single one.

"Div, you can't—" Rebekah starts.

"I'm going," I insist. I reach across the cafeteria table and grab her hands. I feel them shaking a little, and give her fingers a reassuring squeeze. I visited the Women's Center here on campus with her earlier. To talk. To get all this...*awful* off my chest.

There was something about talking to someone about everything, all that's happened, all that I think is *going* to happen, that felt...good. Right. Particularly with a person who claimed they've never played a video game in their life.

It gave me perspective. There's a whole world outside my bubble. All I have to do is let it pop.

I close my eyes for a moment, soaking in the oddly comforting sounds of the college cafeteria. The never-ending din of voices, conversations that sound friendly and jovial, all around me, pushing back against the welling sadness that keeps trying to envelop me. The food here isn't that fantastic, but it's free, thanks to Rebekah. And with everything shutting down, with no access to my channel and social feeds, I'm taking every free thing I can get.

The money isn't gone. It's not like it vanished overnight. But I know it's not going to come back any time soon, not until I restore my channels. And who knows how long that's going to take.

And if I even want them back.

I open my eyes to see Rebekah shaking her head.

"But you saw what they said they're going to do," she presses back, withdrawing her hands from mine.

"It's a public place, Beks." The words feel just as hollow and fake as the ones I tried to say in her counseling session. That I'm fine. That it'll be okay. Because I'm just as worried as she is. About the appearance. About our plan. "They aren't actually going to do any of that. Besides, I jacked up my speaker fee, and for some crazy reason, the convention folks agreed. It'll cover what we need for my mom's last class. I'll be able to register for a course or two at County. I'll be free. From all of this."

I force a smile and sweep my hands around and into the air. "It'll be my grand public sign-off. The end of the great D1V!"

Rebekah starts crying.

"Aw, come on, everyone in here is going to think I'm breaking up with you," I tease.

"Sh-shut up," Rebekah sputters out, a laugh mixing with the tears. She wipes at her face. "Besides, you kinda are. I'll miss our stream."

"Yeah, but it's not like that," I remind her. "We'll still stream together for fun and hang out and game all the time."

"I know. But I'm allowed to be worried about you. I'm allowed to be scared."

"You are. You absolutely are," I say, recognizing the words I know she learned in therapy. "But I can't let these people think they're in control of me. I won't let them have this hold over me. I just won't."

Rebekah nods.

"Any word from Aaron?" she asks, looking off to the side, like she's trying not to have this conversation.

"No," I tell her. "But that's not entirely unexpected. He doesn't really have a way to reach me. I kind of want to wait until all this is over to talk to him, anyway. You know?"

"He might be worried about you," she points out, and I swear, it's as though the words are physically hurting her to say out loud. She grits her teeth as I give her a look. "Stop it. I care about you, so... I guess...by some weird osmosis... I care about him, too."

"So it's just science?"

"Just science."

I suddenly remember that I *do* have his email. At least, his game email from *Reclaim the Sun*. It would be easy, really. A quick, "Hello, I'm okay," using someone else's account while mine is down. Maybe make a new one, a guest account. But I want this finished first. I mean, I found his home address all too easily when I wanted to send him the VR headset. Surely the trolls could find him, too.

I want to keep him safe.

I change the subject. "By the way, I talked to Detective Watts, and you don't have to come if you don't want to," I say. Rebekah immediately looks up at me, aghast and glaring.

"Oh *hell* no," she says emphatically. "You don't get to go

without me, do this without me, and leave me an anxiety-filled mess at home. I'm there. We are in this. What's her plan, anyway?"

"Yeah, about that—"

A couple of college kids walk by, blatantly staring. They both have retro video game shirts on, *Space Invaders* and *Centipede*. They whisper to each other as they pass our table, glancing back at us over their shoulders.

I pull the sunglasses off.

"Damn it," I mutter. "Maybe I should dye my hair. Or cut it. I should cut it."

"Please, that would break your mom's heart," Rebekah protests, shaking her head.

"We're a family used to such things," I say, staring at Rebekah's hair.

Blood orange.

That could work.

I pull out my phone and scroll to Detective Watts's number. I stare at the screen for a beat, taking a deep breath.

"Div?" Rebekah ventures.

"It's just…" I bite my lip. "Once we do this, there's no going back, you know?"

"I don't. You haven't told me what's going on." Rebekah snorts. "You act like we're going to war."

I look up at her.

"We are."

The bell on the door chimes, and I glance up, spotting Detective Watts looking around the café. I raise my hand and wave at her.

"Wow, you weren't lying about the Misty Knight–esque detective," Rebekah whispers. "She's so cool."

"*You* be cool," I whisper back, grinning.

Detective Watts strolls over, a small scowl on her face as she weaves around chairs and tables, finding her way to ours. She grabs a chair and pulls it out, the metal making a sharp squeal against the hardwood floor, and takes a seat.

"Do you want anything?" I ask.

"Hi, I'm Rebekah!" my friend pipes up, looking a bit awed.

Oh my God, Beks.

"I'm good," Detective Watts says, her eyes still scanning our surroundings. "The names for the places you and your friends hang out, I swear. Couldn't we have just gone to Starbucks?"

"What's wrong with Brew-ti-ful?" I ask with an innocent smile. We decided to relocate for our meeting with the detective, and the café, situated fairly close to Rebekah's campus, also doubles as an art gallery. It's a good place for an open mic, a cup of coffee, or to sit down and plot out the downfall of a cyber mob.

At least, in my opinion.

"I can think of several things." She crosses her arms and leans back in her chair. Her eyes flit over to Rebekah. "Are you okay?"

"Hmm? Yeah!" she exclaims, nodding vigorously.

"Okay, well…" Detective Watts pulls out her phone and a little notebook from inside her jacket. "Are you ready?"

"Yes." I exhale.

"Great." She looks back and forth from me to Beks. "Here's the plan."

20

AARON

"Pass the red pepper?" my dad asks from across the kitchen table. I grab the little shaker and hand it over to him, watching as he douses his pizza slices with the stuff, to the point where I'm convinced his pizza is going to make a crunching sound when he bites into it. The layer of pepper flakes coating the cheese looks like chain mail armor.

I stare as he takes a giant bite, closes his eyes in contentment. As if he can feel my stare, he waves a finger and says, "Don't you judge."

"I'm not, I'm not," I say, even though I am. For the pizza. For the game and the digital archive of letters. His secrets.

I look over at Mom, who's busy cutting up pieces of pizza into smaller triangles for Mira, who sits there and pouts over it. Her arms are crossed as my mom presents each tiny slice to her.

"Come on, Mira," my mom nudges, pushing the little pieces closer to her.

"Why can't I have big slices?" Mira whines. "I'm big enough."

"She probably is," Dad comments. There's a little sweat on

his forehead, and I can't help but smirk. Despite the years of over-seasoning, he can't fool me. The red pepper does have an effect on him. "Let her try a big slice."

"Fine," my mom says with a sniff. She takes a slice out of the box and places it in front of Mira, who gleefully picks it up and squeals as the cheese slides off the slice and onto her lap. Mom levels a glare at Dad, whose mouth is tightly shut, holding back a laugh.

"I'm…sor…ry…" he sputters out before laughing uproariously. Mira joins in, clapping, and a soft smile sneaks its way onto Mom's face.

I roll my eyes and grab another slice of pizza while Mom fusses over Mira, picking cheese off her lap and taking the cheeseless slice for herself.

"Dad, I hate to ask this, but…" I glance over at my mom, who looks up at me, her eyes narrowed, and I know this is going to end up being a *thing*. "Look, there's this event in the city tomorrow, and I really need to go. It's for my writing. I know it's last-minute."

"Writing. I think you mean *video games*," Mom says sternly.

"I'd argue it's the same thing," Dad says, shrugging.

"GamesCon," I continue, surprised by my dad's defense. "There's a video game showcase and all, yes. But I need to be there to ask questions of people who work in the industry, about writing for games."

"Hmm, isn't that something you can do through email?" he asks, taking another bite of his red pepper–crusted pizza.

Email. I try not to glare.

"Or at college?" he adds.

"There's…" I exhale. "There's a girl."

My mom drops the fork and knife she's been fussing with, the silverware clattering on the table.

"Oooooh," Mira coos.

"*Really* now?" My dad grins, laying his slice of pizza down. His puts his elbows on the table, glancing over at my mom and back at me. "Alright, you can go. I'll handle the office."

"This is not the way to teach him responsibility!" my mom protests. "What are these games preparing him for?" She turns to me with a determined expression. "If you go, you're fired."

"Great!" I exclaim. "It's not like I wanted the job, anyway!" Hurt flashes across her face, and I sigh. "I just don't understand why you're so against all this."

"Because I don't want them taking advantage of you!" my mom shouts, and then turns to Mira quickly, flashing her an apologetic look. "It's okay, it's okay." She glances back at me. "Aaron, we've had this conversation before. That boy, that studio, still hasn't paid you, right?"

"Well—" I start.

"When your father was working in his restaurants, you know what would happen sometimes?"

"Darling, you don't have to—" my dad tries to chime in.

"No, we're talking about this *now*," my mom insists. "Sometimes he would be working well past his time, and they'd say he would get paid, but he wouldn't. Or on holidays, when he was supposed to get overtime? He never did. Just empty promises again and again."

I look at my dad, who shakes his head and looks down at his plate.

"Dad?" I venture.

"It's true." He clears his throat. "Your mom doesn't want these people taking advantage of you the way they...took advantage of me." His eyes meet mine. "Sometimes, when people know you really need something, they'll hold it over you. To control you. It's their way of pushing you around, without really doing what they promised."

"The work for Jason is just... It was supposed to build my

résumé. If I get a real job, in an office at a studio, that sort of thing won't happen," I say hopefully. "Right?"

My mom looks at my dad, her mouth a thin line.

"What?" I ask. "What is it?"

"Aaron, I've read enough about game studios and the career you're pushing toward to know a bit better. That *is* what happens." She stands up and walks over to me, placing her hands on my shoulders. "I just want what's best for you. I don't want…"

She looks at my dad and winces.

"She doesn't want you turning out like me," Dad says, shrugging. "What? That's what you were going to say."

My mom leans over and kisses him on the forehead.

"I was going to be a bit more delicate than that." She returns to her seat. "We can circle back to this later. Why don't you tell us about this girl?"

My mom smiles, and Mira gives me a mischievous look. My dad squeezes my arm and slaps me on the back, and I can't help but let out a little laugh.

"The, um. The girl. She's only there on Friday," I say, not wanting to get into too many details. All I need is Mom putting two and two together and figuring out I'm off to see D1V, the girl she wants me to avoid because she's afraid of what people will find when they google me.

"Okay," my dad says, "well, I can take over for—"

Our front door swings open with a crash, and Ryan tumbles into our living room.

My entire family shifts in our seats to look at him, and he scans the living room quickly, eventually spotting us on the opposite side of the room, in the adjoining dining room.

"Ryan!" my mom exclaims. "Are… Are you okay?"

"Hey, Mrs. Jericho, yeah I'm fine, I—"

She turns, glaring at me. "*Someone* didn't tell me we were

having company." She looks back up at him. "Come over here, we've got plenty of pizza left."

"I didn't—" I start, but Ryan hurries over, looking harried and panicked.

"You weren't answering your phone," he pants, taking deep breaths, his voice high-pitched. He glances at my parents. "Evening Mr. Jericho, Mrs. Jericho. Sorry, but... Aaron. You have to see this."

He pulls out his monster of a smartphone, which is practically the size of a tablet, and taps something on the screen. He hands the phone to me.

I almost drop it on the table.

It's a post on ManaPunk's website—the one that I wrote all the copy for and penned all the blogs for, by the way. The news update is all about their upcoming appearance at GamesCon's Indie Game Showcase, featuring the game Ryan and I had worked so hard on and promptly been fired from.

Stop by ManaPunk's booth to try out the next indie RPG hit, THUNDERTAIL. With stunning artwork, beautiful music, gorgeous prose, and unique, innovative gameplay that blends a randomly generated dungeon crawler with a powerful narrative, it's the next level in indie role-playing games! We'll have plenty of swag to give away, so you can show off your excitement for the game at home!

All the artwork in the post was clearly from Ryan, the finished illustrations and the like. And that post, that copy—I'd written that. I mean, I couldn't care less about the actual blog post; it was just a blog post, after all.

But that gorgeous prose bit? That was *mine*.

Fury fills me. "I can't believe he used your art without permission," I tell him.

"It's the stuff I gave him that day in the café. And it gets worse," Ryan says, scrolling down some more. After the line break on the blog, there's a link to purchase posters of the finished illustrations, in full color.

"You have *got* to be kidding me!" I exclaim.

Ryan looks at my family nervously. "Mind if I steal him away for a second?"

"You already have," my mom grumbles.

"Excuse me," I say quickly. I dart off with Ryan into the living room and up the stairs to my room, where he scrolls all the way down past the event details and the poster links.

It's a video.

A trailer for the video game.

He clicks it, and the voice-over starts. In addition to all the familiar graphics and artwork in the game, the voice that's speaking…it's reading my words. *My* introduction to the game, *my* prologue. The beginning that *I* wrote. The characters I spent so many hours trying to breathe life into appear on the screen, renders of Ryan's artwork, speaking the words I'd written. A story Jason said he hated and tore apart time and time again.

Here it is.

It's this weird mixture of pure excitement and joy blended with crushing disappointment and anger. Jason fired us. *Both* of us. He didn't pay us anything for any of this, and yet here it is in the game, in this demo he's going to use to try to sell his new title to a bigger publisher at the showcase.

"I've been emailing and calling him and Laura all day," Ryan says, taking the phone back and sliding it into his pocket. "Nothing. And you know the two of them are glued to their phones at all times."

"They're not answering on purpose," I say slowly.

"Yup."

There's a pause, a beat in our conversation.

"So…what do we do?" I ask.

He pulls out two tickets for GamesCon. For Friday. Tomorrow.

"It was sold out," Ryan says, waving the tickets, "but I found these for sale on Facebook this morning. We got lucky—it's not like we can rely on our former exhibitor badges. Something tells me they aren't going to be waiting for us at registration."

There's a sense of elation in my chest, swirling about with a sinking feeling of…well, feeling foolish. What was I going to do tomorrow? Just show up, demand to be let in to an event that's been sold out for months? Ask for my exhibitor badge, when chances are Jason got rid of it a long time ago or gave it to someone else? I didn't even know if Jason was planning to give us badges in the first place, not that it mattered now.

"We're going," Ryan says, handing me a ticket. "You and me. Save our world, save your girl?"

"She's not my—" He shoves me. "Hey!"

"For a writer, you really don't have any kind of flair for the dramatic, you know." He plucks the ticket out of my hand. "I'll hold on to these—you pack. Résumés, business cards, all that fun stuff for when we're done disrupting society. We're heading there first thing in the morning. What time is her panel?"

"I'm not sure." I shrug, trying to look casual.

"Are you really trying to convince me that you don't have the time and panel location memorized or tattooed on your body somewhere?" Ryan asks, eyebrows raised.

"It's at 11:00," I say, somewhat sheepishly.

"Perfect. We get there, confront Jason, and then?" He gives me a pointed look. "What exactly do you have planned during D1V's panel? I mean, if there are some trolls there to cause trouble and heckle, we can't exactly beat them up or anything."

"Uhhh…" I think for a moment, remembering that saying D1V seems so fond of.

Don't read the comments.

"I've got a pretty dumb idea," I say.

"Of course you do." Ryan grins and pulls me in for a hug.

After I finish packing, I head downstairs to do the dinner dishes. I'm scraping pizza cheese off a plate when I feel someone's eyes on me. I glance over my shoulder and see my dad hovering in the doorway, looking pensive and awkward.

"Hey," I say, turning back to the sink, peeling a piece of mozzarella off in a long, terribly satisfying pull. I flick it at the garbage disposal, and toss the plate into a bin of soapy water. "Thanks for, um, helping back there. With Mom."

"Aaron," my dad says, taking a step into the kitchen, his feet heavy against the floor. He pauses. "I know. I know that you know, that is."

I whirl around, my heart pounding, suds flying off my hands. Dad wrings his wrists, his cheeks flushing. He looks… embarrassed. Caught.

I clear my throat. "How long has it been going on?" I ask, leaning against the kitchen counter. The sharp edge digs into my back as I quietly add, "Does Mom know?"

"Your mom?!" My dad scoffs, and then laughs. "God, no. No, no way. And it's been…ten years, maybe? Twelve?"

"Twelve—" I start, then cut myself off, my lips trembling with fury. How can he laugh about this? Act like…like it's nothing? "Dad, you need to talk to her about this. You need to do it before I do."

"Please, Aaron, she wouldn't understand." He shakes his head. "You see how she is with you."

"Me?" I ask, completely dumbfounded. "What do I have to do with it?"

"I just..." He takes a breath. "I always saw myself doing something more. Having something a little more for *myself*, not just working with food, and now, this." He looks off to the side, toward the door that leads into mom's practice. "Ever since it started, it was sort of my thing. My secret."

"It's not fair to Mom. To the family."

"It's really not that big a deal, Aaron," my dad says dismissively.

"Not that... Dad, you're having an *affair*!" I spit out, anger brewing up in my chest. "You can't just expect me to—"

"A what?!"

I look beyond my dad, through the door frame, and into the dining room. There, looking totally stunned, is my mother. She walks over, slowly, her eyes wide, the way people in a horror movie do when they're approaching something terrifying. My dad turns to her and then back to me, his expression morphing from carefully awkward to utter bewilderment.

"Aaron, what the hell?" he pleads, rubbing his forehead.

"What is he talking about?" Mom asks him, her voice trembling.

"Damn it." He exhales. "I am *not* having an affair."

"Then explain all those letters on the—" I start.

"Oh my God, I've been writing fan fiction!" Dad bursts out. His face turns bright red as I stare at him, and he laughs awkwardly. "I saw that someone had opened a bunch of my old Word documents on the office computer, and since your mother hadn't brought it up, I figured it was probably you."

My stomach drops.

The overdone letters, with all that flowery language—they weren't actually *for* anyone?

"Fan what?" my mom asks. "I don't understand."

"I've been…trying to write a fantasy novel," my dad says, sounding terribly embarrassed. "Some of my old coworkers…old friends, from the restaurant, they all play this online game. *Ultima*. It's old, but it has these chat room clients, and we catch up sometimes in there. And I write stories set in the world we play in."

While my dad seems to have a good sense of humor about all of this, the swirl of guilt inside me feels awful. I've spent so much time feeling angry at him. Feeling so disappointed, all over nothing. "So those letters—"

"Epistolary works for me," Dad says, shrugging. He glances at Mom. "Sometimes I write on the office computer. Or play the game with my pals."

My mom continues to stare at him for a beat, then looks at me.

And then, suddenly, she can't stop laughing.

"I feel like I should be mad at one of you, or maybe both, but I'm not quite sure where to start," she says, still chuckling. "Do I get to read this novel?"

"Well, I mean, it's not a novel *yet*…" My dad shrugs. "I'm just sort of practicing." He glares at me. "I wasn't really ready to talk about it yet."

"I'm…sorry?" I say, wincing, unsure of what to say here. I feel terrible.

"An affair. Honestly, Aaron." My dad laughs, but then his eyes narrow, and he studies me, his expression curious. "So, wait. You believed the letters?"

"Well, yeah," I mutter.

"Hmm." He touches his beard thoughtfully. "Maybe I'm not too bad."

"Letters?" my mom asks.

"Yes. There's a character in the game that my character is married to." Dad grins. "Inspired by you."

"Oh great," I groan.

"Do you want…" He tilts his head at the door to the office. "Do you want to read them?"

My mom smiles softly. "I would love to."

Dad gives her a goofy grin, and the silence stretches just long enough to start feeling super awkward.

"Still here, guys," I say, waving an arm around, feeling flustered.

Mom laughs and walks over to give me a hug. "When you get back from your convention, I want to read your story," she murmurs. "If that's okay."

"Mom—"

"No, let me finish. I've been…tough on you about that," she admits, pulling back and biting her lip. "I know I have been. I just… I don't want your passion to be what wears you down, Aaron. That's the quickest way to stop loving what makes you happy."

I nod jerkily, feeling a little teary. "Thanks, Mom."

"That story." She points at me, then takes Dad's hand. "Don't forget."

The two of them disappear into the office, and I return to scrubbing the plates. I can't help but think how lucky I am right now. This silly, quirky situation with my mom and dad felt like it was on its way to going someplace way darker, and I'm so grateful it didn't.

My mind drifts to D1V, and all the stories we haven't shared yet. I don't know nearly as much about her as I'd like to. About her life, her family.

I want to tell her this story.

I want to make her laugh.

I want to be the person who writes long, overly flowery letters about her, using fan fiction as an excuse.

I drop the final plate into the sink and grit my teeth against the storm brewing in my chest.

I need to do something. Help her somehow.

So that's exactly what I'm going to do.

Mana Punk Newsletterr	Catch up at GamesCon, demoing our latest	9:44 p.m.
Microsoft Home	Xbox Deals This Weekend, GamesCon Special	7:43 p.m.
Det. Nikki Watts	Tomorrow.	4:30 p.m.
The Vox Populi	You are NOT welcome.	2:42 p.m.
The Vox Populi	Show your face. See what happens.	1:08 p.m.
Lee Lamar	Time to talk with Engadget?	9:36 a.m.

I close my phone. I've got access to my email account again, but catching up on yesterday's emails isn't exactly helping to get me excited for today's trip to GamesCon.

Not at all.

I'm fussing with my hair and makeup in the bathroom, when my mom peeks in, the door creaking open slowly.

"Divya, I really wish you'd reconsider going," she says with a heartbreaking look at me. "And your hair. All that beautiful hair. The last time you cut it was—"

"Freshman year," I interrupt, meeting her gaze in the mirror for a moment. "I know."

I cut off most of my hair last night with Rebekah. My shoulder-length dark locks are now all short and pixie-like, styled a lot like hers, but with less of a giant swoop on the side. I've got it dyed a blood orange with shocks of red and yellow throughout, which make the fake yellow-framed glasses I'm wearing as a disguise look even more fierce and intense. I blink a few times, my face awash in color. Bright hair, pastel glasses, green eyes.

It's hard to recognize the person in front of me now. I love the glasses, the hair is fun, and I feel like a character out of a fantasy novel, ready to do battle.

Final Fantasy (D)1V.

Come at me, bros.

"Are you sure this is a good idea?" my mom presses, following me out of the bathroom and into our living room. She flops down on the old couch, the one that sinks and hurts my entire body. I think about how, after the panel, I'll have just enough to help pay for her last class and maybe find some used furniture. I've still got my savings, and while the speaking fee isn't exactly a wild amount of money, it's enough to get us right over the edge with what I've already got saved. She fidgets about, trying to get comfortable, and I shake my head.

"What?" she asks, leaning back into the cushions.

"Nothing," I say with a huff. "I need to do this, Mom. Not just for the speaker fee, which will put an end to all of *this*." I point over in the direction of my bedroom, toward the computer. "But for you and for myself. All the blogs are talking. No one thinks I'm going to show up. Everyone thinks I've disappeared. They'll see. They're all gonna see. And then they won't. 'Cause then I *will* disappear."

"Your friend is going with you, yes?" she asks, struggling back to her feet. "Rebekah? The one with the hair—you know, I can't even call her that anymore, because now you're also the-one-with-the-hair to somebody." She grins, and I hug her.

"Yes, she's coming," I say, letting her go. "I'm meeting her at the convention. She went early to get the table set up, and to…" I chuckle, thinking about Rebekah waiting in line at the crack of dawn to meet some of those comic book heroes of hers, like Kate Leth and Delilah S. Dawson and Fiona Staples. The perks of being an exhibitor. "Get some autographs before the lines start."

"Promise me you'll be careful," my mom insists, grabbing my hands. "Keep a low profile, don't say anything that'll get you into trouble."

"I will, I promise." I give her hands a final squeeze, and head toward the door.

My heart feels a bit heavy. Not because of what I'm about to do, but because of what I've already done.

It's the first time in my life that I've ever truly lied to her. I *can't* be careful, not today, and I know it.

I hustle down the stairs of our walk-up, my boots thundering against the old rattling steps, and burst out the front door into the early sunlight. The sun is barely out and about, but people certainly are, bustling down the sidewalks to get to whatever day jobs demand they work such hours. I change out my glasses for my sunglasses, eager to avoid running into anyone who might also be heading to the convention and might somehow recognize me.

I briskly walk toward the PATH train that'll eventually take me into New York City, first making its way in the opposite direction toward Hoboken before turning around and heading where I want to go. An annoying delay, but worth it for paying just two dollars to get there.

My phone buzzes, and I pull it out, peering at the screen from under my sunglasses.

There are a few messages waiting, but nothing I'm not expecting.

Detective Watts 6:03 a.m.
Did you get my email? I'll be waiting for you at the convention center. At the first sign of trouble, you call me. Text me. Whatever. I'm here.

Rebekah Cole 7:01 a.m.
Are you on your way yet?! I've got the table set up and I MET KATE LETH OH MY GOD SHE IS SO COOL AND I CAN'T EVEN.

I smile, a bit of hope fluttering in my chest, and look up at the PATH station just a few blocks down the road. I take a deep breath and keep moving.

Today's going to be hard.

I open my inbox and load yesterday's message from Detective Watts. I read it quickly, my heart hammering in my chest over every single word. For a minute, I think about emailing Aaron, to tell him about our plan. It's not too late to make a random account, send him a quick message in the game. But he would just worry, and that wouldn't help anything. I'll message him after it's all over. Besides, I want to keep him safe.

Because today it's finally happening.

I make my way through the PATH station and onto the platform. I take a deep breath and exhale as the train rumbles closer, the station hot and humid, as I try to keep my cool.

It's happening.

And I won't be stopped.

22
AARON

I plug my phone into the bus's outlet and lean back in the soft cushioned seat. There's a weird smell coming off it that I'm trying to ignore.

"We really should have taken the train," Ryan grumbles, pushing his seat back and awkwardly squirming about in what I assume is an attempt to get comfortable. "And do you really need to charge your phone already? Don't you have a power bank with you, too?"

"Hey, best to play it safe." I shrug.

"Or what?" Ryan scoffs, settling in and closing his eyes. "Just take a nap, enjoy our smelly ride, and maybe get off your phone for a minute." He grins. "How's your arts and crafts?"

I glance over at the plastic tube I've got leaning against the bus wall, a long clear bright blue thing made for holding posters.

"It's not arts—" I start.

"I still think it's a bad idea. Getting all theatrical," he says with a yawn. "I love you, but wake me up when we get there. And set your alarm. I don't want to end up in Boston or something."

The cheap UltraBus we're on goes from Philadelphia up

to New York City, and only charges a whopping five dollars. Plus, you get free Internet and places to charge your gadgets. The downside is that it can be kinda slow, it's hard to find seats, and sometimes the buses aren't as clean as they could be. And sometimes the Internet doesn't work. But I'll take a five-dollar, slightly uncomfortable bus ride over paying for the pricey train any day. The Amtrak is all kinds of expensive, and even if you do the New Jersey Transit & SEPTA— Philadelphia's regional train—combo, traveling from Philly to Trenton and then Trenton to New York City, it ends up being almost fifty bucks.

And besides, since the gig with ManaPunk is officially over—not that Jason had paid us—I'm saving as much as I can until I manage to line something else up. If I blew every dollar on a nice train ride, it'd be a really long summer with absolutely no spending money.

The bus roars to life just as Ryan starts to snore softly, and I know I should seriously do the same. Catching the 6:00 a.m. ride meant being up at nearly 4:00 a.m., which wasn't all that difficult, since I couldn't sleep at all.

But I keep staring at my phone. And the social media feeds. I wonder if D1V is out there somewhere, looking at the same threads I am. Seeing what I'm seeing. What those Vox Populi idiots are posting about her. The awful photoshopped images, the GIFs that replay her defeat again and again, the terrifying threats that seem to follow every article that hints about her appearance at the convention.

The video clips of what they did to her mother.

The attack in the arcade.

The comments upon comments upon comments.

I adjust the plastic poster tube and try to get comfortable in my seat.

She'd once said to me, in our string of texts together, to

just ignore the comments. Don't read them. Don't pay attention to them. But I can't do that. Whether it's these messages
about her, or all the positive responses to Jason's announcement of his game, using our stolen art and words...it's all I
can do. Read comment after comment.

And that's what I'm going to do, this entire bus ride.

Read the comments. And let the frustration consume me.

23
DIVYA

"Sorry, says the pass is invalid."

The muscular security guard scanning badges inside the convention center hands me back my pass, and I immediately thrust it back.

"That's not possible," I insist, wiggling the laminated piece of plastic at him, the little red and yellow flags on the end stating "exhibitor" and "speaker" flapping about. "I'm a guest here."

"You and everyone else," he retorts, scanning the badge again and making a face.

"Come on," I groan as he hands it back with a shrug. He gestures for me to step aside and starts welcoming in other people. I fuss with my phone as a few other convention goers make their way in, more than a handful casting sideways glances at me. Yes, hi, my pass didn't work, let's all stare.

Finally, the GamesCon website loads. It takes what feels like an eternity, standing here with random eyes on me, and the cell service being absolutely garbage inside the convention center. I swipe along the rotating banner on the home page, and there I am.

"Hey." I reach out and tap the security guy's shoulder, noticing a large, fully detailed and colorful *Chrono Trigger* tattoo on his biceps featuring the anime figures from the game's cinematics, as opposed to the classic, old-school Super Nintendo sprites. He barely glances at me as he finishes scanning in someone else.

"Listen, you can head over to registration when—"

"Look, okay?" I hold up my phone to show him the landing page on the convention website. Right there in the shuffling banner there's a big ol' photo of me. I mean, it's a picture of me with different hair and another look, but I think it's still clear it's me. Maybe?

He squints at the phone and at me, looking skeptical.

"Yeah, I don't—"

"Wait, wait." I rustle in my bag and pull out my wallet, showing him my license. "See? The names match."

He takes his time studying my ID while I tap my foot impatiently. Finally, I say, "Look, you gotta cut me a break here. I have a panel and I won't get to it on time to—"

"Alright, go ahead," he grumbles, gesturing at the entrance, clearly annoyed.

"Thank you, thank you!" I exclaim, hustling by. "Frog is the best character, by the way!" I shout, turning around. He glances back over his shoulder, and a sliver of a smile pulls along the edges of his mouth.

I shuffle my way into the convention building. The Javits Center in New York City is a sprawling mass of glass and marble and steel beams, and the morning sun pierces the long, open hallways that lead to the different floors and massive halls containing these events. It's still early, so the fans aren't yet swarming about the inside, and there are hardly any lines at the registration tables. But once everything officially opens, those lines are going to be a monster, and I would be stuck at the back, waiting with everyone else.

The lines outside were enormous, making a slow crawl around what looked like the whole city block. I felt my heart beat wildly as I passed by some of the guys standing in that line, wondering if anyone was here for me. And not in the good way.

I hurry up a set of stairs that has a massive sticker coating the surface, so it looks like a set of bricks from any number of *Super Mario Bros.* video games, and head toward the exhibition hall, where yet another security guard waves me by and into the actual convention.

As angry as I am at this scene that I've tried so hard to be a part of, I can't help but feel elated about being here. A rush of joy courses through me as I make my way down the grid-like walkways between vendor and exhibitor booths. A massive exhibit that's practically the size of a house boasts the Sega logo, with some new games being tested out on gorgeous gigantic HD screens. There are a bundle of booths selling things along the aisle, stuffed plush recreations of various Pokémon and other bits of recognizable video game pop culture, like Pikmin and weapons from the *Final Fantasy* games.

I keep an eye out for the number and letter combination that Rebekah gave me for where our booth is sitting. Well, more like a table. We're situated somewhere near the Artist Alley, with a bundle of other speakers and indie artists exhibiting prints, dishing out autographs, and selling books and other swag.

I edge my way past the Archaia and Boom! Studios comic booth, a large black square of an exhibit with tables surrounding it, selling a number of comic books, both video game tie-in related and not, from *Adventure Time* to *Ladycastle*. I finally spot Rebekah's bright hair at a table situated beyond the giant cube, next to someone who looks like an illustrator and a table with what appears to be a bunch of podcasting equipment. With a flourish, Rebekah unravels something that looks like a giant blanket and starts to arrange it on the table.

I hurry over just as she finishes smoothing it out.

"Oh wow," I drawl, taking a step back.

Rebekah looks up and smiles, then moves to join me, her hands on her hips, clearly admiring her handiwork. "Not bad, right?"

"Who designed it?" I ask. The black sheet draping over the front of the table is decorated with an Angst Armada logo, a little spaceship from *Reclaim the Sun* crossed with a balled-up fist, the name of our clan emblazoned over it. It's orange and gold and furious looking, and I love everything about it.

"Remember that player, Maggs?" Rebekah asks, grinning. "She made it. Sent it on over. Said good luck today. And that's not all we've got."

Rebekah walks back over to the table and pulls out a box from underneath, setting it on top of the kinda-shaky table. For a place that charges so much money to exhibit, you'd think the rental furniture wouldn't feel fit to fall apart. She opens the box and dumps the contents out onto the table.

Pins. Hundreds and hundreds of pins.

The beautiful enamel looks spectacular. "Angst Armada" is written in stunning golden script against a black star-filled sky on one pin. Another has an illustration of one of the *Reclaim the Sun* ships, blasting off, flames erupting from the thrusters on the wing and tail. There are even some patches thrown into the mix, which read an array of things, from "Space Trash" to "Blast Like a Girl." A pin that says "Log On, Fight Back" immediately catches my eye, reminding me of that email from the Oculus publicity director. I scoop one up and pin it to my shirt.

Then I quickly pocket one of everything else. I can't help it—I just love all the designs Rebekah's put together.

"These are free for me, right?" I ask with a wink.

Rebekah offers me a weak smile and sits down behind our little table. Compared to the podcaster and this illustrator, and with all the other exhibitors around us, our offerings look pretty sparse, but it's still something I'm feeling way too damn proud of.

"What's wrong?" I ask, pulling up a chair next to her. "This all looks so good. Did you get the autographs you wanted?"

"Oh, you better believe I did." She pulls two comics out of her bag, both shielded in plastic. There's an old issue of *Ladycastle* signed by Delilah S. Dawson and the first issue of *Hellcat* signed by Kate Leth, which also has a few little doodles on it.

"I got a few *Adventure Time*s signed, too," she says as she stows the comics again, shaking her head, her eyes set on the pins and patches on the table.

"Hey," I say softly. "This looks great. Why do you look like you're beating yourself up?"

"It's just…" She waves her hand at the other booths, who all have huge signs and elaborate displays. "This is probably the only time we'll ever get to do this, right?"

"I don't know." I shrug. "Maybe. You could start a channel, you know. You've got a lot of followers, too."

Rebekah gives me a look. "After everything we went through? *You* went through?" She shakes her head. "I don't think so. But we'll see. Whatever. I'm allowed to be bummed and have conflicting feelings about this."

"I know." I wrap an arm around her shoulders for a moment, then lean back, just taking everything in. The sounds of the convention floor. The people running up and down the aisles in a hurry, but everyone's eyes alight with something. There's a joy here, and it just vibrates in the air everywhere you look, from the vendors to the people who somehow snuck in early, to the folks working the floor on behalf of the convention center.

It's a building full of my people.

And at the same time, it's not.

Somewhere in the mix are those who think I don't deserve to be here. Who have made it a point to try to keep me away. To scare me away. To push me out of my favorite places, in video games, on social media, in real life.

And to those people, I've got a message.

I'm here.

And I'm not afraid.

24
AARON

"We would be able to sneak around this place a lot easier if you didn't have that," Ryan grumbles as I struggle to catch up with him, weaving in and out of the crowd on the convention floor. I'd been to a few conventions like this before— New York Comic Con, some smaller ones in Jersey City and Hoboken. So this isn't my first one by any means, but it is my first time carrying a giant poster tube that's making it hard not to crash into people.

"I need this!" I exclaim, hurrying behind Ryan and bumping into a few cosplayers wearing outfits I don't recognize, one with a bright white fake wingspan that would be the envy of any real-life angel. "You'll see."

"It has a strap!" he shouts. "Just sling it over your back!"

"I don't trust it." I hold the tube closer as I move around a group of people. "Someone could smash against it."

"Fine. Do you remember where the booth is for Mana-Punk?" Ryan asks, looking around. "There's no way Jason sprung for a big display this year, that's for damn sure. And when is D1V's panel, again?"

"Not sure, and the panel starts at 11:00," I say, craning my neck to try to see anything in the swelling mobs of people. "I really can't make out a single booth name. He's probably with all the indie game developers."

"Let's check the map on the website. Ugh, never mind," Ryan complains, putting his phone back in his pocket. "There's no service in here. Of *course* there isn't. Look at all these people. Come on, let's go bug one of the information people—"

And then I see it.

"There!" I point toward another row, almost dropping the tube. "See?"

A few rows away, the ManaPunk logo pops up above a bunch of other little booths, a few indie developers' logos surrounding it. I can see Jason there with Laura, excitedly talking to people walking by, extending eager handshakes and doling out postcards. All around the booth is Ryan's artwork. His fantasy world. All the characters he helped draw and bring to life.

And behind Jason and Laura—the demo. An enormous flat screen is playing the opening chapter of *Thundertail*, the definition so clear you can see even the tiniest of details on the characters. The cinematic plays through, and I can almost hear the voice of the narrator, but it's as clear as anything in my head regardless. I wrote those words. I know them.

And they belong to me.

I move to make my way over when something familiar catches my attention. On one of the gigantic circular columns that jut up throughout the convention floor is a large sticker, sporting the silhouette of some kind of spaceship. It looks a lot like the kind of vessels you can get in *Reclaim the Sun*, and overlaid it...

"Vox Populi."

"Oh no," I moan, hurrying toward the pillar.

"Aaron? Hey!" Ryan hustles after me. "What is it?"

"Look." I jerk my chin at the sticker as we approach, and now that I'm in front of it, a wave of anger surges through me. I look down the aisle to the right and off to the left, and I can see more of them, in between the throngs of people weaving about, stuck on the pillars, mixed in with flyers and other stickers.

"You know what's interesting?" Ryan says, distracting me from glaring down the aisle.

"Hmm?"

"Look." He points at the Vox Populi sticker and the other stickers and posters next to it. "It's under all this. Already."

"So?" I shrug. "What's—"

"That means it was here earlier. *First*." He reaches out and starts to pick at the edges of the sticker, finally getting an edge up. A bit peels off and rips, barely making a dent in getting the thing off.

"Guess they got here to paper the place early." I shake my head and lean in to give peeling the sticker a try. A little more comes off, but it still rips, leaving a trail of white against the gray paint—

"Hey!"

I turn around, and two guys are standing right behind me and Ryan, arms crossed, dressed in jeans and plain T-shirts. One of the guys has a chain necklace on, like something out of the early 2000s.

"Hi?" Ryan ventures first, then turns away and starts picking at the sticker again.

"Uh, Ryan…" I say hesitantly.

"You're going to want to stop doing that," one of the guys says, taking a step forward, narrowing the already small space between them and us. Ryan whips back around, his eyes narrowed.

"Listen, you sentient can of Axe body spray—"

"No, you listen." He reaches out and shoves Ryan away from the pillar.

"Hey!" I move in between the two of them as Ryan recovers and presses up against me, absolutely ready to push by and get himself beaten up. "Everyone just calm down."

"We're fine," the other guy speaks up, the one with the chain necklace. "But you two better mind your own business."

He reaches for something in his back pocket and pulls it out quick, making me and Ryan flinch. It's another sticker, and he laughs with the other guy before leaning over and slapping it on top of the one we were trying to peel away.

"Everything okay?" A third guy walks over, dressed a bit more typically conventionesque in a *Final Fantasy* T-shirt, the hint of some kind of tattoo peeking out near his neck. He exchanges a look with the two trolls and then eyes us, a flash of recognition washing over his face.

"You." He points at me with a sly smile.

"What?" I ask, glancing quickly at Ryan.

"You're the boyfriend," the guy continues, giving his friends a playful slap on the back. "You don't recognize this guy? From the videos? The texts and pictures?"

He looks back at me, grinning.

"Nice of you to show up." He digs for something in his pocket, and I wince again as he pulls out another one of those stickers.

And then he slaps it across my face.

"Enjoy the show," he sneers at me, then all three of them dart off.

I peel the sticker from my face, the glue ripping at my stubble and skin. These are seriously heavy-duty stickers—that must be why they aren't coming off the columns.

"Ugh." I crumple the sticker up and whip my hand around to get it off, shaking it into the trash next to the pillar. "That was...so not great."

"Are you sure we should be here?" Ryan asks. There's a slight tremor in his voice.

"Not really," I stammer out. Then thoughts of D1V float through my head, and I exhale. "But we have to be here. Not just for her, but for us."

I nod in the direction of ManaPunk.

"Yeah. Yeah, I know." He clears his throat. "Okay."

I start walking over, when Ryan grabs my shoulder, pulling me back.

"What now?" I groan.

"I'm sorry, have you even thought this through at all?" he asks. "What are you going to do? Ask Jason nicely to turn it off? Run over there and just steal the prototype? Rip the computer out, knock over the television? How are you going to get it all away from him? From Laura?"

"I'll figure something out."

"No. You won't," Ryan says firmly. "You'll run over there with this crap on you, this tube that looks like an oversize quiver of arrows, and fuck it all up. Or those Vox Populi bros will catch wind of us walking that way and interfere somehow."

He leans against the pillar and exhales.

"Here's what we're going to do."

I nudge my way through the crowds over to the Mana-Punk booth, where several people are milling about, talking to Jason and Laura, or maybe just trying to get a look at the demo. I get it. ManaPunk is a popular indie. People know the name, know Jason. It's enough to break my heart, seeing that booth without me in there. I wanted people to know me the way they know him, I guess. This was supposed to be a huge moment for me and for Ryan, and instead, it's all about him.

I squint, looking around the booth and the area surrounding them, for anyone else who might be one of the Populi. But how would I tell, anyway? Dressed kinda plain, looking like a bro...that describes a lot of the people meandering about.

They could be anywhere.

I steel myself, taking a deep breath, and inch closer, just as Laura locks eyes with me. She smiles, and suddenly, it's like I'm looking at someone I don't even know anymore, a stranger. I'd had this strange drive to try to...what, protect her from Jason? When all the while, I'm pretty sure I needed protection from her. I'd thought we were friends.

She nudges Jason and says something, and he looks at me, his face aghast, like he's seeing a ghost.

A small sense of victory courses through me. At least he knows he did something wrong. That's what his expression is telling me.

"Aaron!" Jason exclaims, his tone nervous. He inches a little in front of the television playing the demo, as if that's going to hide it from me. "Good to see you. Come on over!"

"I saw the video, Jason," I say, taking a step toward the booth. "The trailer. Online."

"Ah, yes, that." His eyes dart over to what I'm carrying. "What is that? Part of a costume or something?"

"Don't try to change the subject," I say, fidgeting with all the stuff bundled under my arm. "The video. The demo. That's my story. My words. Ryan's artwork. You tried to set us against each other. You tried to trick me into signing that contract and just giving you my work, and then you used it anyway."

A few people appear to be listening to what I'm saying, and Jason starts to look extra nervous. I spot someone take out their phone, maybe shooting a video.

"Jason, we were friends," I press, and for a second, I feel my lip start to quiver. There's no way in hell I'm going to cry here, right now, in front of him. "How could you do this?"

"Hey, Aaron, come on. Take it easy." He looks around and lowers his voice. "Look, I was desperate. I needed something ready to showcase. I was still going to like, work on getting contracts and all with you two. Let's talk about this somewhere else."

"Here's the thing," I say, taking another step toward him. I'm right up against the booth's table now, and I grab one of the postcards with Ryan's art on it. "It's fine. It's all fine. In fact, I'm ready to sign the paperwork you sent over. I printed it out and brought it with me."

"Wait, really?" he asks, his whole posture shifting immediately. "That's great! I never wanted any of this to get complicated. You know? And I heard that your streamer girlfriend, or whatever she is, I heard she's not doing it anymore? Got rid of her videos or something?"

"Yeah, it didn't quite go down like that, but she's speaking today about it. And she's not my girlfriend," I add. I glance around for any of the Populi, as the last thing I need is to be recognized again.

Out of the corner of my eye, I see the curtain behind the television swish back and forth a little, the black fabric separating. Ryan's hand and eventually his head peek through. He locks eyes with me and nods.

"Well, maybe after all that dies down, you can circle back?"

Jason ventures. The genuine tone in his voice is there, and it kills me. He doesn't sound like someone who stole my writing, stole my and Ryan's art. He sounds like that old friend again. The cool senior I met when I was still a freshman. The knowledgeable hero I looked up to all these years. A mentor.

"Maybe... Oooh, maybe you could write under a pen name?" he suggests, his smile wider, his enthusiasm unmatched. "We can figure something out."

"Yeah, maybe." I shrug noncommittally. It actually doesn't sound that terrible. Ryan, meanwhile, is fussing around with the back of the console box that's connected to the television, and appears to be having very little luck with it. I see him gritting his teeth as he tugs at something, and for a second, the massive television wobbles. Jason must have felt something, and he starts to turn around.

"What about Ryan?" I ask loudly, trying to regain his attention. He turns back to me, his focus recaptured. "Can you bring him back in, too, maybe?"

"Yeah, definitely," Jason says, smiling. "As soon as that friend of yours disappears. Don't get me wrong, I feel bad for her and all, but I have a business to run."

I try not to glare at him, but I don't think I'm successful, as he cocks an eyebrow and tilts his head.

"She doesn't have to *disappear*," I say, feeling the anger boiling up again. "She doesn't deserve that. She—"

And then I see it.

There's a Vox Populi sticker stuck inside the booth.

"What the hell, Jason?!" I push by him and point at the thing, stuck to one of the posters against the fabric curtain. "What is this? You know who those guys are?"

"Oh, calm down, they're just a bunch of gamers playing pranks."

"Pranks?!" I'm shouting. "They attacked her *mom*, Jason. How could you do this?"

"It's our audience," he snaps back, his voice a little more hushed now. "It's my livelihood. I don't know her, and I'm sorry, but I don't care. Now, do you and Ryan want to make money, or not?"

Something behind the curtain flutters.

There's a loud groaning noise.

And the television begins to pitch forward.

"Jason!" I shout. "Look out!"

With a crash, the massive screen plummets to the floor, taking half of the booth with it. The cords, the curtains, the thick plastic pipes holding it all together, all colliding down on top of Jason and Laura. Pieces of Ryan's art go fluttering everywhere, the postcards exploding into the air like a magician tossing playing cards into the wind.

People all around us are screaming.

I stare for a moment, mouth wide open, and look in horror at Ryan from across the destroyed booth. The console is in his hands. It's one of those super expensive gaming and development PCs, one I know Jason uses to develop his games. It has to be worth thousands. He smiles sheepishly and ducks behind the one remaining curtain, disappearing from sight.

I bend over and dig through the bits and pieces of the booth, a number of other convention-goers with me. Jason and Laura are cursing up a storm as we haul them out of all the debris.

"Fuck!" Jason shouts, looking at the booth in pieces. "That television was worth two grand!" He storms over to what's left of it and digs around under the fallen curtains and pipes. "Where's the—"

He looks up at me, suspicion dawning on his face. "Did you come here with Ryan?" he asks coldly.

"What?" I scoff. "No. What's wrong? Are you okay?"

"He said on social media, and I quote, 'If ManaPunk is showing that demo, I'm going to steal that shit,'" Jason says, taking a step toward me, fury in his eyes. "Where is he?! Where the hell is my demo?!"

"Jason, come on. It's probably under all that stuff," I say, taking a step around him.

"Do you have any idea how much those computers cost?!" he shouts, eyes scouring the debris.

As Jason bends down to sift through the curtains and pipes and cords, I take off, running madly through the crowd, holding my poster tube above my head.

"Aaron!" Jason shouts. "Aaron, get back here!"

I'm weaving in and out of people, keeping an eye open for any sign of security, Jason, or the Vox Populi, when my phone vibrates. I duck behind a line of people waiting for what will inevitably be some very disappointing Philadelphia cheesesteaks from a food stand, and notice I've got only a few minutes to get to D1V's panel across the building.

I start running. I can't miss it.

She needs me.

Suddenly, I think back to Laura, working with Jason. The person I'd thought I needed to defend, hadn't needed me at all. I'd spent so much time thinking about trying to save her that I never considered she didn't need saving. That I was the one who needed saving, from people like *her*. People like Jason.

What if I'm wrong about D1V, too?

But this is different, right? Right?

I shake my head, my thoughts running wild, and hustle out into the main hall, squeezing past what feels like a thousand people until it opens into a large open space.

"1R," I say to myself, again and again, checking my phone

several times as I descend an escalator toward the meeting rooms. They're massive spaces, big enough to hold a full wedding in, or maybe a panel about *Firefly*.

I find the hall for D1V's panel. There's a large sign outside it, detailing the panels going on in the room that day and the times. One about *Sailor Moon* fandom happened way earlier this morning, another about writing strong female characters just got out, and now D1V's event.

"Harassment in Video Game Culture & Women: A Conversation."

I glare at the names on the list. It's still like three dudes and then D1V. How is that a balanced conversation at all?

I move to walk into the room, when a large burly man stops me.

"Quick pat down, sorry," he informs me.

"Wait, what? What for?" I ask.

"High-profile guest, lots of threats surrounding her on social media." He pats me up and down, quickly, clearly disinterested and not doing a very good job. "Nothing I'd consider creditable, though. Those trolls are all the same. All talk, no action."

I try not to glare at him, but he must catch it.

"Problem?" he asks, pulling out his phone and fussing with something on it.

"No," I say. "Thanks."

He mumbles something in response, and I push through the door into the room. Inside, most of the chairs are full already. The stage is all the way up in the front, the guests just taking their seats. Some guy up on the podium, bald and full of tattoos, is fiddling with a few papers and making small talk with one of the male panelists sitting at the table. Another dude is next to him, looking at his phone, and then…

I squint.

But it can't be.

There's a young woman sitting there, but her hair is a mixture of colors. Blood orange, with splashes of yellow and dark red, like her hair is on fire, with golden glasses and...

She looks up and across the room.

Green eyes.

I can see them from here. Bright, piercing.

D1V.

She must have changed her appearance after everything, something I certainly can't blame her for. Must have made navigating the convention floor much easier, but now she's onstage. Everyone can see her; they all know who she is. I feel my breathing grow short and heavy, and I look around for a seat, settling on one between the very back and very front. Smack in the middle, where hopefully she can see me if things go poorly.

I think about the security guard and turn around to spot a bunch of people just wandering in. I think I can make out his outline by the door, still on his phone, but I pretend that I'm not seeing that. He's paying attention. He isn't being careless. Everything is going to be okay.

My heart is hammering in my chest. All these people. All those threats. The threads upon threads and comments upon comments from people who have no idea who this amazing girl is. Or how amazing she is.

I glance over at the walls, the loose paneling connected with hinges and broken up with seams, easily foldable and movable to make the room bigger or smaller or—

And there they are. Vox Populi stickers.

Just a few, but they're scattered all about the sides. I stare at some of the people lining the walls. Did one of them put the stickers there? Did several of them? How well were *they* searched?

Damn it, I should be doing security here.

More attendees shuffle in, filling the rest of the seats, and before I know it, the hall is full, with a bunch of people standing in the back, leaning against the flimsy walls. I'm one seat away from the middle row, with a short kid filling the chair in front of me.

Perfect.

I reach down for the plastic tube I brought, and the contents that are rolled up inside. Everything looks innocent enough, like posters or swag you'd get at any convention.

I'm ready.

The bald man at the podium blows into the microphone a few times and looks over at the panelists. I can't take my eyes off D1V, who sits there, so strong, so resolute. I don't see a single crack in her bravery, and my heart soars.

I wish I could shout something.

Tell her that I'm here for her.

But I sit back. And I wait. I don't want one of these security guards misconstruing my actions and kicking me out of the place. And besides, after watching Laura at the booth…maybe D1V doesn't actually need me here? I look at the plastic tube again and start to feel a little silly for even having it with me.

"Hello, and welcome," the bald man says into the microphone, and the audience quiets down. I see a few people pluck phones out and hold them up, recording. "I'm Thad Folkward, author of *The Dangerous Lives of Men*." There's a smattering of applause from people up in the front, and I can't help but scowl. This is the guy they chose to moderate a panel about women in video games?

"It's an honor and a privilege to be here today, speaking to these fine creators. I'll introduce everyone, starting directly next to me. First, we have Solomon Gray, the art director over at Ravenfox Games."

He drones on, introducing Solomon as my gaze darts around the room. Everyone looks... I don't know, not suspicious? Normal? I'm not really sure what I'm looking for here, other than people who look angry. But they're all fixated on the stage. Some with cameras, others with phones, some just watching, entirely caught up in the moment. I note a few guys who are dressed rather plain, like the dudes who pestered me and Ryan out in the corridor, but they aren't really any different looking than anyone else.

I turn my head slightly, and there, leaning against one of the walls, is Rebekah, D1V's streaming partner. I wave in her direction, and for a moment, she breaks focus with the stage and sees me. I wave a little more and point at myself, mouthing "Aaron" at her.

She scowls and gives me the finger.

I smile.

Rebekah from the Angst Armada just flipped me off.

That was awesome.

"Next to Solomon we have Arthur Reginald, lead programmer at Shiftcore Games. Some of you might know his work from titles such as *Armor & Sleep*, or perhaps his even more famous work, *The Fall Out*." The applause is a little louder this time, more intense, and I shift my attention to the stage to see what the big deal is. The man holds his hand up and says thank-you into the microphone.

I catch my breath. It's time for D1V.

"The young lady who follows, many of you may have spotted in the news lately. It's my great pleasure to introduce

streaming and Glitch sensation—in her first appearance ever,
I believe—D1V!"

Applause thunders in the hall, and my heart races. A few
people in the front stand up, clapping, their hair an array of
colors. It looks like a small army of girls, each with patches
emblazoned on their jackets. I can't quite make them all out,
but there's something uniform about the logos.

I can already tell I want to be friends with every single one
of these people.

"We're here for you, D1V!" one shouts over the roar of
the audience.

"Commander!" another cheers, raising her hands in the air.

"Okay, okay," the MC says, a smile bright on his face. "Let's
get started." He pulls out some kind of remote and pushes a
button, and a large screen lowers behind the panelists. D1V and
the men turn to watch as a bright blue splash of color appears.

"Before we officially begin," he continues, and everyone
on the panel turns back to face the audience. "We have a special bit of footage from Solomon and Ravenfox games. Who
is ready to see the first bit of gameplay from… *Twenty Thousand Leagues*?!"

The audience roars again, and I can't hide my smile, despite
the circumstances. The much-hyped ocean exploring game
inspired by Jules Verne has been making waves in the press
for months, and I've been dying for some more ocean exploring ever since I played through the *BioShock* series on Steam.

I lean back a little in my metal folding chair. I'm allowed to
enjoy a little of this, right? I find myself wishing Ryan were
here. He'd love this preview.

The room goes black, the lights shutting off with an audible
snap. Several people in the audience gasp, and the darkness is
broken by the glow of multiple cell phones. People hold them

up, little lights in the black, and as the footage starts, hundreds of smartphones are set to record.

This is going to be all over the Internet, and I'm thrilled that I actually get to be here for it.

Music swells, epic and intense, a symphony. The projector screen shows a boundless ocean, surprisingly empty except for little fish flitting back and forth. Some kind of horn sounds in the musical score, deep and ominous, and a vessel courses into view.

A voice-over booms, deep and dramatic, as the shadowy outline of a submerged vessel begins to materialize.

"In an ocean where—"

The lights flicker back on.

The audience buzzes with voices, several people shouting in protest as Thad fusses with the remote on the stage. I look to D1V, who's craning her neck toward the projector screen, just as confused as everyone else is.

"Sorry!" Thad shouts, holding his hands up, trying to calm the audience down. "Let me just—"

Snap!

The lights are off again.

There's a brief sound of celebration from the audience, but it dies quickly. Almost instantly. And I immediately see why.

The screen. It's gone black.

With the exception of two letters in the middle of it, a white line slicing down between them.

V | P

The Vox Populi.

They're here.

"Boo!" a voice shouts from somewhere nearby. A shadowy figure stands up across the aisle.

"The Vox Populi will rise!" screams someone else near the front of the room.

"Someone get the lights!" Thad yells from the stage.

"Boo!" another voice chimes in, louder. A guy behind me. I turn around, and in the little bit of light shining in from the outside near the walls, I see Rebekah shove him. I stand up, wanting to rush toward her, but suddenly there's a massive chorus of booing, echoing from all around the hall. And a strange… I don't know, a rustling sound, coming from everywhere around me. Like someone fussing with a backpack or a jacket, only times several dozen.

After what feels like forever, there's another loud *snap*.

The lights crack back on.

It's easy to spot what the rustling was now. Multiple guys around the room are sporting bright white shirts with a black V | P logo right in the middle, matching the one on the screen.

They're everywhere. They were here the entire time. Just hidden among the audience.

Yet as scary as that is, it takes everything in me not to laugh at the fact that all these guys took their shirts off and changed while the lights were out.

It feels…ridiculous. And sad.

Several guys around me get to their feet and start to take slow, meaningful steps forward. My heart pounds in my chest, a sense of urgency mixed with fear coursing through me. Are they going to come for me? Or are they heading toward the stage?

I take my badge and tuck it inside my shirt, hiding my name. I don't know how D1V does it up there, on display for everyone. I try to steel myself, to find some strength for her, and I reach down and grab the plastic poster tube.

Behind me, I can barely make out that one security guard, the man who was on his phone, but I see him grab the guy tussling with Rebekah and throw him out of the hall.

A masked face appears on the projector screen, still easily visible even with the lights on.

WE ARE THE VOX POPULI.

There's a roar of cheering scattered throughout the crowd.

WE WILL NOT BE SILENCED.

And suddenly, it's complete pandemonium.

Security guards seem to erupt out of nowhere, shoving their way through the swelling crowd to the stage, where they form ranks around the panelists. The army of dudes surges toward them, all looking enraged at…what? What is it about a girl being popular on the Internet that pisses them off so much?

Some of the Vox Populi who were behind me shove by, and I look at the floor for a moment, afraid they might see me. Somehow recognize me.

When my eyes flit back up, D1V is still standing on the stage, resolute, serving up a powerful glare.

She's so brave. My God.

"We are here to have a civil conversation," Thad says angrily into the microphone. "If you cannot be respectful, we will have to ask you to leave, or remove you by force."

"*She* should leave!" one of them shouts. "There are better streamers in the community. She's taking up space. She's taking ad money from those who deserve it!"

"And who are you?!" D1V roars, snatching a microphone from off the table, feedback thundering after her voice. "Who are you to say that?"

It's the first time I've heard her voice in person. She's fierce, enraged, inspiring. It takes everything in me not to be knocked back onto my chair.

A number of women in the audience cheer loudly around me. The chorus of shouting grows louder and louder, the boos of the trolls battling with the cheering. D1V tosses the microphone aside and is yelling at someone in the crowd, while the Vox Populi surge against the security guards. All the while, the girls in the front who are there to support D1V shout back at them.

Then someone throws a bottle.

It smashes against the stage, and I hear it shatter across the hard surface. One guy next to D1V—the Shiftcore Games dude—puts himself in front of her. The girls standing in the front grab at the Vox Populi members, and a few of them charge up onto the stage, gathering around D1V.

D1V lunges away from the girls and the game developer, scooping the microphone up again.

"Now!" she yells. "*Now!* It's happening! It's happening!"

What…who is she shouting for?

It's happening?

The emergency exits off to the side of the hall suddenly burst open, and a flood of police officers descends upon the Vox Populi hard and fast. There's shouting and protesting as they're surrounded, and the rest of the audience explodes into chaos when one of the trolls is hit with a Taser, his loud scream piercing the hall.

The surge of people in the hall is horrifying, and I scramble toward the middle of my row, trying to avoid getting trampled. Other attendees push and shove their way down the narrow aisles between the folding chairs, some just kicking the chairs aside, scrambling over the metal. They're falling over one another, hurtling for the door, and the floor around me is littered with comics and tote bags and posters.

I push my way through to the other side of all the chairs,

knocking over a bunch as I flee from everyone pummeling their way toward the exit. The aisle opposite is mostly clear, and I weave in and out of people, making my way up front.

When I finally reach the stage, panting and clutching my poster tube, the girls in D1V's Angst Armada are gathered around her. The Vox Populi have been dragged from the room, and one of the police officers is talking with Thad—a woman with thick black hair and a dark blazer. A detective, maybe? The two remaining panelists, looking a bit shaky, each take a moment to say something to D1V as they get ready to leave, and she bows her head gratefully at them.

I start to unscrew the top of my poster tube. It's now or never.

"Hey. Hey!" shouts one of the security guards. He's a bit younger than the rest, looks like he might even be a gamer. "What are you doing?"

"I'm a friend," I protest, looking up at the stage. D1V is wiping tears from her face, thick lines of black trickling down her cheeks.

"Prove it," he challenges.

My heart races, and I feel flush all over. "I—"

"Hey! Hey, YouTube!" he shouts up at D1V. I glare at him. *YouTube? Really?* "You know this guy?"

D1V glances down at me, but not before scowling at the security guard who called her "YouTube." Her piercing bright green eyes seem darker now, with the smeared makeup around her eyes. She blinks, looking confused for a moment, then shakes her head.

"Alright, buddy, let's go," the security guard says, shuffling me along.

"Wait, wait!" I say, reaching into the tube I've been carrying around with me all morning.

"Slowly!" he barks, putting a hand up.

"Come on, I don't have—" I huff, not wanting to say something stupid, and pull the first sheet of paper out from inside the tube. I unfurl it. It's cut out in a speech bubble, with text inside.

I hold it up, the text facing D1V and the stage.

"D1V!" I shout. "You always say 'don't read the comments.'"

She looks down at me again, perplexed.

"Read these."

A boy is standing in the middle of a dissipating riot, holding up a sign.

It's like a scene from *Love Actually*, a movie my mom makes me watch with her every December. Except a small militia of undercover police officers just busted up a giant ring of online trolls, cyber stalkers, and sexist harassers, so this isn't exactly a moment for surprise romantics.

But there he is, with a sign.

"Your videos inspire me to try and be a livestreamer one day! My mom says when I'm old enough to have an account, she'll help me. She says you're a good role model."

The boy drops the sign, which flutters to the floor and curls back up into a tube shape as he awkwardly pulls another one out for me to see.

"I don't have a lot of friends at school, but when I'm with the Armada, and watching you on the livestream, I feel like I have a community."

He does it again. The paper flapping to the floor, the next one unspooling loudly.

"I know you're having a hard time right now, but you should know that you're an inspiration to us geek girls everywhere."

He drops the third sign and digs into the tube, trying to pull out another. But it looks like it's stuck. He looks from the tube to me, the tube to me…and tosses the plastic thing over his shoulder. It hangs in back of him, looking for all the world like a sword.

He's far from the stage, so it's hard to make him out.

But it's in the way he's looking at me.

In his awkward movements.

The over-the-top, unnecessary kindness.

And I instinctively know it's him.

"It's okay, girls," I say to the Armada standing around me, their hair an array of colors, their faces hard and angry as they stare at the boy. I push gently away from them, their hands leaving my arms and shoulders. I hop off the stage and nudge some of the fallen chairs aside, nodding at the convention's security guards as I pass them.

Until he's right in front of me.

"I thought you'd be taller," I say, trying to hide my grin.

"You changed your hair," he replies, not hiding his. He reaches out, but quickly stops, pulling his hands back. "Sorry. Can… Can I?"

I can't even speak.

Instead, I reach out to grab his shaking hands.

And in that moment, he becomes real. Out of the headset and into my life.

"Those signs were really dumb." I smile as he squeezes my hands in his. "Aaron."

"I know." He grins again. "I thought you might run into trouble. I was just going to hold them up in the back for you. So you wouldn't forget who you are. What you mean to people."

He pauses and swallows hard, suddenly looking shy.

"I didn't want you to forget...what you mean to me."

Oh, my heart. This boy.

How could I possibly forget?

I'm overwhelmed. Between the Vox Populi showing up, and now him, I am a sea of emotions.

I look over at the police officers, who are taking statements from some of my Armada girls. Detective Watts is there, her arms crossed, watching everything and speaking into what looks like a small recorder. She's got her eye on me and Aaron, and her watchful gaze is so welcome in this moment.

"I wonder if it's only going to get worse now," I say, turning back to him. "Once this hits the news, someone else will take their place. I saw everyone out here, with their phones recording. There must be a hundred videos online already."

"Maybe," he says. "But more people will be afraid to do that now. And more people will stand up. Right? I mean, they have to. Look at all this."

He looks around, surveying the hall. And I see it, too. The chaos. Stuff everywhere. Chairs all over the place. The result of frightened people.

But then there's the Armada.

My girls on the stage, and the handful that are trickling back into the auditorium.

I see them, with their wild, brightly colored hair, hairstyles that clearly weren't meant to just match me—since no one saw me like this before today—but to match my commander, Rebekah. She strolls over with them, leading a few dozen girls and a couple of boys.

"So…we sold out of the pins." Rebekah gestures at the crew following her. "They cleaned out what I had left on me." I see her patches and buttons already stuck and pinned on outfits and bags and belts. "At least we have that."

She glares at Aaron.

"So, this is him?" she asks me.

"This is him," I say with a small smile. Aaron gives her a little salute and a crooked grin.

"Hmm. I'm not impressed." She brushes by us, onto the stage, where she starts passing out some remaining patches to the girls up there. Aaron turns to me and laughs.

"She likes you," I say, grinning.

The door to the hall bursts open with a loud *bang*, and a familiar-looking guy storms in. I can't seem to place him, but he immediately sets his eyes on Aaron.

"You!" he shouts, hurrying over. He grabs Aaron, pulling him away, holding him by the collar of his T-shirt. "Where is it? Where the fuck is it?"

"Whoa, whoa!" Two of the police officers jump off the stage and seize the man, who I now recognize as Jason, the ManaPunk games guy. I've seen him in plenty of articles, his style and look distinctive enough.

"What's going on here?" one of the officers asks.

"This guy stole a development computer out of my booth," Jason says, pointing accusingly at Aaron. "With a demo of a game on it that belongs to me."

"Is this true?" the officer asks. One of the convention security guards meanders over, saying something into his walkie-talkie.

"Well, yes, most of it," Aaron says, looking over at me with a shrug. "He had material in the game that he hadn't paid for, created by me and my friend, with no plans to pay us for it. He had no right to showcase it, so we took it."

A few people hustle over, their phones out and recording. I notice their press badges and catch glimpses of the websites they're here for. *Polygon. Kotaku. Giant Bomb.* Some of the outlets who have covered me in the past. I wonder what sort of piece they're going to write up about what just unraveled, or what's already online. What they tweeted, what videos and photos they posted.

And what they're about to make of this situation.

"I…" Jason looks from Aaron to the officer to me, and then at those press badges, as if one of us is going to magically understand his stance on whatever is happening. "Look, it's a bit of a misunderstanding, really." He's talking more to the press people than he is to anyone else, and I can see it. "How about, um, how about you keep that computer, and we call it even?"

He stares pleadingly at Aaron, who looks completely taken aback. I am, too, honestly. Those things are expensive as hell. But I'm guessing whatever bad press he's fearing right now outweighs the cost of that PC.

"Um. Are you serious?" Aaron asks.

"Yes. Totally." Jason nods jerkily. "And I'll take the writing and art out." He glances at the press people. "It's just— It's not what it looks like."

The journalists glance at one another, and I can practically see this guy's career going up in flames right in front of me.

"Sure," Aaron says cheerfully. "Done."

"Good, good." Jason brushes himself off, hands shaking. "We're not working together ever again, though. Don't call me."

"Fine by me," Aaron retorts.

Jason mutters something under his breath, glancing at the cop and Aaron, then storms off out of the hall. The reporters hustle back to the edge of the room, their eyes set on their phones as they type away. A few of them follow after Jason, and I wonder what kind of follow-up questions this guy is about to get hammered with.

"Hey!" an angry, deep voice shouts.

I turn to see an older guy storming toward us.

"You can't silence the Vox Populi!" he snarls.

Aaron moves to shield me from the man, and the guy takes a swing at him. Aaron's plastic poster tube clatters to the ground. My heart pounds as Aaron moves to strike back, two of the police officers bounding back over, but I push Aaron aside, reach down, and swing the poster tube up in an arc at the man's head.

It connects with the most satisfying *thunk* I've ever heard in my life.

He goes down hard, his body clattering against the folding chairs, and the security guards and police officers quickly surround him.

Aaron looks back at me and smiles.

"That was amazing," he says, a little breathless.

"I know." I smile, lifting one shoulder in a half shrug.

"Hey, I've got an idea," he says hesitantly, reaching out to give my hand a squeeze.

"Me, too," I whisper, dropping the poster tube.

I don't let him kiss me, though.

I kiss *him.*

RECLAIM THE SUN: CHAT APPLICATION

D1V: Guess who?

AARON: New chat application, who dis?

D1V: Oh, hah hah hah.

AARON: Welcome back.

D1V: How was the trip back to Philadelphia?

AARON: Not bad.

AARON: Ryan says hi. He's currently trying to put the computer on eBay.

D1V: Wow, can you even do that?

AARON: I think so, but it keeps getting taken down. Not a good enough rank or something.

AARON: Hopefully his dad will do it? I dunno.

AARON: How are you?

D1V: Still shook-up. Got my social account access back.

D1V: But I don't know.

D1V: I'm not sure I really want any of it anymore.

AARON: I hear you, but isn't that letting them win?

D1V: Maybe. I'm torn. I might just get off of it altogether.

AARON: Makes sense, I guess? Whatever you're comfortable with.

D1V: Oh my God, this is the part where you ask for my phone number.

AARON: Oh.

AARON: OH.

D1V: Too late.

D1V: Goodbye forever.

D1V: I hope you have beautiful children someday.

AARON: Nooooooo.

D1V: [D1V has signed off]

D1V: ... Okay, ready? Write it down.

26
AARON

After clearing the hard drive, Ryan's dad put Jason's Mana-Punk computer up on his eBay account with Buy It Now at $5,000, and even at that price, the bidding started almost immediately. In the end, we wound up netting a glorious $6,000.

It wasn't nearly as much as Jason had always promised us, but my half will certainly help buy some books on coding and the software I'll need to create my own games. Maybe I can even build a little website, work on a tiny studio my last year of high school? I could get some of the software at a discount on Humble, maybe? Steam?

I've got time. And this time, I'll definitely own my story.

AARON: So.

AARON: Would it be weird if I like, came to visit?

D1V: Am I still saved as D1V in your phone?

AARON: No...

D1V: You can't see me, but I'm making a face.

AARON: I'll fix it right away, promise.

DIVYA: And as for the other question, I don't think so?

DIVYA: Would it be weird for you?

AARON: No. Not really.

AARON: I'd like to...you know, maybe go on a...

AARON: You know, like a date.

AARON: A date type of thing.

DIVYA: Wow, I am swept off my feet. Like, clean off.

AARON: Good, good. I was rehearsing that for hours.

DIVYA: I can tell.

DIVYA: Also the answer is yes.

DIVYA: If you bring me flowers though, I will slay you.

27
DIVYA

"Streaming for fun isn't as...well, *fun* as it was before," Rebekah grumbles.

"Come on, be happy for me," I whine into the phone, even though I know she is. Mom's last class is paid for, and I've got enough to register for two courses at County, plus some funds leftover after selling some of my gear. With no plans to return to streaming professionally, I traded in my gaming PC and curved monitor for something smaller.

I pet my new little laptop, which can run most modern games—barely. I have to turn the graphics down. But I don't mind.

"I am, I am." She chuckles. "And your little pal Maggs is doing great, running the channel now. Way to pass the torch."

I smile. I knew Maggs would be perfect.

"When are we gonna get online next?" she asks. "The feeds are exploding, and I'm out of patches again in the shop. You might not be the leader in the Armada anymore, but you're still a figurehead."

"So I'm your queen?" I ask innocently.

"Stop it."

I pause for a moment. "Beks," I say at last. "I need some time. I think you do, too."

"I know, you're right," she relents. "But can we try for once a week? A lot of my friends who play *World of Warcraft*, they at least do weekly raids."

"That I think I can manage." I smile.

The doorbell rings, and I smile harder.

"Still on to go flea marketing for vintage games tomorrow?" I ask.

"If you aren't still on your date, I am." Rebekah laughs.

"You're the worst," I say. "Love you."

"You, too," she says. "Have fun."

I rush downstairs, and there's Aaron, in real life, waiting for me.

On any other Tuesday, I'd be preparing for my stream. Talking back and forth with Rebekah. Going over sponsorships, trying to figure out who we had to bring up, link to. What products to potentially show off. Where we might go raid, what the plan might be. It might have been in *Reclaim the Sun*, or any other massive multiplayer game. *Destiny. Halo. World of Warcraft.*

Today, I'm going out with a boy who likes me.

One who just took a bus across New Jersey to go on a date with me.

I grab his hand, and we walk away from my apartment building. The wind blows, and the warm sun shines down on us.

Reclaimed.

★ ★ ★ ★ ★

ACKNOWLEDGMENTS

This book came to life during a strange time.

My wife and I had moved from our home of nearly a decade to a new city, in a new state. And then we did it again. So many of my friendships became virtual. In a way, this book explored that and what it meant to be so close to people who were far away.

So, first, to my Richmond, Virginia, friends.

To Bill Blume and Phil Hilliker, for that writing retreat. That's where this story was born, a messy first draft written in a week full of writing with no cell reception. And to the rest of that Richmond crew: Rebecca Jones Schinsky, Bob Schinsky, Amanda Nelson, Gwen Cole, Sarah Glenn Marsh, Adam Austin, Beth Sanmartin, David Streever, Kristi Tuck Austin, Anne Blankman, Chelsea Washington, and Kelly Justice at the Fountain Bookstore. Thank you for making a new place feel like home, if only for a year.

To writer friends like Olivia A. Cole, Akemi Dawn Bowman, Kelly Jensen, Sangu Mandanna, Samira Ahmed, Lauren Morrill, Lily Anderson (you were right about the title!), Kat Cho, Thomas Torre, Patrick Flores-Scott, Marieke Nijkamp, Blair "Two Sheds" Thornburgh, Ashley Poston, Sam Maggs, Heidi Heilig, Lauren Gibaldi, Summer Heacock, Jessica Conditt, Whitney Gardner, Sarvenaz Tash, Katherine Locke, and Jeff Zentner—thank you for your endless pep talks, late night brainstorming, and friendships.

Dear friends Preeti Chhibber, Swapna Krishna, Darlene Meier, Miguel Bolivar, Rob Perdue, Mikey Il, Tim Quirino, Brian Lim, Chris Urie, Dario Plazas... Your friendships inspire me every single day. My Michigan friends, who edited away with me in sleepy cafés and bookshops—Lillian Li, Erica Chapman, Darcy Woods, and Rebecca Fortes.

My colleagues and friends at P.S. Literary, especially Carly, Curtis, Kurestin, Amanda, David, and Maria. I don't know how you deal with me.

Mom and Dad, for putting up with me as I dragged old computers into our basement as a teenager, frequently breaking them and our home computer in my pursuit of knowledge. That part of this book is very real.

My rock-star agent, Dawn Frederick at Red Sofa Literary. You were right. You knew we'd get here one day. Thank you for believing in me when I seldom believed in myself.

The entire team at Harlequin and Inkyard Press, especially Lauren Smulski, Rebecca Kuss, Gabby Vicedomini, Laura Gianino, Quinn Banting, Bess Braswell, Brittany Mitchell, Connolly Bottum, Stephanie Van de Vooren, and Natashya Wilson. And Mary Luna, for the gorgeous cover art.

And, as always, to my wife, Nena, and son, Langston. In a universe of trillions of planets, the only place I want to be is here with you.

Need more Eric Smith rom-coms in your life?
Turn the page for a sneak peek at his next book,
You Can Go Your Own Way!

The playfield is truly the heart of every pinball machine. All of the player's goals are right there, splayed out in front of them. And like life, it's up to you to find a way to reach them, with the tools you're presented. In this case, it's a ball.

—*The Art and Zen of Pinball Repair* by James Watts

The sound of collective screaming and a massive crash shake my entire workshop, and I almost stab myself with a piping hot soldering iron.

"Adam!" my mom yells from inside the arcade. If another pack of junior high kids from the nearby Hillman Academy "accidentally" flipped over a machine trying to get it to tilt, I am going to lose it. I grip the iron, the cracked brown leather wrapped around the metal handle squeaking a little against my skin, and shake my head, trying to refocus. Maybe I can finish this before it's time to pick up that custom piece—

And another crash rattles the walls. A few parts tumble off my shelves, tiny intricate pieces of metal and glass, bits of copper wire, all clinking against my table.

I attempt to catch a few of the electronic pieces, trying not to burn myself with the iron in my other hand, and then a hammer falls off the perforated wall of tools in front of me. It collides with a small cardboard box full of pinball playfield light bulbs, and I wince at the small crack and pop sounds.

"Goddammit," I grumble out. I toss the soldering iron aside and try to clean up the mess. At least those light bulbs are like, ten bucks a dozen on arcade wholesale websites. But pinball machines sure do have a *lot* of lights.

"Adam!" This time it's Chris. "Dude, where *are* you?"

I'm about to bolt from the workshop when I remember Mom is out there. I reach for the latest read I promised her I'd finish—*We Built This Gritty* by Kevin Michaels, a book on launching small businesses by an entrepreneur here in Philly that one of her colleagues is teaching at the county college—and immediately yank my hand back. The soldering iron had gone right in between the pages when I tossed it, and the book is already smoking. I pull the iron out and set it aside and flap the book around wildly, little wisps pooling up from inside the bright orange book. I flip it open.

It's burnt right down the middle. Great. Something tells me she won't be able to trade this back in at the campus store.

I glance over at The Beast and give the forever-in-progress Philadelphia-themed home-brewed pinball machine a pat, the glass still off the surface, wires and various parts splayed out over the playfield. My well-worn copy of *The Art and Zen of Pinball Repair* by James Watts sits smack in the middle of everything. I've still got a way to go before I can try playing Dad's unfinished machine again, but if anyone is gonna get me there, it's Watts. If I could just get a free chunk of time in between the studying and the arcade and the—

An array of swears echo from inside the arcade, snapping me back.

Right. Chris. Mom. Chaos. Potentially broken and nearly irreplaceable machines worth thousands of dollars.

I unplug the soldering iron and place it in its little stand, like a quill pen in an inkwell. I wedge the now-toasty book under my arm and take a few steps to pick up some speed, to get a little force, and I push my shoulder against the dark red wooden workshop door. I push, gritting my teeth. The splintering surface presses into my arm, stinging with the pressure, until finally the wood squeals against the frame, shrunken in and wedged together due to the sharp Philadelphia winter.

The whole workshop is like that, really, casting a major contrast to the polished, well-kept-despite-its-years pinball arcade. The cracked workshop table that is *way* more rickety than it has any right to be, tools showing their age with hinges that refuse to move and metal pieces falling off shrinking wood and weak plastic handles, vintage pinball parts that *maybe* still work, a concrete floor with a surface that's chipping away, revealing dirt and dust, light bulbs I don't even remotely trust. My sad excuse for a drafting table sits off to the end of the workshop, and I've never really used it, preferring to fuss with plans right on the messy workshop table, next to all of Dad's scribbles.

We could clean it up, have this room match the rest of the arcade. But I love it. It reminds me of him.

The door swings open suddenly and hits the wall inside the arcade with a loud bang.

And it *is* absolute chaos here.

A bunch of little kids are rushing outside, and I see a couple of adults gathering coats and their small children, who are likely about to join the exodus. The afternoon light that's pouring in from the wide open front door and our large plate glass windows lining the wall make me wince. The glare hurts only slightly less than the idea of customers hustling out of here on a Saturday, easily our best, and *only*, solid day during the wintertime off-season. Especially now, at the end of the year, with so few days left before we close for the New Year holiday.

People don't come to pinball arcades in the winter. Well. Maybe they do, but not when your arcade is located near all the tourist stuff in Old City, all the college students are away on break, and you don't serve any alcohol. No tourists, no college kids, no booze, no pinball. It's a neighborhood for expensive restaurants and niche boutiques, old-timey candy shops and artisan pour-over coffee. Not an arcade with a poor excuse for a snack bar inside that mostly serves soda, chips, and reheated chicken tenders and fries.

If it wasn't for the upcoming Old City Winter Festival, I'm not sure we'd be able to keep the lights on come January.

"Mom?!" I shout, looking to the back of the arcade. "Chris, what is—"

But then I see it.

On the other side of the arcade, my mom has her hands on her hips and is glaring intently at a handful of twentysomething guys who are sheepishly milling about near one of the windows. And Chris is trying to lift up a machine that's currently tilted over, the glass that would normally be covering the playfield shattered across the ground. Another machine is tilted over, leaning against a support beam.

"What the hell?!" I snap, kicking the workshop door closed and storming across the arcade. My thick black boots squeak loud against the worn, polished hardwood floor, all the imperfections of the ancient Philadelphia wooden boards permanently glossed in place. A few more guys, these ones my age, weave around me, fiddling on their phones and oblivious. Bits of glass crunch under my feet, and I glance down at a bumper, red and black and looking like one of those crushed lantern fly bugs that litter the city sidewalks.

"What happened?!" I ask, tossing my burnt book onto the floor. I nudge the tilted machine upright and then bend down to help Chris, who is straining to move the machine on the floor. I manage to wedge my fingers under the side, carefully tapping the metal, trying to avoid any extra glass, and lift. Chris lets out a groan and I grit my teeth as we push the machine upright, and it nearly topples back over the other way, but Mom reaches out and stops it.

"*They* happened." Mom nods back at the guys who are standing about awkwardly. "Any updates there?" She points at one of them, and that's when I realize they're all sort of keeping an eye on one vaguely familiar-looking dude in the middle, who is fussing with his phone.

"Just a second," he grumbles out, and he flicks his head to the side, his emo black bangs moving out of his eyes. I can't help but squint at him, trying to place his face. Half his head is shaved, and he has this sort of Fall Out Boy look that would be cool, if he and his pals hadn't clearly destroyed a pinball machine in my family's arcade. A splash of anxiety hits me in the chest as I realize I'm not sure what game has been totaled, and I turn to look at the machine.

Flash Gordon.

I exhale, relieved that it's not one of the more popular or rare games in the arcade. But still, it's a machine from the '80s. One of the first games in the industry to use the popular Squawk & Talk soundboard, a piece of technology that is wildly expensive to replace, since it isn't made anymore. That's the sort of pinball trivia both Chris and my mom tend to shush when I start rambling too much, telling me "that should be a tweet," which translates to "shut up" in the nicest way possible. I'm almost positive that's the reason they pushed me to get the arcade on social media—to have a place to share those musings.

The machine didn't deserve this, even if that awful movie maybe did.

"How much is it going to cost to fix?" the familiar guy with the hair asks. He must catch me staring at him, 'cause his eyes flit over to mine, irritated, and I look away, focusing back on the machine.

I pluck at some of the glass on the surface, nudging around some of the broken obstacles on the playfield, and feel a sharp sting in my hand. I quickly pull away and spot a thin line of red trailing along my palm.

"Adam?"

I glance up, and my mom, Chris, and Emo Hair are all staring at me expectantly.

"What?" I ask, focusing back down at the machine and then back at all of them.

"The cost," my mom presses. "That machine. How much do you think it'll cost to fix all of this?" She gestures at the floor and shakes her head, her mouth a thin line. All that brewing frustration that she's trying to bury down. Kids mess with the machines often, and we've certainly had a few hiccups like this before, but I've never seen her looking this wildly angry. I didn't even think she *liked* that machine.

"Oh." I swallow and clear my throat. "I don't know. It depends on how bad the damage is?" I scan the playfield and then the side of the machine, which has a sizable dent in the steel that I can probably hammer out. But the shattered glass, the pieces, and who knows what's going on inside it. I think back to Watts's *The Art and Zen of Pinball Repair*, my holy tome, written by my hero.

If you think it's broken, it is. And if you think it's going to be cheap to replace, it's not.

I stare at the broken glass.

"You know what, how's a thousand dollars?" the familiar guy holding the phone asks. He looks around at his dude friends, their faces awash in expressions that are essentially shrugs, each nodding at him. "Everyone Venmo me $200 after this, if you can, or I'll kick your asses."

Some of the guys laugh while the rest break out their phones.

"Why?" scoffs one of them. "You're the one with the money."

Emo Hair snorts out a laugh and shakes his head, and glances back up from his screen. The fact that all of them are so relaxed about that much money irks me. The arcade is barely scraping by these days.

"What's your Venmo?" he asks, looking at my mom and then at me. My mom and I exchange a look. He huffs. "How about PayPal? Apple Pay?"

"I mean…we could take a check?" My mom shrugs, wincing. One of the bros groans like this has somehow physically *wounded* him, and before I can say anything, my mom snaps a finger at the guy. "Hey, you five are the ones who broke this machine. If I want you to go get that thousand dollars in a burlap sack full of coins at the bank down the road, you'll get it."

"Sorry, ma'am," one of them mutters.

"Just Venmo it to me," Chris says, pulling out his phone. "I'll hit the bank and get it taken care of, Mrs. Stillwater." He glances at my mom and shakes his head at me. I know that look. He's about to force another freaking app on me, and I don't think I'll be able to talk about pinball on Venmo. It was bad enough when he tricked me into joining Pinterest, convincing me it was a pinball thing.

He steps over to the pack of guys, and they're all looking at one another and their phones and his, and I really shouldn't be surprised that he knows how to handle this. Him and his apps. I wish he'd just run the social media for the arcade, but he says it wouldn't sound "genuine" or something. If typos make someone genuine, I am *very* genuine.

A year behind me at Central, a junior, Chris has this whole Adam Driver look about him. Same sharp cheekbones and bits of facial hair, only a little shorter and with thin square glasses, and as geeky as you can get without actually being in a *Star Wars* movie. My best friend since I was eight, and our only employee in the off-season, as everyone is either a college student heading home for the break or a fellow local high schooler who has no interest in working over the winter.

He nods at the guys, looking at his phone.

"Alright, I got it," he says and then turns to us. The bros stand there for a beat.

"You can leave," my mom snaps and points toward the door.

"Right, right," the familiar guy says and gestures for the rest of his pack to follow. They amble out of the shop, their feet crunching the glass on the floor in a way that makes me feel like it's on purpose. I take a step forward, but Chris reaches his arm out, his hand pressing against my chest.

I glance up at him, and he just shakes his head.

I huff and bend down to sift through the glass and pieces of machine, while my mom disappears into the back office. There are some bumpers on the ground, and a few small white flags, little targets meant to be knocked down for bonus plays, are scattered about like baby teeth. The glass, though, that really bothers me. A good sheet of playfield glass can go for a little over a hundred dollars, and while I know that's not *technically* a lot of money in the grand scheme of things…we don't have that much to spare these days.

Jorge over at NextFab, the makerspace that Chris practically lives in when he isn't here, has been great at helping me replace some parts, as well as teaching me how to build some of my own, which is way more helpful than YouTube tutorials. But a whole sheet of glass? Bumpers with *intricate* circuitry and copper coils? That's not something easily 3D printed, especially when he keeps doing it for free. And I don't know how much of that I can manage in my workshop. Or afford, for that matter.

I look around the dirty playfield for the remaining flags but...dammit, they are nowhere to be found. At least the backglass, the lit up artwork on the back of the machine, isn't damaged. Flash is still there, looking dead ahead at me, alongside Dale and the...ugh, wildly racist Ming the Merciless.

Hmm.

Maybe the machine *did* deserve this.

Chris squats down next to me.

"Want me to grab the broom?" he asks, picking at a broken bumper.

I look back to my hand. The line in my palm is ugly but clean. I flex my hand a little, and the cut widens, and I see just how far up and down my hand it goes. I wonder if I'll need stitches or if it'll scar.

"Sure." I clear my throat and both of us stand up. I glance toward the arcade's exit, the place now empty, as Chris walks over to the snack bar. "Must be nice," I say, "being able to drop that much money without thinking about it."

"Yeah, well, not like his dad isn't good for it."

"His dad?" I ask, peering over. Chris's behind the bar, some paper towels already scattered out in front of him, a broom in one hand. Heat lamps keeping fries and onion rings warm tint his face a reddish orange for a moment before he ducks back out.

"Well, yeah?" He shrugs, walking over. He places the paper towels in my hands and nods at the cut. "Apply pressure." He starts sweeping, moving bits of glass and broken parts into a small pile. "I swear, one more incident like this, and that is what's gonna make me finally try to get a job at the maker-space. Or a coffee shop..." He looks up at me as I stare at him. "What? You know I can't work in here forever, bro."

"What do you mean 'what'? I know *that* part." I laugh. "Who is his dad? You're just gonna leave the story hanging there?"

He nearly drops the broom but reaches out to grab the handle.

"Are you serious?" he scoffs. I shrug and he shakes his head. "Adam, that was *Nick*. That's why I thought you were so mad, looking like you were about to charge after him and his goons." I shrug again. "Jesus, Adam. Nick *Mitchell*."

The stress on that last name.

Mitchell.

It sends a shock through my entire system, and I turn to look at the exit, as though he and his friends might still be there. I tighten my hand into a fist, and the pain from the cut sears through my palm, lighting me up through my forearm. And I swear, for a moment, I can feel it in my head, bouncing around like a pinball against bumpers.

Nick.

Whitney Mitchell's brother.

Did he even recognize me? Did he know this was our arcade? Back when me and Whitney were supposedly friends, before high school changed everything, I don't think I ever saw him come around. But I saw him all the time at school and before her dad's career took off, when we'd play at Whitney's old house in South Philly. And when we were kids, everyone had their birthday parties here at the pinball arcade. With so many mutual friends and the like, he had to have been in here at some point. Until they forgot about us, like the entire building was just one giant toy that fell behind a dresser.

"Alright, well, I can tell you know who he is now," Chris says, walking back toward the snack bar. He grabs some more paper towels and thrusts them at me, nodding at my hand. I look down, and the paper wad is an awful dark red, soaked through from my rage. "Go take a seat. I'm gonna get the first aid kit out of your workshop."

"What about Flash Gordon?" I ask, glancing back at the messed-up machine.

"It's a problematic racist relic. Who cares? Come on." He laughs, reaching out and grabbing my shoulder. "Besides, if you want some replacement bits, I'm heading to the makerspace tomorrow—we can rummage for parts. Go grab a seat." He nods at the snack bar and walks off. I turn around and pull my phone out, snapping photos of the broken pinball machine. The scratched-up metal exterior, the dented places around the playfield. I bend down and snap pictures of some of the crunched glass still on the floor, the broken parts scattered in a neat pile thanks to Chris.

I stroll over to the arcade's snack spot and sit down, Dad's last great idea for the place. The chairs aren't exactly the pinnacle of comfort, but it's what my family could afford when we first put this spot in here, and the hard wood digs into my back. It's still passably cozy enough that local writers will drop in to play a few games, drink our bad coffee or nurse a soda, and spend the day staring at a blank screen while scrolling through Twitter instead of writing.

I sigh and glance up at the wooden shelving that looms over the café corner, a shabby chic display that Chris's parents helped build. Tons of mason jars, full of coffee beans and loose leaf tea, illuminated by strings of white Christmas twinkle lights, sit on nearly every shelf. Decor meant for hip college students and artsy creatives in West Philly, pulled from a Pinterest board someplace and made real. I think it looks pretty, but if Gordon Ramsey made an episode about our arcade's little food corner, it would just be a twenty-eight-minute scream.

Chris walks around the side, a little first aid kit in hand, and gestures for me to give him my hand. I hold it out and he glances back at the Flash Gordon machine.

"Real shame," he says, wistfully looking at the shattered game.

"Yeah." I nod. "I took a bunch of photos to post—"

Pssssssst!

There's the sound of spraying, and I scream, yanking my hand away. I glare at him, and he's sporting the widest grin I've ever seen, a bottle of spray-on rubbing alcohol in his hand.

"Argh!" I groan. "Why!"

"Kidding, fuck that game." He laughs.

"You could have *told me* you were going to do that!" I shout. He tilts his head a little at me. "Fine, you're right—I would have made a scene over it."

"Everything okay?" Mom's in the doorway to the office, peeking out.

"Yeah, Mrs. Stillwater," Chris says.

My mom scowls at the two of us before breaking into a little smile, but that expression disappears as her line of sight moves toward the broken pinball machine. She closes the door, and I look back at the exit to the arcade again.

"And I'm gonna need you to stop it," Chris says, reaching out and grabbing my hand, slapping a large Band-Aid on my palm. I wince and suck air through my teeth, and he just gives me a look. He pulls out some of that gauze-wrap stuff and starts to bandage up the big Band-Aid, keeping it pressed to my palm. "That guy isn't worth it, that machine isn't worth it, and that family definitely isn't worth getting all riled up over."

"He *had* to have known this was my place," I grumble. "Whitney probably *sent* him here."

"Oh, come on," Chris scoffs. "I'm not her biggest fan either, and I know you two don't get along, but she isn't some nefarious supervillain, sending her *henchmen* here. When was the last time you even talked, outside of snarky social media posts? You like pinball, she likes playing *Fortnite* and *Overwatch*. Not exactly a blood feud."

"I'm not even sure she's into the video games at her dad's places or whatever," I grumble. At least, she wasn't into video games when we were kids, always so irritated when we'd retreat inside to get in games of *Halo*. "Besides, you don't understand." I shake my head, trying to chase away the memories of that summer before high school and those first days wandering the halls at Central. Her and her new friends, leaning against their lockers, matching jean jackets and bright lip gloss. She was like an entirely new person, and the way she laughed with them when I walked over to say hi…

"Anyway." I clear my throat. "I wouldn't put it past her."

"You need to spend more time worrying about the people who are there for you and less about those who aren't," he says, fastening the gauze together with two little metal clips. "Maybe go on a date with someone or something."

"How do you even know how to do this?" I lift my hand up, flexing my fingers, ignoring the dating question. There's no time for that, between the arcade and school. If I kiss a girl by the end of my senior year, it'll be a miracle.

"Please, my dads are carpenters and you know how I spend my free time," he says. "It's best to be prepared in case someone loses a finger at home or in the shop or at the makerspace."

I laugh and again find myself looking toward the door. I let out a long exhale through my nose.

"You think we're going to get anyone else in here today?" Chris asks. "It's just, you know, maybe I could duck out early to go work on stuff?" There's this beat of silence that doesn't need to be filled, and I sigh.

"I think we both know the answer there, right?"

I lean back in my chair a little, the sharp pain of the wood digging into my back weirdly comforting, distracting me from my hand and thoughts of Nick and Whitney and that whole terrible family. This is why no one but local writers ever seem to want to sit here. Even groups for birthday parties or the handful of events we get at the arcade, small local businesses hosting get-togethers after hours, avoid the hardened chairs.

"Do you need to talk?" Chris asks, and I glance back at him. "I mean, I can hang a bit longer if you need me." He digs around in his pocket and pulls out a little candy bag and waves it at me, the plastic crinkling. Swedish Fish. Not the regular kind either, the tropical sort, with orange, pink, purple, and off-white fish in the mix. He shakes it until one drops out onto his hand, and he holds it up between his fingers. "I grabbed a bag at the CVS before I came over here, for my dads. Didn't realize *we'd* have to use it, though."

"Oh God, no," I whine. "If you're gonna do that to me, just leave."

Whenever Chris's parents want to talk about "big feelings," they break out these Swedish Fish candies. Have something important to say? Out comes the candy. It's usually something critical that might make someone feel upset, but it's the way you're feeling, so it's good to get it all out. Then pair it with something that makes you feel good while you're hearing something that might make you feel bad.

It was a tradition Chris first told me about when we were really little, and one that's been ongoing. I'm not quite sure why Swedish Fish are the candy of choice, but I'm guessing it's because you can buy them in bulk at the South Philadelphia Ikea. He's since introduced it to me and all our friends.

Tell someone how you feel, let them eat the candy and take in all those thoughts and emotions. Or, give someone the opportunity to say how they're feeling, and take it all in. Simple enough.

I hate it so much.

"I hate this so much," I grumble and pluck the fish from between his fingers.

"Listen," he says, reaching out and closing my good hand around the candy. "You're upset. You're thinking about Whitney and the Mitchells. Nick and the boys. Both of those sound like terrible West Philadelphia indie rock bands. And you're thinking about maybe going on Twitter and saying something snippy on social media. That what those pictures are for? Yeah?"

"N-no." I barely stammer the word out. "It's for...insurance."

He gives me a look.

"You're the worst." I glower at him.

"Don't go online, it's a waste of your energy," he says, nodding at me. "Save your online presence for posting your pinball puns and facts. Now, eat your candy."

"No." I glare at him.

"Fine, fine." He smiles, shaking his head, and pulls out his phone. "I'm gonna head off to NextFab. You behave."

"Ugh, can't you just work on your weird woodworking coffee things in the workshop?" I groan and gesture toward the red door on the other side of the arcade. "Then you could just be here all the time."

He laughs and then sighs. "What are you going to do here without me?" he asks.

"Hmph." I huff. "Probably have a meltdown on the regular."

He reaches over and taps the screen of my phone, and my

eyes flit up to him. "Don't do it, and you'll be fine," he says and then bends over to grab his backpack. It's this beaten-up leather thing that looks straight out of an old movie. I half expect to see it filled with old books tied together in beige string, but I know it's just full of woodworking tools, and depending on the day, some glassblowing stuff. It's not lost on me that my best friend spends all his time creating beautiful new things out of nothing, while I stress over repairing machines older than I am every single day.

He walks out of the snack bar and toward the door but stops and turns around.

"And hey, if you need to talk." He throws something, and I reach out to catch whatever it is that is flapping its way toward me. The plastic bag of Swedish Fish makes a loud crinkling sound as I grab it out of the air. "Text me, but I'm gonna want pictures of you eating your candy. It's important that you trust the process."

He's out the front door, and I'm alone in the arcade with his candy and my phone.